Michelle Carter has received fellowships from the National Endowment for the Arts, Stanford University, the Fine Arts Work Center in Provincetown, Massachusetts, and the Cité International des Arts in Paris. She has published short fiction in *Playgirl, Grand Street,* and various literary magazines, as well as in the anthologies *20 Under 30* and *The New Generation.* She has been a Jones Lecturer at Stanford University, and is currently Assistant Professor of Creative Writing at San Francisco State University.

ON OTHER DAYS WHILE GOING HOME

— *Michelle Carter* —

PENGUIN BOOKS

PENGUIN BOOKS
Published by the Penguin Group
Viking Penguin Inc., 40 West 23rd Street,
New York, New York 10010, U.S.A.
Penguin Books Ltd, 27 Wrights Lane,
London W8 5TZ, England
Penguin Books Australia Ltd, Ringwood,
Victoria, Australia
Penguin Books Canada Ltd, 2801 John Street,
Markham, Ontario, Canada L3R 1B4
Penguin Books (N.Z.) Ltd, 182–190 Wairau Road,
Auckland 10, New Zealand

Penguin Books Ltd, Registered Offices:
Harmondsworth, Middlesex, England

First published in the United States of America by
William Morrow and Company, Inc., 1987
Reprinted by arrangement with William Morrow and Company, Inc.
Published in Penguin Books 1988

1 3 5 7 9 10 8 6 4 2

Lines and phrases from Grateful Dead lyrics are excerpted throughout
this work. The author very gratefully acknowledges the role of the band and its music
in fueling and firing the writing of the book.
Permission to quote from the following lyrics is gratefully acknowledged:
"Cassidy" by John Barlow and Bob Weir, copyright © 1972 by
Ice Nine Publishing Company Inc.
"Box of Rain" by Phil Lesh and Robert Hunter, copyright
© 1970 by Ice Nine Publishing Company Inc.
"Your Cheatin' Heart" by Hank Williams, copyright © 1952 renewed 1980;
Hiriam Music 50% U.S.A. only; Acuff-Rose/Opryland Music, Inc. 50% U.S.A.,
100% World Outside U.S.A., 66 Music Square West, Nashville, Tennessee 37203.
International copyright secured. Made in U.S.A.
All rights secured.
Portions of this work appeared in vastly different form in *Grand
Street* and *Negative Capability*. The Prologue appeared in
slightly different form in *Shankpainter 24*.

LIBRARY OF CONGRESS CATALOGING IN PUBLICATION DATA
Carter, Michelle.
On other days while going home/Michelle Carter.
p.   cm. — (Contemporary American fiction)
ISBN 0 14 01.0972 2
I. Title.   II. Series.
PS3553.A782605   1988
813′ .54—dc19   88–17453

Printed in the United States of America by
R. R. Donnelley & Sons Company, Harrisonburg, Virginia
Set in Fournier

For my parents,
Lizabeth Carter and Millie Duckson,
and my godfather,
Al Graf

The author would like to thank John L'Heureux for years of invaluable support. Many thanks to the Stanford Writing Program and the Fine Arts Work Center in Provincetown. Special gratitude to the tireless readers who offered love and strong words: Deborah Gordis, trusted friend; Ehud Havazelet, the writer next door; Gerald Flaherty, who helped turn an idea into a story; Jessica Coope, especially, for knowing what matters. And to Mark Cioc, beyond thanks, still: thank you, with love.

Come, wash the nighttime clean
Come, grow the scorched ground green

—JOHN BARLOW

From the back of the office I watched my aunt Marie at the counter, waiting on two men dressed like women. I was sitting at the back desk printing names on file folders, which was my job because I made neat capital letters.

The men looked less flashy than others like them who'd been into the office. They had on gray skirts and dark blazers, and felt caps with net veils that fell loose around their hair. The taller one was signing papers, and the other one was holding a man's suit on a hanger. Their friend had been arrested in a dress the night before, and they were trying to talk Marie into bringing him the suit for the arraignment.

"Co-signer," Marie said.

The shorter one handed the taller one the hanger and took the pen.

"What did you decide?" the taller man said. He held the suit out to my aunt.

"I don't know," she said. "They probably won't let me give it to him. In a case like this they'll give him jail garb for the hearing."

The shorter one stopped reading and they both looked at

13

my aunt. Everybody knew jail garb meant a bright orange jumpsuit, colored for easy spotting in case the prisoner tried to bolt. Everybody also knew jail garb never helped anybody look less guilty. The tall man kept holding the suit out to my aunt.

"What time is the hearing?" she said.

"Tomorrow," he said, "ten."

My aunt took the hanger and slid the suit over the counter. "I'll do what I can."

"Thank you," the men both said.

The shorter one went back to reading the forms. I looked straight through them to the front of the office and sounded out the words painted on the glass. The three of them standing there blocked some of the letters, but I knew those backwards words by heart:

S'ILLEZARF

LIAB

DNOB

I used to play make-believe by thinking up meanings for the words read from inside. The right-way spelling, FRAZELLI'S BAIL BOND, didn't mean a thing to anybody at school anyway. For a while I pretended that S'illezarf was a kind of dwarf who'd come to us for liab and dnob, which were kinds of bread we baked in the back room. Then one day a dwarf really did come into the office, and he wasn't any more fun than the usual traffic.

The taller one gave Marie a lot of money and the two men left the office. Marie shut the bills in the cashbox and put it all in the locking cabinet. When I was littler, she would have taken this opportunity to explain that those were both men, they dressed like women, and there was no point in thinking anything about it. I was ten years old by then so I figured she knew I'd heard enough of that, and I was pretty much treated like an equal around the place. Except by the people who came in off the street and looked right through me like the two men in the office just did. They'd stared straight across the room to the clock on the back wall, like I wasn't sitting right in front of it.

A delivery boy came in with our dinners from the Inn Justice down the street. Marie paid him and gave me my hamburger and fries in a paper wrapper all soggy with grease. It looked too disgusting to open, let alone eat. Marie broke another hamburger into mutt-size bites and pushed the plate under her desk. Mr. Hoops woke up and started pushing the dish around the floor. Marie sat down with her hamburger and the *Court Reporter*. I tore open two foil packets and squirted ketchup all over my fries.

"At Sharon's yesterday we had home-cooked soup," I said.

Marie didn't look up from her desk.

"Turkey soup. Made right from the bone."

She turned a page of her paper.

"Is that what you'd like?" she said. "Me in an apron like Donna Reed?"

I watched her at her desk, her reading glasses at the end of her nose. She had on a white skirt and pumps, and the bulky red sweater I'd gotten her for Christmas the year before with the twenty dollars she'd given me to spend on her. She looked like anybody's mother at school, was just as nice as anybody's mother too. Except that she wasn't mine technically, she was my father's sister. My mother was long dead, my father long gone, God knows where. As far back as I could remember, I'd had a vague sense that I shouldn't ask Marie too much about any of it. Asking, I knew, was likely to make her feel like I didn't appreciate all she'd done, like it hadn't been enough.

"I don't want you to wear any apron," I said. "It's not that."

But Marie didn't ask me, What *was* it, she just kept eating her hamburger. Through the front window I saw Jotta heading toward us from across the street, cigarette in hand. Jotta said she'd bring me something when she came in to work tonight, and I'd been waiting all day to see what it was. She didn't have her usual raincoat on, and her red hair flew out behind her. I pulled the rubber band from my ponytail and ran my fingers

15

through my hair so it fell loose like Jotta's. She usually wore it up because it was too frizzy, she said. It did have a look of having been brushed too often.

When the front door opened, Mr. Hoops ran out from under Marie's desk. He barked and snapped at the counter gate when Jotta pushed through it. She held her cigarette up out of his reach.

"Hello, sweetie," she said to him.

"We're eating late," Marie said. She pinched off another few bites of her hamburger and handed the rest out to Jotta. I snatched it away from her.

"Jotta can't have that," I said.

"What do you think you're doing?" said Marie.

"Jotta's vegetarian this week," I said.

"Give that back," Marie said.

"You're right. I better stick with these," Jotta said, and grabbed my bag of fries. Marie took her hamburger back.

"What's with the ketchup?" Jotta said.

Marie was still glaring at me over her glasses. Jotta perched herself on the high stool at the counter. She was dragging each french fry along the edge of the bag to scrape the ketchup off.

"Lay off me," I said without looking at either of them.

"Tell it to Donna Reed," said Marie.

"Donna wouldn't care," said Jotta. "Donna's got crow's feet to worry about."

"Lay off her too," I said. They laughed. Not that Donna Reed really counted. But if Donna Reed had been real, she would have been just the kind of woman Jotta would have hated.

Jotta had this thing about kids and babies. If she went into a restaurant and spotted one at another table, she'd turn and walk right out again. As for Donna, Jotta would say she had no use for the kind of woman who'd stay home all day picking up toys and cleaning baby vomit off her shoes. Marie was always telling me to bring friends from school over. I could just see Sharon and her mother walking in this dumpy office in their fancy homemade dresses.

"Well," I said to Jotta, "where is it?"

She looked blank for a second. "Honey, I'm sorry," she said. "I'll bring it in tomorrow."

"What's that?" Marie said.

"I told Annie I'd bring her something today," Jotta said. She shielded her face with one hand and mouthed some words to Marie.

"I don't know," Marie said. "You think we could fit that through the door?"

"Fit what?" I said.

"I was more worried about what she could feed it," Jotta said.

"We'll feed it Mr. Hoops," I said.

"Shame on you, Annie," Marie said. "That dog loves you."

An old couple came into the office. Mr. Hoops ran out from under Marie's desk, and Jotta asked the couple if she could help them.

"What did she tell you it was?" I asked Marie.

"Settle down now," she said. "She'll bring it in tomorrow. Behave."

I gathered up my hamburger and headed for the back room, which was what we called the little apartment where Marie and I lived. I'd been wondering all day what Jotta was bringing me, and now I was supposed to wait until tomorrow. The hallway smelled like dog piss because that's where Mr. Hoops's newspapers were. Marie took Mr. Hoops in on a bail when I was eight. "A teacup poodle," the man had said, "for the little one to love." He'd bent down at me and held out his hands, cupped like the man in the Allstate commercial. But instead of a little house, there was this tiny, hairless rat of a thing, which I hated from the first night it kept me up yelping and carrying on till dawn. It would nip at my heels when I'd walk by it, and piss in my dresser drawers when I'd leave it be. But Marie and Jotta and half the people in the city would kootchy it and koo it and feed the damn thing hamburger.

"I don't want it," I told Marie the day after the real Mr. Hoops first brought it in.

"He didn't bring it for you," she said. "He owes me a lot

17

of money. The dog's collateral. Half a grand."

Fine and good, I understood that. All of which was to say that the hallway between the office and the back room was generally pretty rank, and I tended not to do anything about it until Marie started threatening to put the papers in my bed. The real Mr. Hoops never did return.

I opened the hall door onto our kitchen and was hit right off with the lovely blue-green tint of Marie's white sink. The day before at her house Sharon had taught me thread sculpture, which you could do any number of ways. You could pound nails into wood and connect them with different colors of thread. Or soak thread in paint and drag it over paper. Or let the paint dry on the thread balls and see what shapes they hardened into. Over the course of the day while Marie was in the office, I'd tried them all and used the sink to mix my paint. At Sharon's house it all had been fun somehow. Here everything seemed to turn into mess and trouble.

I put down my hamburger and hunted under the sink for some Comet, but all I could find was ammonia and a bottle of Pine Sol. I threw a lot of each into the sink and started wiping it down with a dishrag. Soon the blue and green started to lift, but then something was stinging the Jesus out of my nose. My hands were burning too, so I dropped the rag and ran cold water full blast onto them.

I looked out over the room, which was like a living room except that I slept there too. It was a disaster area. Wood and paper scattered over the sofa bed, paint cans and thread all over the floor. It looked like so much to do, especially with my hands feeling tender and my head pounding from the smell of it all.

I lay on the sofa bed, waiting for my head to clear, curling my fingers and stretching them slowly out again. I remembered the hamburger I'd left by the sink, realized I hadn't eaten anything since yesterday. The cleaning stuff made me feel strange. Then there was the mess and how mad Marie was going to be. My head wouldn't clear. There was Sharon's mother cooking in her cotton dress and slippers, the two men in the office looking through me at the clock, Jotta not bringing my present for me. It wasn't like her to make a promise and then forget all about it. She used to forget her promises all the time when she was drinking. Now she was always on some kick or other, some group or book or hobby that she thought would turn her life around.

I sat up just to see how it felt. I picked up my guitar from where it was leaning against the arm of the sofa and started to run through all the notes I knew, from the bottom E string up to the fifth fret A on the high E string. Jotta had given me the guitar a few weeks before. She'd gotten it for herself, for her music therapy group, where everyone took home an instrument they didn't know how to play, then reported back once a week on what they learned about life from music. Jotta lasted only a couple of meetings. It all ended the night she'd shown up at the back-room door with the guitar, a bag of peaches, a carton of Camels, and a jug of maple syrup. Her hair was windblown out of its ponytail and stood out straight around her face like the spikes on the Statue of Liberty. Her tan raincoat was buttoned top to bottom and hung straight to her knees. It was her uniform whenever she gained some weight in her belly, which was the only place it ever seemed to go.

She'd thrown the guitar down on my sofa bed and said that no therapy group in the world could do her as much good as a big greasy waffle with peaches and syrup all over it. She dug a lot of stuff out of the back of the kitchen cabinet, and we mixed up some batter and poured it sizzling into the waffle iron. We sat up most of the night, eating and laughing and listening to Jotta tell stories. She told us about her first and last guitar lesson with the seventeen-year-old junkie from Mission Street and about the people in her music therapy group, showing up with their horns and recorders and banjos, playing "Little Brown Jug" like their next sensible move depended on it.

I put the guitar on the floor and stood up. My head was still stinging, pounding. I couldn't stay in the back room and keep breathing in the smell of the cleaning stuff. I went out to the hallway, but the dog smell got to me there. I decided to check out the front office, maybe try to coax Jotta into fessing up about her present.

Marie was at the file cabinet when I opened the office door.

"Where's Jotta?" I said.

"Home. Tom snaps his fingers and Jotta jumps."

"What did Tom want?"

"He called here, which he should know better, from Jotta's apartment, where he's got no business, to say he was sick, which has been common knowledge for years."

"I thought Jotta wasn't married to him anymore."

"For all the goddamn good that does," Marie said. Tom was the only person I knew who could make my Aunt Marie swear.

I pulled myself onto one of the high stools at the counter, craned my neck to see as far down the street as I could.

"She's home, Annie," Marie said. "She wouldn't be lolly-gagging on street corners with Tom waiting."

I put my attention to the pictures under the counter glass, started outlining each one with smudges that disappeared seconds after I lifted my finger. Since the pictures were right up front for anybody to see, I always thought they must have been important moments to Marie, though I couldn't figure out why. There was one of her wearing a stiff blazer and fluffy collar, shaking hands with a bald man in a shirt and tie. Though her mouth hung open like she was retarded and the man's eyes shone like a dog's eyes in headlights, she kept the picture at the counter because the man was mayor once. There were other official-looking photos, pictures Jotta called the Monkey Suit Series. But there was one picture that was different from all the others.

In a yellowing snapshot near the wall, a younger Marie sprawled on somebody's lawn—we didn't even *know* anybody with a lawn, so that was strange enough. She was wearing jeans and a sleeveless shirt that fell off one shoulder so her bra strap showed. I'd never seen Marie in jeans, and I'd never seen her hair grown long like it was in the picture. I'd tried to steal the picture one day, when she'd gone out on errands and locked up the office for half an hour. I'd fixed my eyes on the sidewalk-gray Hall of Justice across the street while I wedged a pencil under the heavy glass, then slithered an index finger toward the picture. Just when I'd touched one corner and was starting to nudge it loose, old man Black Robert passed by and tapped on the glass. I'd torn the corner jerking my hand away. Looking at the picture still made me feel queasy, since I knew the day would come when Marie noticed the tear.

Marie slammed the file drawer. I could tell she was upset and that it had something to do with Jotta and Tom, but I knew she wouldn't explain if I asked her about it.

I hopped off the stool and headed for the back room again. The Tom Cleaver business confused me. Marie and even Jotta would talk like they hated him, but he had bright green eyes and a quick smile. He used to give me rides on his motorcycle, which Jotta always made me swear not to tell Marie. He'd race me up Market to Polk Street, right onto Lombard and down the zigzag block. The first time I was only seven or eight. He pulled up next to me and Jotta on a sidewalk in Chinatown, switched off the engine so he could whisper and coo in her ear. Soon she softened enough to whisper and coo back. Out of nowhere the bike burst into a roar again, without him seeming even to touch it. He patted the seat behind him and told me to hold on tight.

I curled my fingers around two of his belt loops and buried my face in his jacket. It was black and hot with letters and patches sewn on the back, and it smelled like the sheets when Marie hung them out to dry. On the first turn I was dead sure I'd fall. When I didn't, I opened my eyes.

"Look," he yelled, and pointed to a row of chickens hanging by their feet in a storefront window. Then he pointed the other direction, where an enormous bony fish had been cut from gill to tail and stretched inside out on a wooden rack. I rode a long time with him, not even thinking about falling or getting the tangles out of my hair. I couldn't make any sense of it, of

21

Marie's not wanting Jotta to be with Tom. I could see just riding and looking at the things he'd point to, going fast as a rocket for the joy of holding on.

The ammonia and Pine Sol smell still hadn't left the back room. I wanted to take off somewhere, maybe go on over to Jotta's. Marie would raise hell over the mess anyway. I thought I might as well shoot the works and leave by myself without asking. I knew the streets, and it was only seven-thirty, still daylight out. Besides, maybe Marie could shrug it off, but I was going to find out what Jotta had for me.

It was too bright out. The sun was about to set, but glared up from the gravel lot behind the office. I stood there for a minute trying to focus. I headed for Folsom, then cut a couple of blocks out of my way to make sure I wouldn't end up anywhere on Bryant Street where Marie could see me through the glass front of the office. It was exciting to be so bad, to mess up to where I couldn't stand it anymore, then just leave and hit the streets on a real-live mission.

I came out on Bryant at the Sixth Street crossing, walked up Sixth a block to where old man Black Robert worked most of the day, parking cars. Years ago he worked with another guy who was called just Robert, since he wasn't black. Robert was long gone, but Black Robert was still Black Robert, even though there was no one to tell him apart from anymore.

A lot of summers I'd helped the old man at the parking lot by writing down license plate numbers on his yellow lined clipboard, but I hadn't spent much time over there that summer. I almost walked by quick with my head down, just in case he saw me and called to tell Marie I was out. But no, I thought, no point in that. What's the fun in being bad if you just go slinking around?

I stopped in front of the driveway, spotted him sitting on his stool in the back. He was all decked out in his usual overalls and the black leather cap over his white hair. His sweetheart

Gloria was on the stool next to him. Gloria's skin was a shade darker than his, but her hair was just as white. She always seemed to be draped in foreign rugs that she belted around her waist, though she wasn't any smaller there.

They both smiled and got off their stools when they saw me.

"Slow today?" I said.

"Oh, yeah," Black Robert said. "Can't complain."

"Your aunt," Gloria said, "she busy over there?"

"Sure," I said. "She's usually busy with something."

"Earthquake this morning," Black Robert said. "Three-point-five."

"I guess," I said.

"You and your aunt," he said, "you hear anything over there? Would've been quite a rumble if you'd've heard it."

"Didn't notice anything," I said.

He went on talking about the article he'd read about earthquake scientists and whether little quakes helped put off the big one or meant that the big one was that much closer. I didn't understand what Gloria had been doing with him all those years. She lived up in Sacramento, where she was a very big rental car lady. Black Robert had been after her for years to marry him. Her career was still too important to her, she always told Marie.

I finally cut in on Black Robert's earthquake lecture and asked if he'd seen Jotta.

Gloria looked away, watching the cars turn left onto Bryant. Black Robert looked down at me.

"Since when you worrying over Jotta?" he said.

"I don't know, since today," I said. "She came in the office for a while. Tom called and said he was sick. She was going to bring me something today."

"Tom Cleaver? Foolish woman. She ever learn? What you doing out here by yourself anyway? Your Aunt Marie know you're out here by yourself?"

"Yeah, and I got to go," I said, but I felt so funny from all his serious talk that I just stood there and stared at my sneakers.

Gloria put her hand on his shoulder and nodded back toward the office.

"We got something for you," she said. Gloria always had a way of cooling things down, something I loved her for whenever Marie was getting scrappy.

She went inside the glass-walled office and got a grocery sack from off the desk. When she opened it and held it out to me, I probably showed my disappointment. There were cupcakes, dozens of them, all yellow and without any icing.

"Been taking up cooking," Black Robert said.

"They look kind of plain," I said.

"James Beard call them Florentine Pound Cake Delights," he said. "Thought it might be a nice bonus for my all-day customers. So far they haven't much taken to it."

"Some kind with flavor would be better," I said.

He looked down at them and nodded. "Try one," he said.

"I don't really like this kind."

"Well you could take them home for Marie."

"Marie just ate."

"Later she'll be hungry."

I kept looking at the bag.

"There's her customers, too," Gloria said.

The bag was at my chest.

"It's big to carry," I said.

"Just going home, aren't you?" Black Robert said.

I walked the wrong way for a block so they'd think I was going home, then cut back toward Jotta's place. It was getting dark, which made it hard not to think about Marie stomping around the office with her arms crossed over her chest. The sun getting dimmer made my head feel better. I wondered if I looked just then to Black Robert and Gloria like Jotta said I did to strangers at the office. I'd complained to her about people looking through me like I wasn't there. What did I expect, she said, when strangers walk in and see some kid sit back there crosslegged like she shits fruit salad.

I headed toward Folsom on Sixth then under the James Lick Skyway, where big gray towers held up the highway going to the tourist part of the city. The concrete trembled with the weight of the traffic, and a cold wind moved the gravel and the bottles around. A group of men crouched in the dark next to one of the pillars. Two of them jerked around when they heard my feet crunch the gravel, then went back to whatever they were doing there.

On the other side of the underpass I came to a place with its windows painted black like it had been shut down for years. Now the door was open, and there was light shining through cracks in the paint on the windows. Across the street, five or six hookers were scattered up and down the block. None of them seemed to be going anywhere, but they all wore high shoes and bright clothes that fit tight.

The two men in front of me were walking so slow that when I cut around them the breeze I made seemed to knock them together. Both had on boots with tall heels and wore shiny black jackets. When I looked up it was like seeing two people with the same white face, both staring down at my bag of cupcakes. I almost handed it to them.

I walked faster. The next street I hoped would be Folsom but wasn't. Old people, some white and some black, were sitting against the sides of the buildings. The sky was getting dark, and the traffic lights and the bars lit the streets red and yellow.

When I did get to Folsom, I had to slow down. I'd been to Jotta's a hundred times, but it had always been daytime and we'd go in Marie's car. I spotted her place before long, between two other old skinny buildings.

Jotta's third-floor window was open, and the wind was whipping the shade inside. I could look through the glass in the front door and see where the buzzers were, but the door was locked and there was no one around to let me in.

A few feet away two old ladies were sitting on milk crates with their backs against Jotta's building. One was wearing a clean yellow dress and slippers just like Sharon's mother's. They both smiled up at me, then turned back to their radio, which was tuned to the Giants baseball game.

Out of the corner of my eye I saw someone dart from the

sidewalk into the line of parked cars. I turned to see Tom watching me from behind a pickup truck. His hair hung wet around his face, like he'd been running hard. I thought how good he'd look in one of those motorcycle movies or on a billboard advertising hair cream or cigarettes. He smiled, like he knew what I'd been thinking. Then he was gone, heading down the street against traffic.

I backed out to the sidewalk and looked up at the window again. There seemed to be a dim light in there, but I couldn't be sure.

"Jotta!" I yelled up. The sound of my own voice made me jump. It was squeaky and high, and it scared me more than the dark men under the skyway had. The two old women looked up at me again. I stood very still, looking at Jotta's window, and they went back to their baseball game.

Through the glass in the outside door I saw a skinny young guy coming down the stairs. I ran up and started shaking the knob like I'd just found it was locked. He came through the outside door and held it open for me.

"Is Jotta there?" I asked him.

He shrugged, dug a key out of his pocket and let me in the inside door.

None of the floors was marked so I counted while I went up, six flights for three stories. The dusty flowered carpet they'd yanked up still hadn't gotten replaced. The nails, the dirt, the holes in the bare wood looked worse than the old rug had.

I was out of breath when I got up to the third floor. I knew Jotta's door by the bright orange and black bumper sticker from when Marie ran for Assembly. GET THIS WOMAN IN THE HOUSE, it said along the top, then FRAZELLI and 11TH DISTRICT.

The door wasn't pulled quite shut. I knocked a couple of times, then pushed it open. There was stuff all over the floor: a lamp, an end table, ashtrays. Some of it looked broken. Jotta was lying face down on the couch.

"Jotta," I said.

She turned her face toward me. She hadn't been asleep.

"Is Marie with you?" she said.

26

"No."

I could see only half her face, but what I saw was puffy and worse than from drinking. I couldn't turn and go, and I couldn't keep standing there looking down at her.

"What's it like outside?" she said.

"Getting dark, kind of cold."

She nodded. "Dark yet?"

"Getting dark," I said.

I stuffed my sack under one arm and started picking at the bumper sticker on the door. I could hear somebody next door flipping channels on a TV.

"You play your guitar today?" Jotta said.

"My hands kind of hurt."

"What happened?"

"Nothing," I said.

When Jotta first got that guitar, Marie and I had heard her from halfway down the hall, plucking out E, F, G, A, from her Easy Big Note Method book. Now she was lying on her stomach like a kid would, talking to me without even turning over. What is it that happens to people, I wondered, that they can be full grown and always have to keep starting from the beginning like that.

I didn't know what to say. I couldn't remember why I'd come.

"You ever getting those new carpets in the hall?"

"They promised," she said.

She was still facing the floor.

"Want me to get Tom?"

Jotta jerked her head up. "He's here?" she said.

"I saw him in the street."

"Now?"

"A few minutes ago. Now I think he's gone."

She settled back down.

"Is there anything you want me to do?" I said.

"Turn the radio on," she said.

I put down my bag and stepped over the mess to the clock radio across the room.

"What kind of music do you feel like?" I said.

27

"Just put it on."

The first clear thing I got was the Giants game, the rest was mostly static. I turned the dial the other way and got the ballgame again.

"That's fine," Jotta said.

"The Giants?"

"Fine, fine."

I wanted so much to be able to do something, but I didn't feel like I mattered enough. I set the cupcake bag on Jotta's floor and headed down the stairway. The wind was cold now, but the lady in the yellow housedress was still sitting there listening to the radio. Her friend was gone. The Giants game drifted down from Jotta's window, and baseball was all you could hear.

On Sixth Street only one of the hookers was left. She threw her cigarette down when I walked past, and the sparks flew up around my ankles. What was it Jotta had for me, I was left to wonder. The James Lick Skyway rumbled deep and low above me, booming like one of Black Robert's earthquakes. It would be eight years and a different highway before I'd come looking for Jotta again. She'd be in a greater danger by then, Tom still on the streets, and me to blame.

— 1 —

Six weeks I'd been living with Carter, and Marie still called
me up every day. I usually let her go on for a while—that dull,
newsy talk that saved us from getting hot. We usually stayed
on Marie's turf: detailed recaps of this or that arraignment, of
so-and-so's jumping bail. Tonight's topic of choice was the food
for the wedding—Gloria and B.R.'s wedding, the *only* wedding.
Some people would get less excited about a couple in their sixties getting married. Not Marie. It made the vows all the more
meaningful, she said, by their having waited a lifetime to take
them. Tonight I cut in during the finger sandwich controversy
(whole wheat? rye? sourdough?). Carter and I were going out.

"Where out?" she said.

"Oakland. Some bar on Telegraph."

"These divorced men," she said. "Nothing's too elegant."

"Later, Marie." I started to hang up.

"Jotta says hello," she said.

"You talked to her?"

"This morning. Kathy Fitzsimmons called too, said they
missed you at the graduation party."

"Marie," I said, "you didn't give Fitz my number, did you?"

"This time she didn't ask for it."

"Good."

I pulled the cord till the coils were taut, snapped it against the wall.

"What happened to 'I gotta run, we're going out'?" Marie said.

I heard Carter turn the shower off. I knew Marie was using the talk with Jotta to keep me on the phone. Much as I hated to, I took up the bait. "What else did Jotta say?" I said.

"She asked about the wedding plans, how Black Robert was faring. And she asked about you."

"I can just hear what all you told her."

"Well," Marie said, "she said she's glad it's you and not her that's eighteen."

"And?"

"And she likes Massachusetts. And she and Sam are happy." She paused. "And she's sure she's finally free."

"Free of what?"

I heard her sigh. She hated even to say the name, but out of meanness I forced her.

"Tom," she said. "Finally free of Tom."

Carter was saying that his sister called. Sister lived in Ex-wife's apartment complex and called Carter every time Exwife flossed her teeth. I was waiting for a lull in the conversation, so I could bring up the wedding. Dull as it was going to be, if I could talk Carter into going, Marie's attitude toward him might improve from belligerent to hostile.

I could feel the bartender's eyes on me from across the room. I'd chalked-and-penciled my birth date like my ex-best friend Fitz always used to, but it scared the hell out of me to have to hand over a faked license, especially to bartenders as tough-looking as this one. She must have been in her sixties and she was even skinnier than me, but the kind of skinny that people would call stringy, lean. She had her hair in two gray braids that hung almost to her elbows.

"Judy's battery goes dead yesterday," Carter said. "Late afternoon. Around dinnertime Sister sees this triple-A truck out her kitchen window, hears the guy go up the stairs looking for Judy's apartment."

I was glad it was dark. We'd never been in this bar before, but one of Carter's guitar students said it had a great jukebox, so we had to check it out. There was a lot of weird stuff on the walls, stuff that must have been racy years ago. Fat women doing exercises naked. Nixon hitchhiking. But there was a nice rosy glow from the neon beer displays behind the bar and all around the room. There was a flickering Budweiser sign and an Olympia one with a glowing green forest and a golden river through it. "Knowing Sister," I told Carter, "she probably ad-libbed an orgy or two while she was telling about the tow-truck man."

"Knowing Judy," Carter said, "Sister wouldn't have to ad-lib much."

Carter shook down two peanut bags and ripped them both open at once, like he always did with sugar packets. He started cracking the peanuts and pulling them apart, dropping the nuts into one pile, the shells into another.

Carter was about to turn thirty-five. He was acting funny these days, but I figured he'd get around it. The semester before, when Fitz and I first walked into Senior Writing at Gulliver High and saw him standing up there, I'd asked Fitz right off if that wasn't the prettiest beard she'd ever seen. Fitz just shrugged and passed me a stick of Wrigley's. Carter had strapped his guitar on that first day of class, saying that the best way for us to get to know him was for him to play a few of the greats. The first song came to us from Weary Lemon Watson. "I feel my bones is grindin' down," he sang. "I would hop onto a railroad train, but I fear I'd hit the ground."

Two boys about my age peered in the doorway of the bar. It took only one glare from that bartender to send them scurrying.

The next song was by Shotgun Otis, Carter had said, then lifted the guitar to his shoulder, aimed the neck at us and shouted, "Bang!" Fitz flashed me an oh-brother look when I laughed. "I

31

got no true name," he'd sung, "no mama give me birth. Seems like I was hatched from the cold, dark, witherin' earth." I'd grabbed Fitz's elbow. "Motherless child he ramble," he sang, "motherless child he roam. Ain't nothin' here to tie me to this des'late orphan's home."

Fitz pulled her elbow away. "What's with you?" she'd muttered.

"Listen," I'd whispered. "This teacher. He *knows* me."

An old guy about the bartender's age walked in carrying a big square TV box. A woman trailed close behind wearing the same kind of heavy coat, the same close-cropped hair, greasy, like they combed it with buttered toast. The bartender nodded to them, scooped ice into two glasses and set them on one end of the bar. I couldn't just ask Carter to come to the wedding; I had to make sure to handle it right. I was working on a comment about how the old guy reminded me a little of B.R. even though he was white, but then Carter was back to whining about Exwife.

"This morning," Carter said, "Sister decides to go for a run. She goes downstairs. Eight A.M. The tow truck's still there."

The old couple sat down by the glasses and the bartender filled them almost full with scotch, added a spritz of soda.

"*Eight* A.M.," Carter said, slow and even. "A tow truck, rig and all, out there all night for all the world to see."

He looked down at his drink, saying to it more than to me, "Tow-truck drivers. Jesus Christ."

I scooped an ice cube from Carter's drink and stowed it in my cheek. "So your Ex left you and now she's getting rowdy," I said. "You should've seen the dirt Jotta kicked up when she first split on Tom."

"I am no Tom Cleaver," Carter said. "And Judy's sure as hell no Jotta."

"Meaning what?" I said.

He looked back down at his drink.

"Meaning nothing," he said.

I took a long breath and tried to relax about Jotta. Everybody was always so hard on her, just 'cause she'd spent so long with Tom. I missed the way I used to feel around her—like her rules were all different, like *anything* might happen. I was actually glad that it was me who Marie, Gloria, and B.R. were blowing their stacks over these days. It felt good to be taking the heat for Jotta, even if she was three thousand miles away with her house and her husband and her safe new life. I used to like being with Jotta better than just about anything. Even now, every day, something or other would make me think of her.

One day when I was fourteen, I came to Marie with a list entitled "Evidence That Jotta Is My True Biological Mother." She read the title out loud like a newspaper headline, then went to the desk for her glasses and read the rest to herself. I'd outlined three categories: "Physical Evidence," "Facts," and "Personality Etc." The first listed "Hair (limp, thin, etc.), Hands (long fingers, bony), Paleness, Skinniness (Legs and Especially Arms)." In the "Facts" section were the dates of each of our births, Jotta's whereabouts when I was born, and other statistics that put the times and places right. "Personality Etc." had been the hardest to think how to put into words—I almost cut it out. But I decided that there could be one thing that said it all. "Liking Motorcycles" was what I came up with.

Marie read that aloud and hugged me for a long time. Then she unlocked a file drawer and lined the papers up on the desk: my birth certificate, my mother's death certificate, Marie's adoption papers co-signed by Gloria and B.R. No Jotta.

I asked Carter if I could eat one of his peanuts if he was just going to leave them lie. He didn't answer, so I helped myself.

"Your Cheatin' Heart" came on the jukebox, which seemed real pathetic to me.

Carter wrote a song for Exwife once, just a couple of months before when I'd first started taking guitar lessons from him. It was called "You Rub Me the Wrong Way Baby (But That's Better Than No Rubbin' at All)." He'd taught me how to play it, open D tuning, flat-pick style. That was about the time Marie started getting ugly about me not applying to colleges. She'd rant and scream about my SAT scores and my future till I finally told her, "Forget it, Marie. I got a man to think about now."

You'll walk the floor, the way I do, your cheatin' heart will tell on you. That line always made me picture a little heart with its hands on its hips, screaming, "Hey, out there, wait'll I tell you what she did *this* time." I giggled and then felt silly, because I'd just killed three beers and I didn't want Carter to think I couldn't hold my liquor.

The bartender was back to glaring at me. Her hair was drawn so tight around her face it was like those braids had stretched her smile into pure anger, wide and flat. It was like I'd done her some wrong, just by sitting there.

"She don't want me here," I said. It took Carter a minute to register.

"Quit talking like some old blues picker," he finally said. "You know your grammar—what'd you get on that SAT test?" He was shaking a peanut shell at me. "Seven something, wasn't it? High seven hundreds? You didn't used to talk like that."

I turned and stared hard at the bartender, but she wouldn't look away.

"Did you hear what I said to you?" I asked Carter.

"I heard you. Say it right. *Doesn't,* not *don't.*"

"She doesn't want me here."

"That's better," he said. "That's right."

Carter got up to bring us another round. I told him scotch and soda, and he looked at me and looked at my beer mug, then shrugged.

The old couple at the end of the bar still had their coats on. They had a TV set up right in front of them, right in front of their drinks. The box sat empty on the floor by the man's feet.

I could see Carter talking quiet to the bartender. Was he making excuses for me? I didn't want to stare, but her eyes were still on me, I could feel it.

When Carter set our drinks down, I saw that he'd given

up on beer too. His drink looked just like mine only fatter, and when I asked him why, he said it was a double.

"I can use it," he said.

I didn't argue, he'd been acting so quirky. A couple of weeks before, he'd packed off to this so-called seminar. Three days in Big Sur. Totally on the up-and-up, he'd told me. It was run by the Workshops for the Eighties Foundation, and it was called "Teachstyle/Lifestyle." I couldn't believe how he'd pulled into the carport (after having holed up with this Joni Mitchell type from Eureka all weekend, missing almost all of those twenty-buck-an-hour seminars), and I'd run out to meet the car and saw this bumper sticker, with each letter a different color and a rainbow arching over the words. It said MUSIC IS ENTROPY SPELLED BACKWARDS. I'd looked at it, and I'd looked at Carter, and I'd said, "Carter, *entropy* spelled backwards is *yportne*," which was not what I'd imagined my first words to him would be after our first separation.

Scotch didn't taste like I thought it would. It tasted the way nail-polish remover smells.

"So Sister," Carter went on, "she runs for twenty minutes or so. Then she comes around the block of her apartment just in time to see Judy hop into the passenger seat of that rig, and him, the tire monkey, close the door, climb in the other side, and drive them both away out to tire-monkey heaven."

Carter's scotch was two-thirds gone. "That was fast," I said, and when he didn't answer I thought he must not have known what I meant, so I nodded at the glass, but he didn't look up to see. He took his notebook and pen from his back pocket and started jotting something in it—business as usual, he was lost in a new lyric. I was getting used to it, though at first it would hurt me sometimes. We'd be lying around, or cuddling, and I'd be feeling happy and involved in the moment, and out of nowhere he'd break away and dive for the notebook he kept by the bed. I tried to tell Fitz about Carter's writing in notebooks, but she got all irate and said he was stuck-up. I told her I was moving in with him and she could go to hell and never call me either. I'd decided Carter's notebooks didn't bother me, until I started peeking once in a while. Nothing he wrote ever had a single thing to do with me.

"I've been thinking, Carter," I said. "Have you ever thought of taking up running?"

Without raising his head he rolled his eyes way back to see me, which was sort of scary-looking.

"I mean, you're always saying about how old you feel, like you're a hundred or something. Sister's around your age, and you were just saying about how she runs."

I waited, but he didn't answer. He was making me shiver.

"Stop looking at me like that," I said. "It's creepy."

He looked down at his drink.

"Answer me," I said. "I hate it when you don't answer me."

"Sister's different," he said, and I could tell he thought that was the end of it.

"Different how?" I said.

"She's married, for one thing."

"So what?"

"So she's a wife now, that's what. She's a young married woman in a young married apartment on a young married street on a young married planet."

He drained his glass—scotch, water, ice, all of it.

"And you, you're just so different. For some God-knows-why reason you're just Goddamn old."

He stood and looked down at me. For a man who wasn't tall, he seemed high up right then.

"She's just starting a life," he said. "Babies. New toasters. Plans for vacations two years from now. I"—he pointed to his chest—"am a thirty-five-year-old up-and-coming kid-out-of-nowhere musician with a lot of promise. I have fitted this description for"—he closed his eyes, counted—"twenty years now. Giving lessons and teaching high school. Just for the time being."

He blew his nose on a cocktail napkin on his way to the bar.

An old black man in a checkered jacket was yelling from the far end of the counter at the couple with heavy coats. He seemed to want them to turn the TV around so he could see, but they wouldn't look up. I tried to think of how I could use him as an excuse to bring up B.R., and then Gloria, and then the wedding and how it was coming up soon. But something about the night was making me feel like any wedding was a dangerous issue.

Carter was talking to the bartender again and making her laugh, which really got me. For me he was moody, quiet, on the verge of depression half the time, but give him a sicko ax-murderer crazy-lady bartender and he was a regular Steve Martin. I got a big kick out of watching him though, when he wasn't aware of it—it was like being some kind of Peeping Tom except I just wanted to watch him walk around. Like when he was talking to people like this, or teaching, or playing in clubs. But there were other times too, when we were at home and it was dark except for a little glow from a streetlamp. When he'd turn out the light, I could open my eyes and watch him making love to me. I could trace the outline of his shoulders, his neck, the soft hair that curled around his ears, and look into his eyes with the force of everything I felt. And he didn't have to know.

"There's a story I've been wanting to tell you," he said when he got back from the bar. "Because I'm your teacher," he added, and laughed.

Both our glasses were half-empty when he set them on the table. He'd gotten us both doubles this time.

"I got to sipping on your drink too when I was talking to Emily over there," he said. He sat down hard, not quite in the center of his chair.

I started to say, what's this story about, but he shushed me and held his palm up flat like Diana Ross on that old Ed Sullivan film clip. I was sitting there and waiting, but he was caught up now in some song on the jukebox. He wasn't moving or even looking at me, so after a minute I just turned away because it was making me sad.

The beer signs were looking really pretty, glowing red and green and gold.

Budweiser.

Moosehead Ale.

Lone. Flash. Star. Flash.

I couldn't get it out of my head: Diana on the black-and-white screen, Flo and Mary behind, *think it oh-oh-ver*. I thought of looking for the Supremes on the jukebox, but I knew Carter had no use for those kinds of songs.

"That's by Whinin' Reverend Wheeler," Carter said. "Only decent thing on this machine, though they got some white kid singing it."

Carter sang along with the jukebox, "Lord, I got them low-down blues. Save me from them low-down blues."

"You want to know the first time I ever heard that one," he said. "I was just a kid, not much older than you, sitting in this bar somewhere in Wyoming." He tilted his head back. "Was it Wyoming, I don't know. Somewhere Poppa Dad Treehorn took me. But this song was playing on the box, only sung by somebody real. That was some great bar, all these crusty old codgers matching shots, mostly not saying a word. And all along the walls was this long series of portraits some guy had done, had been doing for years, of all the regulars there—railroad men, Indians, bums and the like. These pictures were pretty sketchy, just black line drawings shaded in with something. But somehow every picture told you everything you ever could have needed to know about any one of those guys."

He started cracking peanuts again, one after another, into two piles.

"When any of those guys dies," he said, "his picture gets a gold star. In the bottom corner, on the glass."

He tossed a nut into his mouth for the first time.

"Is that it?" I asked.

"That's all there needs to be," he said without looking at me.

"I mean, is that the story you wanted to tell me?"

He glanced up at me, a look with nothing behind it.

"No," he said.

Goddamn, that old woman had her eye on me again. I let my hair loose from behind my ears—I heard somewhere that made you look older. There was a movie on the TV, somebody in a wide-brim hat driving a Packard around. That old couple was still just the way they were before, except there were eight or ten empty glasses lined up on the man's side and in between the two of them. The black man had gone. The bartender stared at me.

Carter drained his glass, and I could hear him crunching ice. Then he was back up at the bar and I thought, Just look at that old prune Emily lighten up. It was like somebody pulled some strings somewhere and raised her face about an inch. Her eyes seemed to sparkle. She looked almost pretty.

Diana and Mary and Flo had lifted their index fingers, had shook them in warning: *Think it oh-oh-ver.*

Carter leaned heavy on the bar, both forearms flat on the counter. He whispered something. She rested her fingertips on his wrist when she laughed.

There'd been a time when I'd look at people acting like that and wonder, Were they sleeping together, how long had they been lovers, what stage of the game were they in? But lately I'd figured out that I always picked the wrong people. I realized that all around the world, the people who were lovers were the ones at opposite corners of rooms from each other, at parties, at offices. Their eyes were always turned away, their attention put to anything else.

It seemed like no one had come or gone in a long time. Everything felt still and closed in, like there were no doors or windows. The air was smoky, hot, and thick, nothing moved. A new song was playing, but I couldn't hear what it was. It was on just loud enough to be some kind of noise.

The bartender pushed through the swinging gate and walked up next to Carter. They just stood at first, facing each other, then Carter put out his hand and she took it. She rested her other hand on his shoulder, and he slid an arm around her waist.

39

The woman moved Carter in time to the music. She did the steps and he followed, slow and sleepy. She'd seemed a little frail before, but now her body seemed sturdy, powerful. Her eyes were flashing. She was the strongest thing in the world.

Carter set another scotch in front of me. The ice cubes looked soft around their edges.

For some reason that I didn't know, I felt like I wanted to cry.

"Carter," I said.

He had his notebook out again. He'd laid it right on top of the peanuts and shells and he was writing something. I didn't know how much time had passed. The bartender was locking the doors.

"Carter."

He nodded. I leaned over and saw he was drawing pictures: faces, half-moons, clusters of little stars.

"I had a kind of a story to tell too," I said.

He looked up from his notebook.

"It wasn't a story really," I said. "It was more just something I wanted to ask."

Carter looked back down at what he'd been drawing but didn't put the pen to the paper. "Mine was a not-story too," he said. He waited a minute, then tore the paper out of the notebook. "Maybe both our not-stories can wait one more night."

The bartender's key ring jingled as she circled behind us to the back door. The jukebox was off and I could hear her humming.

Carter put down his pen and wrapped his hand around his scotch. The tabletop was crowded, there were beer mugs, a pitcher, a couple of different sizes of cocktail glasses. I could tell his hand was squeezing hard, but the glass was wider than his grip and the fingers didn't meet.

He raised his drink and held it in the air. I lifted mine to join it.

"To us," he said, and clinked my glass.

"To you," I said, and then, "to Teacher."

I wanted to try to empty my scotch though it was more than half-full. I felt the chill inside my throat, my skin, changing to warm as it slid and then to cool again. I slammed down the glass drained, and waited for Carter to congratulate me. But there was a funny look in his eyes, wet and hollow but scared somehow. I guessed that look was whatever it is people get in their eyes when they're drinking.

Carter wouldn't let me drive. He revved the pedal hard for a long time.

"I think the engine's warm," I said.

He didn't answer. He hadn't said a word since our nightcap toast, except to talk old Emily into slipping him another double. I flipped the heater on. Carter started patting all his pockets.

"What you looking for?"

"Keys."

I pointed to the ignition. He nodded to it and turned the key. It clicked like a stick being pulled across a picket fence.

"You know, Carter, there's probably a lovely black-and-white Oakland cop sitting in his black-and-white car right now with his headlights off, just waiting for you to cruise by doing eighty upside down."

He sighed. "You're worse off than me."

"I drank as much, but there's something with you. You always hold it better than this."

He threw the shift in reverse.

"Carter, let me. Please."

He backed out of the lot without looking behind him, cruised ass-first onto Telegraph without a heartbeat of caution.

"That's it," I said. "I guess you think it'd be pretty manly to wrap yourself around an Oakland telephone pole. I got other ideas about how I want to go."

Carter tried to summon a cocky look, but it only made him look queasy.

"Meaning?" he tried to say, but it came out "Neaming."

"Neaming go to hell." I slammed the door behind me. Carter lowered his head to look at me through the passenger window. I waited for him to throw open the door or to motion me back inside. But he just peered out like somebody looking from the window of a train.

– 2 –

I was surprised when Gloria decided to have the wedding in the city.

"She's going to bus the whole thing down from Sacramento?"

"She knows half of San Francisco," Marie said. "Besides, Black Robert's not getting around so well."

"Jesus, Marie. Why won't you call him B.R. like everybody else?"

"Because it makes him sound like a soft drink."

Gloria was due in town at 5:00. B.R. asked me and Marie to come over at 2:00 to help him get his place in order. Marie had got me up at 8:00 A.M. to go wedding-present shopping.

"Be a sport," she'd said.

We'd sat in the mall lot for fifteen minutes waiting for the stores to open. Marie kept the engine running so she could blast the heater. The exhaust fumes hugged the car, like they weren't ballsy enough to merge with the San Francisco fog.

"You can't pout over him forever," Marie said.

"I'm not pouting. Somebody got me up at dawn."

Truth was, I had enough pout to last me till Alzheimer's set in. Carter had gone to Wyoming. Wyoming. It was ten days since we'd got drunk in the place with the jukebox where he'd danced with the bartender. Nine since he'd staggered home from his night in the Alameda County slammer. Five since his DUI hearing. Four since he'd left for Poppa Dad Treehorn's place in Homer. I'd had to move back to Frazelli's Bail Bond.

"I'm sweating," I told Marie.

"So take off the Arctic overcoat."

"It's *leather*."

Marie gripped the steering wheel like she was revving a motorcycle. "Varooom," she said.

Things continued downhill when the place opened. Ocean-side Mall was like a fun house without the fun. Blue-white light and plastic rubber plants that seemed somehow to be laughing at you. The stale, dry air made my eyes water. There was a car parked in the middle of everything, gleaming red and silver on the slug-yellow tile.

Marie cut left into the first store, Fant-Asia. A thin middle-aged woman with her glasses hung around her neck was raising the chain-mesh curtain. Marie ducked under it and started poking around an aisle of fake Chinese vases. I loitered in the lobby, trying to look uninvolved.

"Annie," Marie called, trying to whisper.

I pointed to a bookstore and waved bye. I thought maybe I'd get a paper—I hadn't checked the horoscopes yet for the day.

"Annie," she said, no whisper about it.

In the next three hours we investigated every store except the Rare Stamp Mart and Family Pet. Appliances. Rugs. German beer steins. Furniture—too impersonal. Nightgowns—too intimate.

"Don't you stop worrying about intimate when you're sixty-something?" I said.

"Lighten up," Marie said. "This is fun."

Around noon she started to linger around the sports department at Sears. I stood my ground in the main aisle, lunch as my ultimatum.

We got the last booth along the wall in the pink and orange coffee shop. I wanted a beer more than lunch. Our waitress was a bouncy blonde with a name tag that said "Kathi." In the time it took her to leave the menus, drop off two waters, take the order, and bring the coffee, neither Marie nor I said a word to each other.

I pulled two sugar packets from the wire basket by the salt and pepper. I shook them down and ripped them both open at once, Carter style. Marie watched me like she saw his hand in it.

"To what do I owe this delightful mood?" she said. "Off in Wyoming?"

"Me?" I said. "Just tired."

"Sorry to hear it. Two-hundred-dollar mattress. You think you'd sleep like a bear."

I shut my eyes. "Marie," I said. "Please let's not get on that."

"Get on nothing. It was a simple statement."

I spooned some ice from the water glass into my coffee.

"It's just that it surprises me," she said. "Not sleeping. What with the bed, the quiet, the privacy."

"Here we go," I said.

" 'Here we go.' The world does not exist to persecute you."

Lately I'd wondered. Carter gone, me in exile—the back room of the back room. I thought of the day a year ago, walking into the office after spending a month with Jotta and Sam in Santa Barbara. Marie was behind her desk, beaming.

"Hey, stranger," she'd said.

The first thing she did was show me my goddamn SAT scores. Second, she led me to the back room and pointed to the outside door. I opened it, but it didn't go outside anymore. It led to a square, dark room with a twin bed, and bookshelf, a chair, and a desk. Third, she said: "Welcome home."

It took B.R. a few minutes to answer the bell. His steps were loud and heavy coming down the stairs. He kissed us both.

"Bless your hearts," he said.

"Mine could use some blessing," I said.

Marie and B.R. looked up at me.

"I feel a sudden urge to advertise frozen peas," I said.

"You're not such a giant," B.R. said. "Marie and I are midgets. You shrink after fifty, right, Marie?" He nudged her with his elbow.

"I have not yet begun to shrink," Marie said. Could she have been fifty? She sure didn't look it. B.R. did, and then some. But he looked good. He had on heavy black pants and a red lumberjack shirt—first time I'd seen him in something besides his old overalls. When Gloria finally agreed to marry him, he'd made a few changes. Turned the gravel lot behind his house into a vegetable garden. And gave up meat. And he told me gently one day: "Let's think of something besides Black Robert for you to call me."

B.R. motioned us up the stairs. His place had always had a musty smell. He had rugs from everywhere—India, France, Spain. The new rug on the stairs was from Pakistan, he said. Marie always claimed he'd saved up and traveled to a lot of those places.

We must have waited five minutes for him to get up the stairs. Marie and I avoided looking at each other.

He stood at the top step and puffed. "I got cinnamon buns," he said.

"We had a huge lunch," Marie said.

"Just made—no mix."

"Got a beer on you?" I said. Marie didn't even shoot me a look, she was that mad already.

"Beer," he said. "No beer. I got other things, I never look."

"We may as well get right to the cleaning," Marie said, but B.R. and I were in the kitchen by then. His joints cracked as he bent down to a cabinet under the drainboard. He started pulling out bottles and lining them up on the floor. A squat brown one you couldn't see through. A tall square one with clear liquid and a label in Italian. He pulled out five or six more with foreign labels. They all needed dusting.

He stopped and scanned the row. "Now this one's Greek," he said. "It's like licorice." He unscrewed the cap off the first bottle in line and sniffed it. "Yep. This one first. You too, Marie."

"I'll pass," she said.

He smiled. "Special occasion."

Marie tried to smile back.

B.R. took three pony glasses from the cupboard. He blew at the dust, frowned, then took them over to the sink.

"Sit," he said.

I sat at the kitchen table. Marie stood with her arms crossed. B.R. dried the glasses and set them on the table. They looked like crystal, with delicate stems. B.R. pulled out a chair for Marie. She looked at it but didn't budge.

"Man can't sit down in front of a lady," he said, "unless she's sitting too."

She had to give in to that. B.R. lifted a *Chronicle* from the stack on the fridge and spread a section out flat on the table. His joints crunched again as he moved the bottles slowly from the floor to the center of the newspaper. Then he sat down between me and Marie with a brimming glass of water. I looked at all the gleaming liquids and colored glass. The bottles were dusty, but the liquor looked clean. I tried not to notice Marie glaring at me through the two tallest bottles.

"Ouzo first," B.R. said. "Just a taste."

It looked like water, and I threw it back in a mouthful. I thought how licorice is not my favorite thing. Then a ball of fire rolled down my throat. I glowed, it felt like.

"Easy there," B.R. said. "Sip."

"Sorry." I took a drink of the water.

Marie's ouzo hardly went down after she put it to her lips. "Sweet," she said, and pushed it away.

"Don't like it? That was Greek. Italy next." He poured the rest of Marie's drink back in the bottle and capped it. He slid the water in front of her.

"Now clear the palate," he said. He knocked off his own ouzo and took the water when Marie finished.

The second bottle was tall and green and didn't have a label.

47

"This was made by a friend," he said. He uncorked it and poured. It was so purple it was almost black.

"Hey," I said, "we never made a toast." I lifted my glass and suddenly thought of Carter. The longing shot through me like the clock-alarm buzzer at 5:00 A.M.

"Well, right you are," B.R. said. He paused a minute, looking at Marie. "You make the toast," he said.

I wasn't sure what exactly she'd been up to all this time, since my view of her was blocked by the bottles. From the tilt of her head she might have been looking through them at my drink.

"Go ahead, Marie," I said.

She raised her glass to B.R. "To the beautiful bride and happy groom." They touched glasses, then turned to me.

"And to Annie's coming home," she said.

"Heah, heah," B.R. said.

I held my glass steady as each of theirs clinked against it.

Our next two drinks were gumdrop colors, orange and lollipop green.

"Takes me back to our Kool-Aid days," B.R. said to me. "You remember the pitcher I kept in the office?" He stopped like he had to catch his breath. Marie was trying to look like she didn't hate my guts.

"To the Kool-Aid days," I said, and clinked glasses with B.R. I wanted every toast to put me one clink closer to Carter. So far each one only made me feel farther away from that table.

"It would take her a half hour sometimes to get a pitcherful out of that spigot. Think it was maple syrup, water came out that cooler so slow, and Annie, she'd stop every couple minutes and change thumbs."

"Which explains the lean and muscular tone of the thumbs you see before you." I made my thumbs strut between the bottles and around the table, hissed crowd noises, bowed my thumbs graciously. Marie was glaring hard at me through narrowed eyes.

"You're drunk," I said to her.

48

"You're an idiot," she said.

"Did you hear that?" I said to my thumbs. They stood upright and gasped.

Nobody made a sound. I didn't think B.R. heard a word I'd said.

"Six years old," he said to Marie. He smiled. "Annie came to the lot one day, six years old, and she said to me, 'I can speak Spanish, Black Robert.' So I said, 'That so?' Annie pointed to a car and said, 'Wheelo.' 'Hmmm,' I said. 'But how do you say this?' and I held up my hand. 'Hando,' she said." Much as I wanted to, I couldn't make myself smile. "Then I pointed out the garage and straight up to the sky. You thought a little longer about that one." He looked at Marie. "Then her eyes lit up. 'Smoggo!' she said." He threw back his head and laughed.

"Quite the little scamp, eh, Marie?" I said.

"Como es lista, esta muchacha," B.R. said.

"Took the words right out of my mouth," I said.

B.R. was rotating the bottles so he could read the labels. Marie had her watch off and was shaking it next to her ear. I raised my glass.

"To smoggo," I said. I downed what little of my green stuff was left. The roof of my mouth ached from all the sugar.

"Time for something special," B.R. said. He cradled one of the bottles in his hands. "Nineteen sixty-seven," he said. "Comet wine."

"We going to drink the stuff or scrub the sink with it?" I said.

"Scrub the sink with you," Marie said. But the sting had gone out of her voice.

"Eighteen eleven," B.R. said. "Big comet that year. And everybody's wine turned out to be the best any of them ever drunk. Comet wines, they call them now."

"And this one's 1967," I said. I took the bottle. "Some big-deal comet that year?"

"Can't think of no bigger ball of fire," he said. Marie cracked a smile. It was the year I was born.

B.R. uncorked the wine and filled our little glasses but forgot to make us sip the water. We all drained our glasses in one swallow. B.R. sat back with his eyes shut. When he opened them, he was looking right at me. Marie was beaming.

"Funny, tastes like wine," I said. But maybe there was something to it. All I wanted was to rise up through the roof, the clouds, and the San Francisco fog and soar above the earth with all its families and houses.

B.R. slowly got out of his chair. He pulled three water tumblers from the cupboard and set them on the table.

"Enough of this tasting," he said. "Comet wine it is."

Marie scooted her chair back and stood up. "Time to get to our straightening."

"You're plenty straight already, Marie," I said.

She almost said something, then turned and left the kitchen. She seemed a little wobbly. I wondered if she felt queasy too, and how much more crap she was going to take from me.

I nodded at the wine. B.R. smiled and poured me a glassful. "Mersee," I said.

He filled his own glass with the same flair, only dripped a few spots of wine onto the newspaper.

"Hey, is that the *Chron*?" I said.

"Only choice in this fool city."

"Today's?" I started to scoot it out from under the bottles.

"Don't believe so. Look up on top the Frigidaire."

The comics page was second to the top. I took it back to the table with me and folded it open to the horoscopes.

"What a smart girl like you reading those things for?"

"Jotta started me on it," I said. "She sent me an astrology book that the man who loves her wrote. Sam knows a lot about the stars."

"That so?" He frowned. "So now she's got you on to the stars."

"Natural stomping grounds for a comet," I said to make him smile. He did. We toasted the stars, and I downed another gulp. Heat was rising from my face and neck. I thought how I could tell B.R. anything.

"So, Miss Annie Asteroid." He slid the newspaper toward

him. "What form of nonsense did the stars shape into when your mama bore you into this world?"

My mama. How could he say something like that without even wanting to be mean?

"I don't look at mine," I said. "I check two for Carter. He wouldn't ever tell me his birthday. I got a peek at his license once, but I was pretty drunk. It was July third or August third, Cancer or Leo. Might help me get a fix on how things'll be up there."

B.R. stood and looked down at me hard. He pulled the bottle toward him, poured his wine back in and corked it.

"You're not having any more?"

He shook his head. It hit me then how much I'd let on.

"You're making me sad," I said.

He looked at my glass. "Maybe one last sip," he said. "For *départ*."

"Day paw?"

"Like in France, in the war," he said. "The final taste of the wine on the palate."

I was drying the glasses when I heard three long bleats of a horn outside. Could we have been drinking that cough-syrup booze for three hours? B.R. had barely left for shut-eye.

Marie screamed in the living room. I dropped my dish towel and ran in, just in time to see Marie's ass framed in the front window, anchoring her inside. She was waving and blowing kisses to a double-parked Lincoln.

"Jesus, Marie. She's not even registered to vote in your district."

Marie waved her arms out the window, then ran downstairs. I was starting to feel bad about mouthing off so much. I knew that being mean to Marie wasn't helping, was probably making things worse. But it came from wanting to push her away—Marie and everything about the world that made me feel like I didn't belong.

I did a quick check of B.R.'s place, which he'd said he

hadn't tidied at all. I opened the door to the room where Gloria would be staying. The bed was made up tight, with a Mexican blanket folded at the foot. The dresser drawers were empty. Not a speck of dust on anything. The wood floor gleamed.

I sat on a chair with needlepoint cushions. Three forty-five by the clock on the dresser. So she was early. Sleepiness was taking me over like a flu. I felt like crawling into that perfect little bed. But Gloria was in the front room calling "Bobby," and it was time to go out there and play tickled-pink-to-see-ya.

There was something about Gloria's face. How long had it been since the first time? I'd just started nursery school. I wasn't allowed to leave school by myself, and it was B.R.'s day to take me home on the bus. Three-thirty, nobody there. I'd sat on the concrete steps by the front office and watched all my friends walk home in twos and threes. It was after four when Jotta pulled up in a shiny white convertible. Her hair made me think of cartoon cats when they got their tails stuck in light sockets.

"Hey, Annie!" Jotta had called. "Check out my new wheels."

I'd walked up but kept my distance. Not even a back seat.

"Where's Black Robert?" I said.

"Gloria came down from Sacramento. She's a rental car lady. Hop in and we'll cruise Van Ness."

I'd looked down at the plastic red interior, the dials, the leather steering wheel no bigger than a dinner plate.

"It looks like a toy," I said.

"It is. Get in."

The wheels screeched, and we sped into traffic. I looked around to make sure nobody I knew was around to see.

"How come Black Robert didn't come?"

"I told you, honey, Gloria's here. She's his lady, you know. Like family."

I'd held my hair down with both hands and squinted against the wind. Jotta lit up a cigarette and turned the radio on loud. I could hear her singing when we stopped at red lights.

We parked in the lot under the skyway. Jotta flashed the parking man a smile and tipped him a buck. We walked slow to the office while she combed the rats out of her hair.

Gloria had been sitting in my chair when we got back to the office, and B.R. and Marie had pulled chairs up next to her. They let out a laugh when we walked in, then covered their mouths with their hands to cut the laughing short.

"Where'm I sending the tow truck to?" Gloria said.

Everybody laughed but Jotta. She rested her hand on my shoulder in a way that made me want her to know I wasn't laughing along.

"Depends on what you want towed," Jotta said, looking meaningfully at B.R. "If it's your car you want, try Sixth and Bryant."

"Parked!" Gloria said. "Such organization!"

I knew Gloria was teasing Jotta in a way Jotta didn't like. But I didn't understand what was underneath the teasing, or that it had mostly to do with the way Jotta had been living her life. It seemed important only that I not laugh along and that Jotta saw. She'd said Gloria was the family lady. That meant she was different from us.

Looking at her now in B.R.'s living room, I remembered what struck me most about Gloria that day when I was four. Gloria's eyes seemed farther apart than any pair of eyes I'd ever seen. I used to wonder if she could see more to either side of her than other people.

Gloria was wearing an Indian print skirt and a rough wool poncho she'd gathered around her thick middle, under her plump breasts. She matched B.R.'s foreign rugs and delicate furniture.

"Gloria," I said, "you're looking just the same."

She looked me up and down. "You're looking like trouble." She laughed and hugged me.

"You smell like the inside of a new car," I said.

"Next year's Lincoln. We just got a fleet."

Marie reached the top of the stairs and dropped two suit-cases in the middle of the room, pretending not to be out of breath.

"You got her well trained," Gloria said to me.

"Guests aren't allowed to work," Marie said. "Especially not brides-to-be." She heaved a breath, picked up the bags again and headed toward Gloria's room.

"So Bobby's hiding from me?"

"I'll get him," Marie yelled from the hallway.

Gloria dropped into a chair and kicked off her shoes. She let out a sigh.

"Long drive," I said.

"Not in one of those things. Like flying a magic carpet." She sat back and started rubbing the bottom of one foot against the top of the other. The chafe of nylon against nylon sounded like the crickets behind the back room at night.

"Jotta still in Massachusetts?" she said.

"From what I hear," I said. "Tom's out on parole, so we try not to talk about her around the office."

"Marie says she's got herself a gentleman," she said. "One who doesn't have a fist where his heart s'posed to be."

"Oh, Sam's just dandy," I said. "They both are. Blissful and cozy and boring and married."

Gloria kept nodding. "There's worse things." She crossed her arms in front of her and closed her eyes, calm as a Buddha. The calmer she looked, the more I fidgeted. Where the hell were B.R. and Marie?

"Hey, Marie," I called. "We got a guest here. Bring out the dancing boys."

"Relax, kid," Gloria said. "I'm an old person."

"You're no more an old person than the day I met you."

"Ha! Was that a day! Remember the first time you saw me? Remember what you did?"

"Started bawling," I remembered in a flash.

"Burst into sobs and ran out the office."

I couldn't think what happened after that.

"You know what you said?" Gloria asked.

I could remember the weight of blankets, ninety degrees out, and sweat seeping into my clothes. Marie had burst in the back room and pulled the covers down, looking worried and mad all at once. I remembered her saying "What's the matter?" over and over.

"No," I told Gloria. "Tell me what I said."

" 'She's the family lady, from the family office. She's come to drive me away because I don't have one.' "

B.R. looked bleary but happy as he ran to hug Gloria. There was a crease on his face from how he'd been sleeping on the pillow. "Glory," he said, over and over.

Gloria stood and B.R. hugged her with everything in him. They rocked back and forth, holding each other. I looked at my sneakers, my fingernails, the snaps on my jacket. She was still the family lady somehow, with a man who'd loved her for half of his life.

"I think we should leave them alone," I said to Marie.

B.R. was still holding Gloria when he called out, "Please, Annie, stay."

Closing the door behind me, I said out loud, "I'll stay through the wedding. But I'm already gone."

By wedding day I'd packed most of my things without Marie noticing. I'd gotten out of all the prewedding hoopla by faking a stomach flu. Marie went off to a bridal shower one night, a party for B.R. the next. Soon as she'd pull out the back lot, I'd climb out of bed and slide my backpack from under it. I had to be careful not to knock around too much, or fat old Buddy who worked in the office nights would come running back to check up on me. Hang on, I told myself. Soon my bedroom would be nobody's business.

Wedding morning I got up at eight and ironed my fanciest

dress. It was white with purple trim around the waist and sleeves, made of some kind of shiny polyester that's supposed to look like silk. Marie had bought it for me two months before, suspiciously close to senior prom time. I wasn't about to go to any silly dance with any of the boys at school. I'd thought once, just for a second, about asking Carter. The theme was "Love Under the Stars." The prom committee had hung glitter-speckled cardboard stars from the gym roof and stuck cotton on the tables to look like clouds. I'd imagined sitting around one of those tables with Fitz and her skinny boyfriend Topher, the fencer (swords, not radios). "Isn't this the cleverest theme?" I could hear Fitz asking Carter. I could see him leaning back in a folding chair, slinging one of his boots right up onto the fluffy table, rattling the glasses. He'd get a faraway look in his eye and start into singing just like Moldy Leroy Green: "Some folks say them stars're shinin' bright; you can lower my coffin by the pale moonlight." I didn't think long about asking Carter to the prom.

I threw the dress over my shoulder and stepped in front of Marie's full-length mirror. I looked a long time at myself in my bra and underwear, then took them off and looked a long time more. I closed my eyes and touched my fingertips to my cheeks, my nose, my mouth. Carter's making love was nothing like the boys at school kissing; his heat was more necessity than happiness. What did he *feel* on top of me? I touched the skin where it pulled tight between my hipbones, curving in, not out like a woman was supposed to. Did he love it because it was rough and hard, because he could bruise himself rocking my hips against his? I slipped on the dress and tied the sash, then loosened it so the dress would fall without clinging.

I reached to the back of my sweater drawer and took out the makeup kit Jotta gave me when I turned sixteen. Jesus, but had I felt silly unsnapping the oval plastic case in front of Marie, Jotta, and B.R. It looked like watercolors inside, with a little brush, a couple of tubes, and a tiny pencil sharpener. I'd felt myself blushing and said, "Give me a break, Jotta." She'd looked hurt for a second. "About time you thought about looking like a woman," she'd said.

I dipped in the patch of purple with the brush and drew a stripe across one eyelid. I blinked a couple of times, which stamped a matching stripe under my eyebrow.

"Two minutes, Annie," Marie called through the door.

The tip of the brush skipped into my eye. "Go ahead, Marie. I'll take my car."

"You don't know where to go."

"B.R. told me."

I could feel her outside my door.

"I'll be there, Marie."

It was fifteen minutes before I heard her tires crunch the gravel. I pulled the backpack out from under my bed to make one last check of my packing job. Marie was probably sure I wouldn't show. I wondered why I hadn't even considered not going.

I reached under the sweaters in the main pocket, tapped the liter of Jack Black I was bringing for Carter. My twenties were still snugly bundled in the hidden zipper pocket, but I pulled them out and counted them one more time. The day before, I'd raided the savings bank where Marie had been depositing my Social Security checks for college. It had taken me over an hour to find the bankbook. I told Buddy I was looking for a prescription. He'd just sat smiling at the front counter in his V-neck undershirt, leaning back on the stool to balance his basketball belly. I slipped the book in my pocket and rushed to the back room to open it. Twenty-one hundred something. I'd expected three times that. Marie couldn't have spent that much on my expenses. I'd earned my own money for my Mustang doing housecleaning for one of Marie's newly divorced lawyer friends. It didn't cost so much to feed me. Two grand was lots more than I'd need to get to Wyoming, and I'd bagged college. But those checks were my only reward for not living like normal people.

The rest of my pack was stuffed with my favorite clothes for every weather condition: two pullovers, five T-shirts, a bathing suit, a slicker. Didn't have to pack my fanciest dress. I pictured myself rolling into Homer in white and purple satin with my eyelids blue. Carter would be standing at the front door, waiting for me with Poppa Dad and all his bluegrass buddies. When I pulled up to park, they'd all see me and whistle. Carter would walk up slow and proud to open the door for me. I'd be nervous because of him not having seen me in a dress before. But he'd be beaming and he'd hold out his arm. My hips'll have rounded out to fill the bucket seat, and in place of my double-A's, two blushing cantaloupes will have bloomed, just from beer guzzling and worry.

Cruising for a space near the church B.R. had picked for the wedding, I recognized every illegally parked car between Fell and Oak. I'd learned on excursions with Marie and her undercover cop friends why they never get ticketed: the two-way hand-mike slung over the rearview mirror was a secret cue to meter maids that the driver was on a hot case, usually lunch or a Macy's white sale. Conbo Bock's El Camino was double-parked in a loading zone. Merrilee Howard's Lincoln Continental stretched the length of the handicap zone and half again. Cab Paxton's BMW blocked one of the driveways to a Chevron station. Fred Booth's Volvo straddled a crosswalk. Joe Edelstein's Honda was the only vehicle with no hand-mike dangling. He'd tucked himself neatly and legally between a flatbed and a van. The needle on the parking meter pointed all the way to sixty minutes.

Twenty minutes of searching put me nine blocks from Pilgrim Baptist. I crossed Divisadero while the wind whipped out the wave I'd put in my hair with Marie's curling iron. At Fell Street where the church was supposed to be, I looked up into the wind to read the twenty-foot theater marquee with foot-high red letters: PILGRIMS GLORIA AND ROBERT AT JOURNEYS END TODAY PRAISE GOD. A fresh-painted ticket booth rose up from the shiny black and white tiles that ran from the sidewalk to the glass front doors.

I was combing my waveless hair in the reflection of an empty poster case when Fred Booth snagged me by the arm, champagne already in hand. Marie called him Fred the Red, for his rosy pink nose and the curly red locks he was always brushing out of his eyes. He was also the kingpin pinko in the public defenders' office.

"Have you *seen* her?" he said.

"My elbow," I said.

He let go, only to grip my shoulder just as hard.

"Has she put on her gown?" he said. "Have you seen her, Annie?"

I pulled my shoulder away. A wave of champagne sloshed onto my shoe.

"I just got here," I said.

He gazed sadly at my wet toes and sandal straps.

"Forget about it," I said.

He turned away sheepishly and slunk back inside. I made a guess about why Fred's nose always glowed. I leaned closer to the poster case to take a final stab at centering my part. The blast of a loud siren not ten feet from my eardrums almost sent me through the glass.

"Tom Cleaver," I screamed.

Tom used to like to sneak up behind Jotta and sound that thing to spook her. Marie said he wouldn't get his comeuppance till the day they blared the siren on the paddy wagon dragging him off for good.

When I turned around, Tom was perched on his bike, almost out of sight behind the ticket booth.

"That damn siren of yours has got to be illegal," I said.

"Out of the mouths of babes flow penal code abstracts."

We were quiet for a minute. "If you got something to say," I said, "come around where I can see you."

"And dirty this lovely tile?"

From my view of the grease on his front tire, I didn't feel inclined to argue. I was just about to dash inside when he wheeled himself between me and the entrance. I was surprised to see him clean-shaven. The beard couldn't have been long gone—

59

his cheeks and forehead were brown, but his chin was gray as the sidewalk. He'd cut his hair so short you could see the scalp. I figured he was well into his forties by then, but the skin on his face seemed to get only tighter, tougher. There were other men in town who were known for the stories about them— brutal stories, savage and cruel. There were plenty of people afraid of Tom, but his was a different kind of power. There was nothing like it.

"You look like hell," I said.

He twisted on his seat and pointed to the letters stitched on the back of his jacket.

"Naturally," he said, and smiled.

I peered in to see if I could get someone's attention if I needed to. Everybody must have been behind the second set of doors.

"Your friends getting married or catching a matinee?" he said.

"It's converted," I said.

He laughed and pointed up to the marquee. "Like the real Pilgrims," he said.

"I guess." I shrugged.

I craned my neck again to see if I could catch someone's eye.

"You need somebody?" Tom said.

I looked down at the tiles.

"Hey, Orphan Annie, it's only me," he said. "I've known you since you were a kitten. I just had to stop, seeing you look so pretty, all dressed up in silk with your hair washed and curled." He smiled. He always did have a way of smiling.

"I don't know anything about Jotta," I said.

"There's nothing you don't know about Jotta. And there's nothing I don't know about you."

"That so?" I said.

"Try me."

"I'll pass. Got a wedding to tend to."

He bowed slow to me, like a cartoon Chinaman. Then the roar of his engine exploded from out of nowhere, so loud it

60

seemed to make the walls swell away from us.

"How come you can always turn that thing on like magic?" I yelled above the revving.

He was smiling when he zipped between me and the ticket booth, off down Divisadero. The tiles still gleamed.

Walking into the church, I was almost mowed down between the entrance and the second set of doors. A yard-high blue-and-white kid-shaped blur disappeared behind the deserted candy counter.

"Troy Bock," I said. "Hot diggety dog."

A blond head peered from around the display case, then pulled back and let loose a volley of giggles and squeals. I took it as inspiration to duck inside.

There were a lot more people than I expected, and not a single one of them was sitting down. The church felt even more like a theater inside than it had in the lobby. The decor was what Marie called Art Yucko: gold pillars along the far walls, a red carpet down the center aisle, a ceiling that rose so high you could hardly make out the gold-speckled stars painted on it. The floor slanted down to a waist-high stage where an altar had been draped with a purple velvet cloth. I was looking around stunned when Merrilee Howard set upon me.

"Isn't it enchanting, Annie?"

"You said it. Where's the curtain the wizard stands behind?"

She laughed so hard I knew for sure she didn't get it. I wondered if they had a class in that at Hastings.

"That's a nice dress," I said. "Or I guess you'd call it a suit."

"I would. Thank you." She reached up to straighten the perfect bow on the string tie around her high-neck collar. She paused and dropped her hands at her sides, like she knew it was perfect without even seeing it. It made me want to run and check the part in my hair again. It's useless, I thought. What

61

the devil could this woman and I have to say to each other?

"How do you know Gloria?" I said.

She laughed just like before. "It was my first associateship in Sacramento. So that would be"—she cocked her head—"five years ago, practically on the button."

She smiled and thrust her finger at me on "button," like someone in a Shirley Temple movie. When I didn't burst into tap dancing, she cut the pixie delivery.

"One of the senior partners wanted to impress some VIP, so he sent me to his old friend Gloria for something dignified to chauffeur him in. 'It's for Mr. Colin Flaherty,' I said to her, leaning on the 'Flaherty' so she'd know it was serious business. She looked at me, I looked at her—it was as if we were saying to each other, 'These are very important men we're talking about.'"

"I bet she's a sharp cookie that way." I was scanning the black faces for B.R., the white for Marie. Merrilee let out that laugh again.

"Gloria sent over this . . . machine, I don't know where she got it. It looked as if something had stepped on it. It had quadraphonic speakers in it, Annie, and flames painted on the sides. I said to myself, 'Merrilee Howard, there goes your career.'"

I thought I saw Marie across the room, leaning against a pillar.

"I'd known this man for a year, I'd never once seen him crack a smile. The day that car was delivered, he spent the whole morning giggling to himself. He and the VIP drove it to Las Vegas."

Cab Paxton was tiptoeing up behind Merrilee, shushing me with his finger over his mouth. The lapels on his white tuxedo seemed to sparkle like the ceiling. I wished I could ask him the secret to the fashion-model wave in his hair. He clapped his hands over Merrilee's eyes. She let out a string of shrieks that put Troy Bock's to shame.

"Merrily, merrily, merrily, merrily, life is but a dream," he sang into her ear.

"Cab Paxton," she said. "Your lack of imagination gave you away."

He jerked his hands back. "Virulence, thy name is woman."

"Cabot Paxton Shakespeare?"

" 'Twas he who stole it from me."

"And misquoted you to boot."

I muttered "Excuse me" and scooted off. I thought how Marie was so hot on getting me overeducated. You lock yourself up with books and papers for the best years of your life. You come out middle-aged and horny, but boy can you talk cute at cocktail parties. I knew these people, I'd grown up watching them trot across Bryant Street from the Hall of Justice to the office. They were good people; they deserved to be happy, and I deserved to leave them.

Hold on Carter, I thought. I'm closer to Wyoming than you know.

While I was wading through the crowd, I felt a tap on my shoulder. It was sad-eyed Conbo Bock, in a rumpled brown suit with a fancy camera around his neck. I cut him off before he could even ask.

"He was last seen in the vicinity of the candy counter," I said, "whooping like a porpoise."

He flashed his too-grateful smile. "Oh thank you, Annie. Troy is so fond of you."

"Kid's got spunk," I said, and Conbo skittered off as only a neurotic single father could.

Marie wasn't leaning against the pillar anymore. I headed toward Fred the Red to ask if he'd seen her. That's when I saw the food. Everything on that table was made to resemble something else—watermelons shaped like baskets, sandwiches cut like stars, pineapples carved to look like women's heads. Fred was helping himself to another glass of bubbly.

"I thought receptions were for eating and weddings were for crying," I said.

His expression turned sheepish when he saw it was me. "How's your shoe?" he said.

"Champagne's good for shoes," I said. "Helps the leather breathe."

He nodded slowly. "Did you get champagne?" he said.

I thought of the eight or so hours of driving ahead of me. "That's okay," I said.

I spotted Joe Edelstein to my right, loading starwiches on a saucer-size paper plate. Marie always called him Flintstone, probably because he was plump and his ties always looked too short.

"Joe Edelstein," I said. "How's that little baby I been hearing so much about?"

"Annie!" he said. He fussed till he found an empty spot on the table to rest his plate, took my hand and shook it like a congressman. He squeezed hard, but his hand was warm and soft.

"So nice to see you here," he said, pumping my hand all the while.

"The baby's put on weight?"

"Six ounces the past two weeks. She's up to seven and two—pounds and ounces, that is."

"That's great," I said. "So there's nothing to worry about anymore."

His face was white, and he looked tired. I wondered why he didn't answer.

"I mean, she's healthy now, right?" I said.

"I don't know, Annie," he said. "It's not just health."

I didn't know whether I was supposed to ask anything more. Joe was looking toward the far end of the hall where nothing was going on. Little Troy Bock was picking pitted olives from a relish tray and stuffing one onto each of his fingertips.

"You can't know till it happens to you," Joe finally said. "You make this tiny little person. You bring it home. It cries all night, all day, it's got diarrhea, it doesn't eat. I woke up one night last week and found Barbara and the baby in the living room, rocking back and forth, both wailing to beat the band.

'What is it,' I kept saying, till finally Barbara tells me, 'She's miserable, Joe. Only thirteen days alive, and she already knows she hates it.'"

I heard myself laugh at that, then tensed my mouth and covered it with my hand. Wasn't everything about babies supposed to be serious? Joe smiled.

"Oh, we laugh about it now," he said. "But it's like I said. You just can't know."

He looked down at his hands, started twisting his wedding ring. His nails were bitten almost to the quick.

"Jesus," Fred the Red whispered. I'd forgotten he was there.

I picked up the plate of starwiches and handed it to Joe. Fred and I watched with admiration while he emptied the plate.

"Have you seen Marie?" I said.

He shook his head, a wedge of rye between his lips. He finished his mouthful and looked at his watch.

"Parking meter's about run out," he said. He dug a handful of change from his pants pocket, piled some melon balls on his plate, and excused himself. I watched him head for his car, for the outside world, where Tom rode the streets and highways, where people lived by moving, not standing still. But Joe would come back and eat a few more sandwiches, smile through the wedding, then go home to his wife. They'd rock the baby and feed it right, like good, decent people, which was what they were. And whenever they felt frightened by what they didn't understand about being alive, they'd draw their baby closer, look deep into her eyes and say: I've found it, my love—look, *there it is*.

It was important to tell B.R. I couldn't stay. I found him in a thronelike chair behind one of the pillars. He had on an old-fashioned tuxedo, with a high starched collar and a stiff bow tie. Troy Bock seemed to be playing a game for him. He'd run and snatch a melon ball and throw it near B.R.'s feet. Next he'd hide behind the pillar and scream, "Whoever stomps on that first wins." Then he'd leap through the air, cowboy boots first, yell "I win!" and run for another melon ball.

B.R. was looking sadly at the melon mush when I walked up. "I think you're losing this game," I said.

He shook his head. "Don't know who'll be cleaning this up."

I squatted beside him, tucking my skirt between my knees. "Where's Gloria?" I said.

He pointed over his shoulder to a closed door off a wing of the stage. Cab Paxton and Merrilee Howard waltzed by to no music.

"You happy?" I said.

He smiled slowly. He straightened his legs in front of him and looked at his shoes.

"Nineteen fifty-eight when I first bought these," he said. "Had Glory in mind all this time. Now wing-tips in fashion again."

It seemed like a long time we didn't say anything more. There were so many things I wished I knew how to tell him.

"You best be sure and say bye to her," he said.

I thought the room was empty when I first opened the door.

"Breaks all tradition, what you're doing," Gloria said.

She looked like a life-size gingerbread woman, sitting in that long white dress on a folding chair against the wall.

"Come spying on the bride in her dress before the wedding," she said.

"This isn't hardly the most traditional day I ever spent," I said. "Church with champagne and melon balls."

She shrugged. "People get hungry." She stood up to smooth the creases out of her dress, started fussing with where it fastened at the back of her neck. "Come lend a hand here, Annie. All these hooks in the back of this thing. Think I was a fisherman. Ha!"

She turned her back to me, and I crossed the room to oblige.

Instead of a zipper down the back there was a long row of tiny fragile hooks, about a half dozen already undone from the strain.

"Never did see a dress fasten together like this," I said. "But then I haven't had much contact with wedding dresses."

"I don't expect it'll ever be your style," she said. "Wasn't mine, till now. Next month I retire. Got to trust my car-renting business to other hands, start spending my days with business of another order."

"Squeeze in a little," I told her.

She sucked in a big breath. Okay, I told myself. On with it.

"It's a nice gathering you're having, and I've had a real nice time."

She let out the breath she'd taken. "Aaaah," she said. "So you're going. And now."

I nodded, though she still had her back turned. "I was going to stay till the end. I don't know what it is."

"That right?" She turned to face me and smiled.

"I hope everything works out. Being married and all."

She shrugged. "Not all that much change in the life, really. Except this damn heavy ring."

She held up her left hand and flexed her fingers. It was the fattest, weightiest-looking gold ring I'd ever seen, with emeralds clustered in the shape of a star.

"Feels like I tilt to the left when I walk."

"It's nice, though. You'll adjust," I said.

She nodded. I nodded back, I didn't know why.

"You know the story of which finger the wedding ring goes on?" she said.

I shook my head.

"Good story, Bobby got it from Athens. They used to argue in Greece about which finger should get the wedding ring, so the smartest Greek in town decided for everybody. The thumb's too busy, he said, the ring would only get in the way." She held up her hand and wagged her thumb. "The pointing finger and the little finger are both too vulnerable." She bent each of those in turn. "The middle finger's too rude, they thought so even then. Which leaves what we call now the ring finger. Which is best 'cause it's most protected."

I smiled.

"There's worse things," she said.

"Nothing wrong with protection," I said. "Guess I don't much feel in the market, is all."

"You'll be fine on the loose." She crossed her arms. "You'll see some places, maybe pick one and live in it for a while. I don't much mind the thought of it."

"Tell it to Marie." I looked down. "I mean, Gloria, would you?"

"Tell her you'll be safe?"

I nodded but didn't look up at her yet. She walked close to me without uncrossing her arms.

"I couldn't say those words," she said, "not to Marie, not unless I believed you're smart as it takes to go about in the world."

I looked into her eyes. It would mean so much to me if you would say those words, I wanted to tell her, and not only because it would comfort Marie. It would mean so much, just knowing you meant it.

"I will tell her," she said.

I gave her a long hug. "I better get rolling," I whispered.

"You better," she said.

When I got to the door, I said, "Your hooks are all fastened."

"I thank you."

I found Marie in the bathroom, teasing her hair with an Afro pick.

"What it *is*, Blood," I said.

She jumped and jerked around. "Christ, Annie," she said.

I said "Sorry," but I had to laugh. She had to laugh too.

"I forgot my comb," she said, and set the pick back on the paper towel dispenser where she must have found it. She had on a dress I'd never seen before. It was silky with a lot of different blues in the pattern, and it tied around the waist with a heavy rope belt.

"You look nice," I said.

"You too."

"I've been looking all over for you."

"Have you?" she said. She went back to smoothing her hair in the mirror, though it was already just the way she liked it.

"I've been kind of a smart-ass lately," I said.

She kept smoothing her hair.

"I guess that's what I wanted to find you to say."

She stopped and looked at me in the mirror. Finally she turned around and hugged me. "If that's all you've got for sale right now, I guess I'll have to take it," she said.

I didn't know why, but I liked her more at that moment than I'd ever liked a person.

She was at the door when she said, "This is a start toward things getting better, isn't it."

"Remember that, Marie," I said.

My hand on the door leading into the lobby, I felt sure of what I was running to, though I didn't yet know the faces and names. But what was it I was running from? When I looked over my shoulder, Conbo Bock was twisting the dials on his camera, pleading with Troy to pose with a pineapple on his head. Like it or not, he was going to get this and more in the background: Cab Paxton trying to teach Fred the Red to waltz. Merrilee fixing her lipstick in a compact mirror. B.R. scraping melon mush onto a paper plate. A wedding like no other, but a wedding nonetheless. The man we called Flintstone counting his change.

– 3 –

There was a charge-a-call phone in the motel lobby, the blue plastic kind you don't need a dime to use. I charged it to Marie, which was the only way I could think to do it.

Carter's voice sounded funny when he answered—I told myself he never sounded like himself on the phone.

"It's me," I said.

"Well, hey there. What's doing?"

"Not much," I said. "Things have been pretty slow around the office lately."

Damn slow. Nine long days since Carter fled San Francisco for Homer. That morning's Cancer had been all about finance opportunities. Leo had said to wake up and smell the coffee. Thanks for nothing, stars.

"You're not too chatty for somebody calling a different time zone," he said.

I shrugged. I wasn't ready just yet to get to the beef of the matter: that I was a full day's drive from San Francisco, where I kept making him roll down the window of his Rambler so I could kiss him good-bye one more time, where I thought we'd be spending the summer together, where he thought I was calling from now.

Three kids in swimsuits ran by the phone booth, snapping bathing caps at each other.

"What's all that I hear?" Carter said. "Where are you?"

"Nevada, I guess. Carson City—no, Virginia City. Wait, which one's the capital? I'm in the other one."

"Nevada," he said. "Whatever are you doing there?"

"Not much. Got a motel room. I just put all my change in this machine they got here, and all that'll come out is Milk Duds."

I could feel his quit-stalling silence.

"I'm on my way east," I said. "And then northbound to Homer."

"You are," he said, and that was all. He gave me directions to Poppa Dad's house where he was staying. I scribbled them on my last deposit slip, which was all the paper I had. I knew I wasn't using up anything I'd likely have much use for.

I'd been too excited to get much sleep. Tossing and turning on that hard motel bed, I kept hearing Carter's voice singing "So Bad Blues," mostly the same line over and over: "Got the blues so bad, can't get no forty winks; try to swallow my whiskey, my throat refuse to drink."

I took the Homer off-ramp around four, two hours ahead of schedule because I'd left before dawn. I would have been earlier still, but I'd pulled off I-80 just over the Wyoming border, where the Green River came bubbling up by a marshy construction site. I had to stop beside it, since it seemed like just about the prettiest thing I'd ever seen. I sat there for more than an hour, watching it skip clean over rocks and around tree stumps, feeling its sting on my heels and breathing its smell.

Carter wasn't home. It was my own fault for showing up early without calling, and I tried my hardest not to be disappointed. Treehorn's house was tall and narrow, with two stories and an attic with a pointed roof and a stovepipe chimney. I tried the front door, back door, and downstairs windows. All locked. So I decided to walk around and check out this town, this promised land that Carter was always talking about. Poppa Dad's house was right off the freeway, and the only glimpse of Homer I'd gotten on the way there was of railroad tracks, a fireworks stand, and a twenty-four-hour beer stop.

Carter had always said that you never knew what might happen in Homer. Once, just walking the street on a Tuesday afternoon, he ran smack into Tennessee Jed McMahon. Spent the next twelve hours shooting tequila with him. The man could sure enough hold his liquor, Carter always said.

I headed off in what looked like the direction toward downtown. Once I got past the trucking yards and warehouses, all I could find were streets lined with tricycles and muddy-faced kids throwing dirt clods at each other. "Depressing," I could hear Jotta whisper, stretching the second syllable long.

I stopped at a minimart for a newspaper and a beer. They didn't card me, so I bought a couple more and headed back to Poppa Dad's place by a different route. Everything on that street looked the same, except for a post office dated 1890-something in sorry need of a paint job. Down the block was a run-down lodge hall with old men sitting around on card table chairs. The lodge had a window on the street with a little brown Christmas tree in it, big as you please in the middle of summer. One old man had a radio in his lap, and it was playing one of those songs by Waylon about Willie, or vice versa.

I was flipping though my newspaper on Poppa Dad's scrawny lawn when I heard Carter's Rambler. I'd have known the sound of that bucket anywhere, but I waited until I heard his bootheels on the sidewalk before I looked up.

"You're early," he said, walking toward me on the lawn. He was wearing his usual jeans and the T-shirt that said "Peatman's Suds 'n' Grill." His beard was fuller, and his arms and cheeks were tanned. His hair looked like it had more gray than before, but that's dumb, I thought, it's been only ten days. I wanted to tell him how much I liked the touch of gray, that it suited him somehow. But that was a comment I knew he wouldn't like.

I stood and hugged him hard, and he hugged me hard back.

73

A rush of tears pressed behind my eyes. I pulled back and patted his stomach.

"You're skinnier."

He looked down at where I'd patted.

"I guess," he said.

The inside of Poppa Dad's place was just like I'd thought it would be, although I'd never met the man. The front room was small and dark with mismatched pieces of furniture lifted from back alleys and garage sales. It all had a peculiar smell to it, sweet and stale at the same time—probably the result of years of jam sessions with people smoking whatever rag weed might have been around that month. On one of the walls hung a framed color photograph of the Seldom Scene—Carter had said they were buddies of Poppa Dad's. Another had a black-and-white poster several feet high, showing a dark profile of a bearded bald man and a caption reading "POPPA DAD," then "Great Falls Memorial Hall" and a date from last year. In the very middle of the room sat a potbelly stove, with a smokestack that rose through a hole in the ceiling. You could look up through that hole and see most of anything that might be going on in the bedroom upstairs.

"Beer or rotgut Canadian whiskey?" Carter asked. I unzipped my knapsack, pulled out the liter of Jack Black and held it up by its throat.

"Should have known," he said, grinning. We went to the kitchen for some glasses and ice, which we always used to open an evening but never bothered with for long.

In the kitchen we clinked our drinks and threw them back. Carter gave me one of those slow up-and-down-the-body looks, but in a sweet way, like you might do to an old friend. He smiled.

"I was just thinking the same about you," I said.

He took me in his arms and kissed me, and though it had been only ten days, my heart pounded all the way to my throat. Then Carter went to the bottle again, and I lifted myself onto the counter and rested my back on a cabinet door.

Carter handed me my refilled glass and stood leaning on the fridge, looking at me.

"Been practicing guitar?" he said.

"You bet. Wrote a song last week. It's real country-western."

I sang him a couple of lines from the chorus: "My eyes do sting with teary drops, but in the onion field of life, you are the tops."

Carter's laugh felt like a birthday present I hadn't been sure I'd get. It made it seem like everything might be okay.

"When I sang my onion song for Marie, she said it was silly," I said. "I told her that CW's supposed to be silly, but she wouldn't lighten up. She don't laugh with me anymore since we've been fighting all the time."

Carter was on the edge of cutting in when I said "She don't," so I said, "You better not be starting in on my grammar, after all, I just got here."

I thought that would make him smile, but it didn't. Would he have smiled in California? Was everything going to be different here? I hopped down from the counter and hugged him. His body was stiff.

"We should talk about you coming up here," he said. "Not that I'm not glad you did."

"Mean that?"

"Sure."

"Then it won't do you any good to talk," I said. "And don't be taking that tone with me. I may be a lot younger than you but I'm also a lot smarter, and I know my own mind."

He was fighting it hard, but he had to crack a smile then. His face relaxed, and he mussed my hair. I realized this was how it worked with us: I acted toughest and surest when I felt the most scared; Carter had a way of making me feel scared a lot.

I sat back up on the counter. "So when do I get to meet this Poppa Dad," I said, "this old coot you moved twice the length of California to piss and moan with?"

Carter turned away and opened the fridge.

"Hard to say," he said. "He runs around a lot. No telling when he'll show."

He was poking his head in the fridge, but he didn't seem to be looking for anything. He opened the freezer and took out the two ice trays and a plastic bucket with some cubes left in it.

"Back last January when you wanted to go to college," he said. "Back last January when you first met me." He twisted one of the ice trays over the bucket.

"Funny, Carter, but that's just what I been saying to myself during the forty-eight hours I just spent on the road: 'I sure do hope the first thing Carter does is give me shit about college 'cause I don't think I've had quite enough of that from Marie.' "

Carter was just dumping the other ice tray into the bucket, like I wasn't there, like someone needed ice. San Francisco or Homer, Wyoming, there was one way I could always force Carter to let me be close. I walked up behind him, slid my hands slowly into the front pockets of his jeans.

"Baby," I said, "put the ice tray down."

He took me by the hand and led me upstairs—a man almost twice my age without a pot to boil beans in, who I wanted only to open my legs to and pull inside me, just so I could wait until he'd fall asleep in my arms. I tried to relax and feel the excitement I usually felt when he clutched at my hips and rolled me against him. But I was remembering standing naked in Marie's full-length mirror, wondering if it was only the roughness he loved.

We both drifted off to sleep for an hour, maybe more. I felt the bed jiggle, and I looked up to see Carter yanking on his pants like somebody had just yelled "Fire."

"Was it something I dreamed?" I said.

Carter gave me a Huh? then said, "I didn't realize how late it was getting."

He ran down the stairs and I heard a knock, which was what must have woke him in the first place. I could hear the roar of a lot of different voices when he opened the door. I leaned out over the foot of the bed far enough to see down through the hole around the stovepipe. Three men passed underneath me, and it sounded like there were more. They were heading for the kitchen with twelve-packs of Bud under their arms.

I was pulling on my jeans when Carter lumbered up the stairs and through the bedroom door.

"Some people are coming over tonight," he said.

"Think so?"

"I told them they could all group here tonight to jam. You didn't give me a lot of notice about this arrival of yours, you know."

Would it have made any difference, I wanted to ask.

I checked things out from the top landing, since I wasn't sure I'd fit in downstairs. There were instruments and cases littered all over the living room: five or six guitars, a couple of mandolins, a banjo, a fiddle. A tall, lanky guy wearing pleated pants and a suit vest was taking the fiddle out of its case. In the corner a pudgy middle-aged guy sat tuning a Martin. What little hair he had was red and stood out over his ears in two stiff tufts. I could tell these guys were the real thing. Guitar lessons or no, I'd look silly even talking with pros like them.

I felt someone watching me and turned to see a big blond guy leaning by the door. He was forty or so, jeans and lumberjack shirt, wispy beard and hair sticking out everywhere. He winked at me and smiled. He had a tooth missing in front.

Carter and the others came in from the kitchen. Some of them went straight for their instruments. The guy in the doorway nodded at the bottom step, inviting me to come sit. Carter and a young guy with a skinny black tie and hair down to his butt were passing the Buds around. Now that everyone was assembled in the room, I realized I was in unusual company in more ways than one: There were no women there.

"I'll levy you a wager," the blond guy called to me up the stairs.

At first I ignored him. But he was smiling so nice.

"About what?" I said.

"Come down, and we'll establish terms," he said. "If"—he raised his eyebrows—"you're feisty as you look."

At first the "feisty" startled me. Then I remembered what I'd figured out in Carter's kitchen about when I acted the cockiest. How did I act when I really did feel unbeatable? I couldn't think offhand of a time I recently had.

I walked to the bottom stair, sat down and leaned back on the step behind me. There were eight men in all, including Carter, and the group varied in age about as much as a group could. An old guy in a Mao cap sat cross-legged on the couch, warming up on a mandolin; I could tell from the licks he was doing that he was damn good. Two guys were sitting on the floor by the kitchen door, one with a pedal steel in his lap and the other tuning up an old acoustic. They both were about thirty, curly-haired, with glasses. I took a double take, realized they were identical, a couple of curly-haired bluegrass-playing twins. The one with the pedal steel was waving his hands around, telling some story to the round guy with the red tufts.

The blond toothless guy who'd challenged me to a bet plopped down next to me on the step.

"Name's Max," he said, and flashed his gap again.

"Annie." We shook hands. He seemed less creepy now than when I first looked at him. Besides, I needed a buddy right then.

The skinny guy with the hair and the tie leaned over us and handed Max a beer. "Your usual, suh," he said. He handed one to me, bowed, winked, and headed for the banjo case.

"People wink a lot around here," I said.

Max laughed. "You got to forgive us," he said. "You spend all your time around catgut and rosewood and guitar pickers, you forget how to talk to a young lady, unless it's with a wink or a song."

Carter was over with the pedal-steel twin and the round redhead, fighting the twin for airtime. Carter was saying he'd played the meanest, raunchiest bars of anybody he knew. The twin, he said he didn't know what kind of trouble people caused over on the coast of California, but up in mountain country they had oilmen and miners and Indians and two state prisons for all of them to bust out of. Their talk had a different tone than B.R.'s stories about the war, or Jotta's wisecracking, or Marie retelling her day. I couldn't quite figure the point of this kind of story-telling, but it seemed a lot more centered on the teller than the story. Whatever it was, interesting it wasn't.

"About that wager," I said to Max.

He frowned, then flashed a wide smile. "Right," he said. He pulled a matchbook from his back pocket, started working the corner between two bottom teeth. "Name your stakes," he said.

"Stakes?"

"C'mon, gal," he said. "You know. What you're putting up, and how much of it you're willing to lose."

"But we haven't said what we're betting about," I said.

He slipped the matchbook back in his pocket, looked at me out of the corner of his eye. "Darlin'," he said, "that's the least of what matters."

Scanning the group again, I realized that none of these guys' faces matched the face of the guy in the poster.

"When's Poppa Dad getting here?" I asked Max.

"Poppa Dad? He's been touring the West Coast the past four weeks. Be rolling in here any day now."

Max started tugging at the duct tape that was holding together the toe end of his left boot.

"You know Carter, right?" he said. "Did you know him back when he was touring with Tennessee Jed?"

I stared back at him. Carter had gone on a drunk with Tennessee Jed, but I didn't think that was what Max meant by "touring."

"Never mind," he said. "Damn sure before your time."

He threw back his head and laughed at something.

"Yessir, Pop might just show anytime. I'd wager tonight." He turned to me, eyebrows raised.

"Bars in Modoc County got their share of Indians too," Carter was telling the twin. "In some of those places they won't give you a bottle of beer out of fear you'll break it across somebody's face. You spend your night drinking out of aluminum cans."

Modoc County, that was way up by the Oregon border. Carter got to California less than a year ago, and I knew he hadn't ventured north of Sacramento.

"He's never been to Modoc County," I said to Max.

Max looked up from his boot. "When he say it was? Seventy-five? Maybe that was before your time too." He winked again.

The old man on the couch was picking out a tune on his mandolin. It was one of those old Stagger Lee songs, couldn't remember which one exactly, but they were all the same to me. Some half-wit was bigger and meaner than everybody else, so two generations of songwriters made a legend out of him. I was waiting for the day somebody would write about Delia De-Lyon's revenge: the day she ordered up a gin fizz, shot Stagger Lee in the balls, and had him dragged off and hanged. Any band that'd sing that side of the story would have my dedication for life.

"How come you all didn't go with him?" I said.

"Poppa Dad?" Max looked away for just long enough that I caught a glimmer in his eye; it was same glimmer as I saw in the eyes of Carter and the twin telling stories. "You know, darlin', he's got his own band, has for years. Wouldn't let any of those guys go, not even for one of us here."

And the Injuns and the miners and the men of oil, sang the old man.

"We got obligations here too, most of us," said Max. "Real professions. Couldn't just up and go."

"Me and Phillip," the twin told Carter, "we played at Coope's Lair, bar way up between East and West Glacier that's got a big Brown Bear tied out back. People come from Kalispell, Havre, Coeur d'Alene, and drink at that place just to get a look at that bear."

The round redhead and the fiddler perked up. The redhead said he'd heard about the place, and the fiddler nodded like he had too.

"I was there," Carter said, and everybody looked over at him.

"Lots of people been there," the twin said.

"Sure," Carter said. "But not this one night. It was just a year or so ago. I was there the night that bear broke loose."

Just a year or so ago, as I recalled it, Carter was in Princeton, New Jersey, and the only thing that broke loose was his wife, Judy Ann.

"What they do 'bout it?" asked Max.

"We all just had to round it up," Carter said.

"Had to wrassle it bare-handed," I said. "Him and Tennessee Jed."

Everybody looked over, including Carter, who looked at me like I was the bear himself. I'd teased him before, even called him on things. But I knew from his face that this was so much worse. It had something to do with us being here, among these men.

"Whose gal is that?" I heard the twin ask his brother.

Carter's look softened to a smile, and I had no clue whatever as to what might happen next.

"That over there's my friend Annie," he said.

The twins nodded hello, the fiddler and the round man smiled and waved, the long-haired guy bowed again, the old man tipped his Mao cap.

"You know about that night up at Coope's Lair?" the twin called to me.

"Annie's a musician herself," Carter said. "I started working with her last January, but she was already well on her way, just needed a little direction. Isn't that right, Annie?" He winked at me.

"And whereabouts did ol' Carter direct you?" said Max.

"Noplace my mama ever had in mind," I said.

Max and the pedal-steel twin hooted, and everybody laughed. That comeback line was as much apology as I was ready to offer.

"Go ahead," Carter said. "Play something for us. Anything at all. Just play."

I shook my head. All the boys started yelling and clapping. How could I play guitar in front of that bunch? I wanted to run to Carter, to beat on his chest for being so mean. He walked over and picked up Max's acoustic. I tried to push it away, but he set it on my lap. Then he leaned over and kissed me soft and gentle, pulled back to look at me with wide-open eyes. It wasn't meanness I saw in that look; it was more just determination.

"Come on, sweetie," he said. "For me. Play."

Though I couldn't play steel strings because they hurt my fingers, and though I'd thought I'd learned something in my few hours with Carter in this strange new place, or maybe because of all those things, I sat up straight and faced the lot of them. "Okay," I said. "I'll show you boys a trick or two."

The old man strummed his mandolin fast to sound like a drumroll. Carter sat on the floor by the couch and rested his guitar face down on his lap.

My right hand was shaking too much for me to jump right in. I swept my hand soft across the strings, thought maybe the B was flat and twisted the peg to sharpen it. They all laughed. I looked at Carter.

"How 'bout that new song you wrote?" Carter said. "Give us a taste of that."

"I don't think so."

"It's a charmer, that one," he said to the group. "It's about love and onions, all at the same time." He winked at the twins, and the two of them started clapping and egging me on. Soon everybody else joined in.

First verse I watched my left hand while I played, trying to press extra hard to stop the strings from buzzing. I did a quick check of the room during the chorus. Most of the men were looking at the floor; the twins glimpsed at each other, then looked away again. I thought about wrapping up, but I'd only played for a minute and quitting would have made me look even worse. I went into the "on my left hand your onion ring" verse, strings buzzing and thumping, and followed it up with the onion dip stanza. They didn't perk up at that one and my fingertips were throbbing, so I stopped before the Irish stew part.

There was a long second of silence when I finished, then a burst of jovial applause. All their clapping and cheering made my embarrassment worse—I couldn't make myself look up at them. Carter walked over and lifted the guitar from my lap. He bent down close to me so the other men couldn't see, then kissed me and cupped his hand over my breast. He could as well have said it then: You have to learn to act right if you want to belong.

The men were getting back about their business. The long-haired guy was tuning up a banjo, and the twin with the acoustic was messing with his finger picks. Carter went back to where he'd been sitting, put his guitar in his lap, but left it face down. He wouldn't lift his head, like he wasn't sure of what he'd see if he caught somebody's eye. I was waiting to see what would happen with the other men, now that Carter had been caught telling tales.

The old man was picking again, and pretty soon the fiddler joined in. The tune had a heavy meter to it; it sounded like one of those old marches where the rebels of the north or south storm the other's fort and win against all odds. The guitar-playing twin jumped in, and he and the fiddler each wrapped the theme around the other's leads at a lively pace. Then they turned the lead back over to the old man. Everybody clapped, and the old man started to sing.

> *Midst the glaciers up in old Montan'*
> *He strode the cliffs with nary a band*

Max set his guitar back in his lap and strapped a cheater across the strings.

No band had he nor gun in hand
'Gainst the greatest foe in all the land

The pedal-steel twin flexed his muscles and did a pose, and the redhead laughed.

The foe had muscle and the foe had fight
The foe had bark and the foe had bite

The long-haired guy started strumming his banjo.

But come the rising sun that bear was gone
By the fearless hand of Carter John

All of them cheered. Even the pedal-steel twin smiled. Carter was laughing, and his face was red.

"C'mon, Carter boy," said Max. "Let's do it."

Carter turned his guitar over and picked up the theme. The four of them sang it again together, ". . . come the rising sun that bear was gone, / By the fearless hand of Carter John."

Pretty soon they all joined in: Max, the pedal-steel twin, everybody. Though there'd been some teasing at first, now everyone was playing in earnest—the song had already outlived the lie. Each man took his turn and either played his own lead or ad-libbed another stanza. Carter stopped looking afraid about anything.

- 4 -

Whenever I drifted off to sleep, a hoot or a strum would jolt me awake. I dreamed Carter and I were lying in front of the house, where instead of scraggly lawn and potholed street there was beach and ocean. I asked Carter to rub my back, so he sat on my butt and untied the strings on my bikini top. It felt good at first, then he bore down and started rubbing with all his strength—kneading, too hard. I couldn't get myself up, and couldn't make him stop. Then there must have been a noise downstairs, because the next I knew I was sitting up with my heart beating fast.

At some point when I was sure I hadn't gotten any more sleep, I realized that Carter was lying next to me and it was getting light out. I sat up, half expecting to find the rest of the boys camped out around me. My head hurt, like I'd inhaled water through my nose. I got up to search the house for aspirin, after throwing one of Carter's old work shirts around me—God only knew who else might have been shacking up in that house.

At the top of the stairs I thought I heard thunder. A few steps down it started to sound more like a bathtub draining. From the bottom step I saw Max slumped in the easy chair by

85

the kitchen door. He had a down jacket thrown over him, and his mouth was hanging open.

I found a family-size bottle of Bayer's behind the coffee mugs in a cabinet over the sink. I downed three aspirin and filled another cup with water to take upstairs. From the living room I could see the sun rising out the front window. I pushed through the screen door and stepped outside for a view of the new morning.

Sitting on the top step of the porch, I thought how this was the closest to quiet I'd likely encounter in the course of my stay. A funny use of the word *stay*. That's what you call a time in your life when it's the one thing you're not allowed to do. You should get the hell out of here, I told myself. And go where? Back to my single bed in the back room? Back to Marie's world of papers and suits and posing with the mayor? So Carter wasn't the man I'd wanted him to be. I wasn't the woman I wanted to be either.

I heard rustling in the junipers bordering the lawn. By the time I looked over, it was quiet again. I was turning to go inside when I heard the same rustling and spotted a flash of dark blue under one of the branches.

I crouched next to a denim-covered leg and parted the bushes, revealing a round, bare belly and a gray-haired chest. Thick, freckled arms were crossed over the face. I gave the leg one good shake, then another. Still no signs of life.

"Hey," I said, and shook the leg harder.

He took his arms from his face and started blinking. He jerked his head up far enough to look down at his bare chest.

"My shirt," he said.

He looked down for a full minute, like if he looked long enough, he might find the shirt there.

"Water?" I said. I held out the glass, and he frowned at it. "You really ought to." He seemed to nod. I put my hand behind his head and touched the cup to his lips. He sucked against the rim of the cup to coax the water into his mouth, but most of the water flowed in two crooked streams down the sides of his

86

beard. When the cup was empty I stood, and he covered his face with his arms again.

I put the cup in the sink and filled a clean one to take upstairs. Carter opened his eyes and touched my hip when I slid under the covers.

"Where you been?" he said.

I rolled onto my side and laid my head on my hands. I slid into deep, heavy sleep with the sun in my eyes, hearing the words I didn't say: Poppa Dad's here.

When I woke, it was twelve-thirty by the watch I'd left on the nightstand. There were voices downstairs—still low-pitched and overly loud.

Through the front screen I could see the backs of three men positioned on the porch. Carter was sitting on the steps to the lawn. Max was slumped in the couch, his outstretched arms almost spanning the length of its back. Poppa Dad was solidly balanced on the short fence bordering the porch. All of them held coffee mugs, all stared ahead at the street like they were waiting for the homecoming float to pass. Whatever I might have wanted to say to Carter, I knew there wouldn't be opportunity to talk for a while. The thought didn't entirely disappoint me.

"Morning," Carter said.

Max looked up and nodded, barely, like each movement pained him. Poppa Dad spun around on the fence and beamed. "A dillar, a dollar, a twelve o'clock scholar!"

"Pop, meet Annie," Carter said.

Poppa Dad bounded off the fence and extended his hand. No don't do it, I wanted to say, but it would've been too late to stop that wink.

"Glad to see you're feeling better," I said.

Poppa Dad raised his eyebrows. I couldn't believe he was going to play dumb, like we'd never met. Did everybody in this town live by lies and posturing? But this man's secret was entirely different from Carter's; his condition at dawn was his own business.

I pointed toward the poster inside. "What I meant was that you look a little haggard in black and white."

"I'll have a word with my makeup crew about that."

I smiled, then he smiled and punched my arm. In a funny way, it seemed like the warmest physical contact I'd had since leaving San Francisco.

"Coffee?" he said. I nodded and followed him back into the house. His walk from behind reminded me of chimps in the circus Jotta used to take me to. His legs seemed unnaturally short to be supporting the heaviness of his arms and chest. But there was a strength to his walk that made me think I wouldn't want to see him coming at me in the dark.

Poppa Dad slid the glass pot out of the Mr. Coffee and held it up to the light.

"Husband's tea," he said. "Weak and good for nothing." He poured it down the drain, opened the fridge, and pulled out a six-pack.

"Guess you missed breakfast," he said, and handed me a beer.

Back on the porch Poppa Dad passed beers to Carter and Max, then mounted the fence again. There was a space next to Carter on the porch step, just big enough for me to squeeze in beside him. I took a step toward it, but a glance from Carter made me stop and put my hands in my pockets. I was slowly learning the rules of this world. In a way they weren't so different from any other place's rules. Number one, you're on your own.

"Ten to one," Max said.

Carter shook his head. "Candy from a baby," he said. "You're on."

Before I could ask what was up, Poppa Dad nudged me and pointed across the street. Two dark men in cowboy hats were driving a motorcycle up a ramp onto the bed of a pickup.

"On the roof," Poppa Dad said.

First I looked to the roof of the house, which seemed ordinary enough. Then I noticed the bottle of beer on the roof of the pickup. The men finished securing the bike and slammed the door to the bed of the truck.

"Count out your bills, Carter boy," Max said.

The men climbed in the truck and started the engine.

"It's not over till that bottle hits the street," Carter said.

The truck slowly drifted forward a foot or two. A hand reached up from the driver's window and pulled the bottle inside. Carter slapped his knee, and Max's head dropped into his hands.

"You're in a slump," Poppa Dad said.

"The stars ain't wimme," Max said.

"Common sense ain't with you," Carter said. "An Indian never wastes his alcohol feeding the concrete."

Poppa Dad giggled, and Max pulled out his wallet. I thought about Carter's speeches in senior writing class about racial tolerance and the human family. Max spread the wallet open wide, held it upside down and shook.

"Like they say in Frisco, put it on my tab," Max said.

I'd just popped open my second beer when I first noticed the siren. It was a long way off, and I vaguely wondered what kind of things people got busted for in Homer, Wyoming. Max had just lost his third wager with Carter (the second involved a cat across the street, the third was over what time it was). I noticed the siren and stopped noticing it. Then it was replaced by an engine roar, and the next I knew there he was, Tom Cleaver, riding his bike past us like Mr. Minding His Own Business, looking straight ahead, slowing at the corner, blinking his turn signal, disappearing onto Main.

I held myself rigid and still, a fixture on a porch on a July afternoon, three men and Wyoming my camouflage.

"Hell's Angels in town," Poppa Dad said. "Must be harvesttime somewhere in Nebraska."

I shut my eyes, trying to make my heartbeat slow. I could have been wrong. Not Tom Cleaver, just some Angel passing through. Then the siren was wailing again, and my heartbeat sped up. Who else but Tom would have a siren in his convoy? When the whine faded, the roar started like before. Tom passed in front of us, just the same way. Looking ahead, slowing, stopping at the corner. Blink, turn, and gone.

"Marie would love it," Carter turned and said to me. "Me, two Angels, and little Annie, and her a thousand miles away." He threw his head back and laughed. It seemed mean for him to be laughing about Marie.

"*One* Angel," I said. "And I'm sure she's shitting station wagons."

The group seemed to quiet conspicuously, like they were considering my remark. Then the siren wailed to life again, growing louder with the roar. And you'd've thought I knew the man inside and out, I was that sure Tom Cleaver was going to do exactly what he did.

Poppa Dad jumped off the fence and stood when Tom drove up, siren blaring, onto the lawn. Carter went from the steps to the porch to stand beside Poppa Dad, which just so happened to take him a few paces farther from the action. Max managed to straighten up where he sat, the picture of don't-fuck-wimme.

The siren died. Tom grinned, cheek to cheek.

"It's Ma and Pa Kettle," he said, "come out to guard the homestead."

Max looked from Poppa Dad to Carter like he was trying to figure out which was which. I walked to the porch steps and put my hands on my hips. "Since when you been tearing up lawns in the Rocky Mountain time zone?"

Max, Carter, and Poppa Dad shifted their stare, in one motion, from Tom to me.

"He's okay," I said. "I know him."

"A true fact," Tom said. "Though I had to ride up into your lap to get you to admit it."

In the next fifteen seconds of silence nothing appeared to change: Tom grinned like he was watching a musical comedy, the men on the porch tried to look like they never needed to breathe. But I was suddenly hot and alive and important, the bear they could never have wrassled down to slip a collar on its neck.

"You got some business with me?" I said.

Tom scooted forward on his seat and patted the space behind him. "There's this matter of a drink we've never had."

Poppa Dad stepped around Carter and stood in front of me on the stairs, facing Tom. "I don't know who you think you are."

Tom shrugged. "I tend not to give it much thought," he said.

"He's okay," I said. "He's all bark, Poppa Dad."

Tom laughed. "Can't believe my ears, you calling somebody Dad."

Poppa Dad wouldn't move away, which made me feel like nobody heard a word I said. I stepped around him, climbed onto the bike and put my arms around Tom's waist.

"Knock off pleading with me to stay, Carter," I said. "Your concern is touching, but I can take care of myself."

Poppa Dad looked at him. "You gonna let her go off with this guy?"

Carter looked at me when he answered him. "You heard her, Dad. She's big on making her own mistakes." He turned and walked inside, slamming the screen door behind him.

"Know a decent bar in this hamlet?" Tom said at the stop sign.

I pointed in the direction of downtown. Several unconnected thoughts hit me one after another as we picked up speed: Carter had said not a word while I climbed onto a Harley behind a Hell's Angel. The wind felt like water, breaking at my face and pulling through my hair. Tomorrow was one of the two days that might be Carter's birthday. I had my fingers dug into the ribs of a man who had nearly killed Jotta more than once.

There were more bars downtown than I'd ever seen concentrated in one place. Tom called out names as we passed them:

"Vaughn's Rodeo Room. Koch's Hole-in-the-Wall. The Desperado. Dave Mac's."

After a few more names I yelled "Okay." We pulled to a stop in front of Colter's Tap.

It took a minute for my eyes to adjust to the dark inside the bar. While I could still make out only shapes and the lights of a pinball machine, I scanned the length of the far wall for the portraits Carter had talked about. But instead of the faces of railroad men and Indians and tramps, all that came into focus was a topless woman spread-eagle on the hood of a truck.

There was already a drink at the place next to Tom by the time I found him at the bar.

"What'd you order me?" I asked.

Tom and the bartender exchanged a smile, then the bartender slid some glasses into a sink of soapy water. He had a dense black beard that he'd reach up and tug every few seconds, like he was checking to make sure it was still there.

Tom raised his shot glass. "Our toast, Orphan Annie?"

I lifted my drink. "To whatever I'm about to subject my stomach to."

"Sugar and spice and everything nice."

The drink looked like weak coffee and tasted like soda pop with a kick.

"You like?"

I nodded. "Now what is it?"

"I told you," he said.

The bartender laughed, sucking through his teeth. He was pumping two upside-down glasses onto cylinder-shaped brushes that were anchored somehow in the sudsy water. Tom slid his empty shot glass to the edge of the bar, tipped it so it fell into the suds.

"Quick and make a wish," the bartender said.

Tom leaned back on his stool and closed his eyes. By the time he opened them, the bartender had set a new shot in front of him. Tom smiled, and they shook hands. I felt like I was watching a meeting of some secret brotherhood.

"What are you doing here, Tom?" I said.

Tom watched the bartender drift to the other end of the bar. He held his shot glass in the air and seemed to be looking through it at something. "The lure of the broken white line, the smell of the asphalt. The fumes in your nose, the sunburn on the part in your hair. The sickening sight of the twisted, broken remains of re-tread tires by the side of the road."

I felt drunker than I should have after half a drink. I was sure a bartender would never have let him slip anything in my glass. I remembered Jotta telling Marie how Tom didn't believe in drugs. Nothing steamed Marie like when Jotta talked about Tom in that tone. Like she wanted to impress us. Like there was something about him that always made her proud.

"Could we talk for real?" I said. "I ask a question and you give an answer?"

"Like in school!" Tom said. "I always did hear you were a hot number in school." He turned on his stool to face me, resting his knees against mine. "First semester, subject A, period one. Shoot."

I drained my drink and set it down. "How'd you get here?"

"Geography. Always was good at geography. Bay Bridge to 80, eastbound, stopover in Virginia City for eight hours, eastbound to Rock Springs, after an irritating little delay at the Green River—"

"You followed me," I said.

"Now *that* is not a question."

I tried to fix on the image of a distant motorcycle in my rearview mirror. Was I only planting it in my memory? But remembering or not remembering wouldn't change his sitting on a barstool so close I could smell the whiskey on his breath, watch his pupils growing big in the dark.

"Next subject, Orphan Annie. I got answers dying to get their turns."

The bartender dropped my glass in the suds and set a new one on the bar. He grabbed four bottles by the throat—gin, vodka, tequila, and rum—and turned them upside down over my glass. I thought of Carter's tearing open two sugar packets at once, but this wasn't the same.

"Why are you here?" I said.

"Ah, philosophy. Might be getting out of my league."

The bartender added a spritz of Coke, gave the drink a stir, and set it in front of me.

"Only on my way to something better," Tom said. "Same as you." The bartender handed him a shot and he clinked it against my glass, like what he'd said had been important enough to toast to.

"You promised no more no-answer answers," I said.

He took a gentle sip from his whiskey and set it down. "An A-plus answer is what that was." He slammed his open hand on the bar. "Mr. Colter, have you got a brew back there for me?"

The bartender lifted a glass to the tap and tipped the handle forward. "It's a funny thing how you figured that out," he said. "Most outa-town folks assume the place is after John Colter, you know, like every tourist lure a hunnerd miles from the park. You're looking at Del Colter. The real thing." He tugged on the beard while foam overflowed the glass.

"I can see you're the genuine article, Mr. Colter," Tom said.

The bartender put the beer in front of him. Tom turned to me and smiled.

"School's out," he said, and drained the glass.

Max, Carter, and Poppa Dad were still on the porch when Tom and I pulled up. I'd imagined during the ride home how Tom and I would roar up onto the lawn. I'd climb off the bike, and we'd exchange a knowing farewell look. "Nice meeting you, boys," he'd say, and roar off down the street before any of them had their wits about them. But now, Tom only eased the bike to the sidewalk and let the engine idle while he waited for me to get off.

"Thanks for the drinks," I said.

He disappeared around the corner with no flourish whatsoever, leaving me to make my own way back to the porch.

94

Not only had I been robbed of sharing the glory of the siren, the roar, and the grand entrance, I'd also been cheated of my knowing look. It seemed, in fact, like that was his intention: to find me in Wyoming just to leave me knowing nothing.

Poppa Dad stood as I walked up the steps. Max winked at me from the couch. Carter was sitting on the fence, looking straight ahead.

"You okay?" Poppa Dad said.

"How could I be anything else?" I said. "How could things possibly be more okay?" I pushed through the screen door like I had a mission inside.

I stood in the middle of the living room, staring into the kitchen. Sooner or later I had to face calling Marie. She'd ask where I was, and I'd probably tell her. She'd ask where I was going. That would be harder.

I heard the screen squeak open and slam shut, felt a hand on my shoulder. I could tell from the weight of it that it wasn't Carter's.

"There's talk of going out somewhere," Poppa Dad said.

"Great," I said. "You boys drive careful."

He gave my shoulder a squeeze, put his hands in his pockets. "He has a hard time caring about things, you know. Soon as something matters to him, he runs away from it."

My eyes were welling up, so I couldn't turn and face him. "Why?" I said. I hung my head and watched a tear fall on the toe of my shoe.

I could feel him look away, uncomfortable now. That seemed to be the one question I wasn't supposed to ask. Poppa Dad reached up and mussed my hair, and I could feel how tangled it was from the ride.

"Tell you what," he said. "I'm only in town a few days, let's do it up right. We'll drive out to the Turf Club, fanciest place in town. Good brew, good view." He reached around to hug me, awkward from the back, trying to position his arms so he wouldn't seem lecherous. We both had to laugh. I turned and faced him.

"Dirty old coot," I said, and grabbed a handful of his shirt to dry my eyes.

"Each Wyoming town you see on the map has a story to tell. Generations of stories." Carter swept his hand out the driver's side window, where dry fields alternated with orderly rows of greens. We drove through a rebel sprinkler that was boldly watering the highway.

"Take Buffalo," Max said. "Please." He nudged Poppa Dad a couple of times.

"Henny Youngman you ain't," Poppa Dad said.

Carter nodded, still waiting to hear the story Buffalo had to tell. Carter didn't seem to have much sense of humor in Wyoming.

"Buffalo's famous for, don't tell me, buffaloes," I said. I turned and propped my elbows on the back of my seat.

"Every inch of fertilized land in Wyoming is famous for buffaloes," Poppa Dad said.

"I got a story for Buffalo," Max said. "It's a true one even. 'Member that pilot who mistook it for Sheridan?"

Poppa Dad and Carter both nodded. Didn't Carter think anybody knew he wasn't a local?

"Seems," Max continued, "that a 727 needs thirty-six-inch-thick asphalt for landing or the wheels tear up the strip, which is what happened when this pilot touched down at Buffalo Airport. He got himself fired, but the folks in Buffalo made him a hero: Wrong Way Such 'n' Such. Fly him in for a festival every year, in his honor."

"That so?" Carter said.

"Wager?" Max said. He winked at me when Carter didn't answer.

The Turf Club was perched on the peak of a hill overlooking the town and miles of farmland. We walked up a flight of steep wooden steps to a deck scattered with director's chairs and tables with red and white umbrellas. A teenage boy in a tuxedo opened the door to the building and propped it open with a wedge.

"Dinner starts in ten minutes," he said, and stretched his mouth into a make-believe smile.

Poppa Dad said we only wanted bar service, and the boy waved us to a table in the corner farthest from the door. Carter and I took our seats under one of the umbrellas. Poppa Dad nudged Max and they both sat on the wooden fence that surrounded the deck, overlooking a golf course.

"I've never seen people perch, lean, and straddle as much as this group does," I said.

Carter was looking off to the irrigated fields next to the parking lot. After a minute he stood up. "They've forgotten us out here," he said. "Beer?"

I nodded. Carter went inside and came out five minutes later with four bottles of Bud. I knew Poppa Dad had sat away from us to give us a chance to talk, so I felt obligated to start a significant conversation.

"Something smells," I said.

"Like shit?"

I took a whiff and held it. "Yeah."

Carter nodded in the direction of the irrigated fields. "Sugar beet," he said. "Most peculiar odor."

We let that discussion settle for ten minutes or so. I could hear Max trying to coax Poppa Dad into a bet over one of the golfers.

"I looked for your portraits in that bar downtown today," I said.

Carter turned to me, blank.

"You know, the pencil sketches that told everything anybody ever wanted to know about railroad men, bums, and Indians. I know it was silly to look—you weren't even sure what state you saw them in."

Carter took a pull from his beer. "The place you went with the Angel."

"Weird bartender in there, owner, I guess. Always doing

97

this on his beard." I tugged at my chin, the way Colter had. Carter didn't look up.

"So your plan is what?" he said. "To keep pushing it and pushing it till you just go up in flames?"

I tried to think of what "it" meant, because his question seemed so serious.

"I don't mean to be pushing on you, Carter," I finally said.

He slammed his Bud on the tinny patio table. My beer might have tipped over if I hadn't been holding it in my lap. I saw Poppa Dad shoot Carter a look. Carter took a deep breath and let it out slow.

"I had to go drink with Tom," I said.

"Had to," he said. "Had to run over and straddle that hot black seat, had to wrap your arms around all that leather."

I felt myself blush. "Come on," I said. "It's not like that. He used to be married to Jotta, is all."

"Used to be," he said.

"That's right," I said. "But he's never really let go of her. There've been some awful times."

A waitress in a short black skirt and tuxedo vest picked up our bottles and set down new ones. Poppa Dad paid her, and they joked around for a couple of minutes. When she walked away she said, "So you're not having dinner?"

"Dinner is a sign of defeat," he answered, and toasted her with his Bud.

I realized I hadn't eaten a morsel of solid food since I rolled into Homer. A charbroiled steak smell was mixing with the sugar beet fumes, which threatened to make me more than a little queasy.

"So tell me some awful times," Carter said.

A long sip of the cold beer calmed my stomach. "The stories blend together, since I never got all the facts. Sometimes Tom would show up at Jotta's place when she wasn't home, maybe call her at the office and tell her he was sick. She'd go home and he'd be waiting for her behind the door. He'd disappear, he'd be back. He's done time, but he always gets off early. Sometimes she's been scared, but it's never lasted long. There was always something about him to her—Tom was just like nobody else."

Poppa Dad and Max were quiet when I finished the story. Then Max pointed at something, and they started talking again.

"I see," Carter said. "So Annie grows up with all this, and at eighteen she says to herself, 'I know what I'll do. I'll get in a car and take myself a thousand miles from home after I don't know what. I don't believe in plans, but if a psychotic wifebeater in leather makes room on the seat of his Harley, I'll be sure to hop on.' "

I heard Max snicker. I felt my face getting hot.

"He's all bark, Poppa Dad'?" Carter almost yelled.

I took a long gulp of beer. "Tom doesn't usually pick a fight or anything, was all I was trying to say."

Carter held up his hands. "I, for one, feel safer just knowing that. Did he happen to mention what he was doing in Wyoming?"

"I asked him that."

"Congratulations."

What was it Tom had said? Something about being on his way somewhere. A young guy in a dark suit and a woman in a chiffon dress walked up the stairs to the restaurant. He stopped at the door and let her walk in first. They both had name tags on.

"He said he was on his way to something better," I said. "He got mad when I said he hadn't answered my question."

"And Jotta is where?"

"Massachusetts."

"A beeline down Highway 80. And worth a short detour to see what info he could dig up."

The steak smell was overpowering the sugar beet fumes. I thought of the family barbecues my old friend Fitz used to have: Dad in an apron, Mom and the kids teasing him about taking hours to get the charcoals going. My stomach growled, and I realized how hungry I was. How could I not have known Tom was using me to get to Jotta?

"I hope I didn't let on anything," I said.

"Might want to give it some thought."

I tried to remember the conversation, but all that came back was the kick from those drinks. A surge of tears was gathering force inside me. I watched some more couples walk in the restaurant in nice clothes, their hair combed and styled. My beer was already warm from holding the bottle in my lap.

"Could we get something to eat, Carter?" I said.

"Is this sinking in?" he said. "You too busy hot-rodding around to see what you're doing to your life?" He exhaled, leaned back in his chair. "I hate to come down so hard. You're not like other people, like the young-marrieds in that fancy steak restaurant. Me neither. That's why I came up to Homer, to get a distance on some of it." He leaned on the table, close to me. "Up here, I got *Wyoming*. I got a place to stay with a *dairy* out back."

I could tell from Carter's silence that I was supposed to be doing something with all this. I swirled my beer, watched it lap the sides of the bottle.

"I need a few dollars to call Marie," I said. "I didn't bring my money."

Carter sighed and handed me his wallet. It opened onto the driver's license: 7/3/51. Tomorrow. I pulled out three dollars and left the table.

The only light in the restaurant came from the candles on the tables and the glow from the stained glass windows. The bartender was helping a waitress load glasses onto a tray. I hoisted myself onto a stool to wait for her to come give me telephone change.

The man and woman in name tags were eating onion soup at a corner table. The woman lifted her spoon, stretching a hot web of cheese to her lips. An old woman at a table next to them dropped a scoop of something white onto her meat. A blackboard on the far wall listed bar appetizers: onion rings, soup, fried cheese sticks, chicken wings.

"Need something, honey?" the bartender said. She rapped her knuckles on the bar while I sifted through the possibilities.

"How much are chicken wings?"

"Two-fifty."

"How long?"

"Already made. You won't miss your train."

She pointed me to a table and said she'd bring them to me. When she left, I moved out of sight from the door. Poppa Dad was right. These chicken wings would be a sign of my defeat. I accepted that as I waited for the woman to bring them.

– 5 –

Poppa Dad shook his head while I pulled rolls of crepe paper from the shelf of party supplies.

"I got the severest doubts about this," he said.

"Green and yellow," I said. "Or green and pink." I threw the yellow rolls back and held a pink one next to the green to check the match.

"It's hard to explain," he said. "I just got my doubts."

I handed him the green rolls I'd been holding so I could forage through the shelf for two more of the pink. "I roll into town with a chip on my shoulder, start mouthing off in front of Carter's friends and hopping onto Harleys. Might've gotten myself messed up but good if Carter hadn't set me straight. 'Bout time I do something nice for him."

Poppa Dad looked down at the green crepe paper and started shaking his head again. "Some people are birthday people, Annie, and some people aren't."

"He'd never tell me his birthday if I asked him," I said. "I got a look at his driver's license yesterday."

"That tells you something," he said, "his not wanting to tell."

"He's shy about displays of caring," I said. "Like you were saying yesterday." I tossed a package of party hats back onto the shelf.

Poppa Dad followed me down the aisle. "I'm not saying anything more on the subject."

"We're different from other people," I said, "him and me."

The hard part was the present. I felt sorry for Poppa Dad, trailing along behind me. He was a lot more good-natured about the whole thing than I'd been the week before, helping Marie shop for Gloria.

First I dragged Poppa Dad through every aisle of Homer's fanciest men's clothing store. A salesman in a three-piece suit followed us around until Poppa Dad told him we'd give him a hoot if we needed his expertise. Poppa Dad had a nice way of getting people to do things.

"I can't picture Carter wearing any of this stuff," I said over a table of sweater vests.

" 'Cept maybe at his funeral." Poppa Dad held a gray vest up to his chest, crossed his arms over it and closed his eyes. "What do you think?" he said.

"Takes me back to my first glimpse of you," I said, and headed for the next aisle.

Downtown Homer didn't have much to offer, but I wouldn't have felt any better if I'd had New York City to scour. We looked at art books, pocket watches, trinkets of every kind and clothing for every occasion. After three hours Poppa Dad sat on a bench in front of the post office. He took one of his boots off and rubbed the toes, one by one.

"I don't know why this is so hard," I said.

Poppa Dad started working toward the ball of his foot. "People who don't do birthdays tend not to take kindly to gifts. Makes it rough on somebody trying to force it."

I stormed to the sidewalk, waited by a parking meter for him to call me back and apologize. When I turned around, he'd pulled the boot back on and taken the other one off. I walked to the bench and looked down at him. He smiled up at me, squinting.

"Two steps to the left," he said. When I moved, my back took the sun off his face. I could see he didn't understand what this party meant to me, why I had to do it.

"Look at me," I said.

"I'm looking," he said.

"Damn it," I said. "I mean, *look*."

Across the street two little girls had stopped to watch me chew out Poppa Dad. When my eyes met theirs, they leaned together, turned, and sprinted away, giggling. What had they been thinking, looking at me?

"Poppa Dad," I said, "when I swagger and strut and puff out my chest, I don't really feel like doing any of those things. Most of the time I don't know why I act the way I do."

Poppa Dad slid his bare foot off the bench, reached out for the boot and pulled it on slowly. I knew he wasn't sure what would be right to say.

"Last August," I said, "I stayed with my friend Jotta for a month. Her husband Sam took me out to a movie the night before my eighteenth birthday. When we got home, he unlocked the front door and made me walk in first. There were colored streamers crisscrossing everywhere. There was music playing and a big banner stretched the length of a wall, with rainbow-colored words: HAPPY BIRTHDAY PISS ANT."

Poppa Dad looked up from his boot. "You come from a long line of hearts 'n' flowers, kid."

"It was then," I said, "it first hit me: things can be just *nice*. Like what people sing about—you know, like Hooker Lee Brown's 'Sweet Jessie' song."

"Right," Poppa Dad said. "As in 'She ain't got no sting, sweet honey she bring.' "

"Exactly," I said.

"Number one," he said, "that's called 'Sweet Jessie *Blues*,' on account of, number two, the guy in the song's looking all over for Sweet Jessie and he can't find her 'cause he made her up."

"That's not the point," I said, and sat next to him on the bench. "The point is, there's a lot more sting than honey about me sometimes. I want to try a different way."

We stood and Poppa Dad put an arm around my shoulders. "Okay," he said. "Have your party, I won't try to stop you. But bear in mind what my daddy used to tell me: 'Always remember, son, no good deed goes unpunished.' "

A block later Poppa Dad stopped walking. "Only one gift I can think of that's a guaranteed hit." He pointed across the street to a liquor store. "Tasteful yet practical. Personal yet shareable between party-ers and party-ees."

Larry's Liquors didn't offer much of anything fancy. There weren't even any aisles to browse, just four walls stacked with the usual brands, and tiny old Larry behind the counter, watching every move. He smiled when I walked up to him.

"Taking the old-timer out without his walker?" he said. "Must be getting careless at the home."

"Them new choppers sure have turned you uppity," Poppa Dad said.

"It's like the toothpaste commercials say," Larry said. "Sex appeal." He flashed a Hollywood smile at me. "May I be of service, young lady?"

"I don't think so," I said.

"Can't know tills you ask.'

"I was looking for something fancy," I said. "For a present. Something special."

Larry crossed his arms in front of him, tapped a front tooth with his index finger while he gave the matter thought. He disappeared behind a burlap curtain, and when he returned he set a squat white bottle on the counter. It was shaped like the crowns they stamp on checkers, topped with a gold ball for a cap.

"After-shave?" I said.

Poppa Dad laughed and shook his head. "I can just see Carter laying back in his bubble bath."

Larry jerked the bottle away from us. "Seems I overesti-
mated the culture 'preciation of both of you."

"What the hell is it, Larry?" Poppa Dad said.

"Chokecherry wine. The best. My brother-in-law up in Big
Piney been making it for years, says this last batch was the
queen of the yield." He set it back on the counter and frowned.
"Don't know where he got these bottles."

I thought of B.R. and all the sweet foreign liquors in the
cabinet under his sink. I'd been too caught up that day in missing Carter to appreciate him sharing his comet wine with me,
calling me his very own ball of fire.

"How much you want for it?" I said.

Larry shook a bag open and lowered the bottle into it.
"We'll charge it to the home, in the old timer's name." He was
still muttering "bubble bath" when the burlap curtain fell closed
behind him.

Poppa Dad didn't say a word as we walked to the car.
When he opened the passenger door for me he said, "I got to
check the gas."

"The sphinx speaks," I said, but he didn't answer. He walked
to the rear of the car and held his hand up to shush me. He
gripped the bumper with both hands, rested his ear on the trunk,
and shook the old Bessie from side to side. It made a quiet
splashing sound, which was what Poppa Dad must have been
listening for.

"Quarter of a tank," he said. He climbed in the driver's
seat and started the engine.

"You're driving this thing where this weekend?"

"New Hampshire, then down the coast on business."

"You and what tow truck?" I said.

Poppa Dad pounded the dashboard till the lights behind
the panel went on. "This car has a *soul*."

"And no gas gauge."

He tapped the dial with the needle pointing to *F*. "It's her job to always tell me what I want to hear. It's my job to know better."

He gave me a significant look which it was my job, and pleasure, to ignore.

Walking up the lawn to the house, I went over the plans with Poppa Dad. He was to round up the bluegrass boys and come get Carter for a quick beer. They were to keep him out till six, which would give me an hour to get the place decorated.

"Got it?"

He shook his head all the way back to the car.

I heard water running when I walked in the house. I found Carter in the kitchen doing dishes. When I put my arms around his waist from behind, he didn't flinch.

"Love them dishpan hands," I said.

"Ninety-nine and forty-four one-hundredths percent pure," he said.

"Whatever that means."

He turned off the water. "That's from a commercial, from back in the sixties." He pulled a dish towel from the refrigerator handle and started drying glasses. My arms seemed suddenly to hang awkwardly from my shoulders.

"So's dishpan hands," I said. "From an old TV commercial."

Carter opened a cupboard and stacked the glasses on the shelf.

"I'm hell on wheels when it comes to dishes, you know," I said.

"Congratulations."

I crossed my arms. "I'm flattered, Carter. That's the second time you've congratulated me in twenty-four hours."

"Guess congratulations have been in order." He shut the cupboard door. I wedged myself between it and Carter and hoisted myself up to sit on the counter. I had to take his face in my hands to get him to look me in the eye.

"I don't know what to ask," I said. "I can't seem to find the right question."

Carter nodded. I kissed him lightly.

"So maybe you could just tell me what's wrong," I said.

He walked to the back door and pulled aside the curtain. "You know I'm not so hot at distilling everything into a news bulletin: 'Carter John experiencing anxiety. Stay tuned for gory details.'"

"So don't distill. Tell me a story. Once upon a time et cetera."

He let go of the curtain and it fell over the window in the door. But he kept looking out, like it didn't matter, curtain or no.

"Have you happened to notice," I said, "how this aloof act is making me feel?" I snatched up the dish towel and pressed it against my eyes, holding the crying back. "Damn," I said, not at Carter, but for all those waifish tears.

"Noticed?" Carter said, still looking at the curtain. "Sweetie, I notice everything."

"Balls." I blew my nose.

He pulled the curtain aside again. "Annie," he said, "do you ever wake up in a sweat in the middle of the night, your heart pounding and your eyes wide open? You sit up in bed, blink hard a few times, and try to remember what you'd been dreaming. But you know a dream couldn't wake you, not like that. It was the sound of your own voice, your own words coming back at you. Or it was something you did that day— you're seeing it over and over like a film loop." He let go of the curtain but didn't make a move, not toward me or away. "Yes, Annie," he said, "I notice how I make you feel. I noticed me making you play that song in front of everybody last night; I also noticed why I did it. And I woke up at dawn today and said to myself: You son of a bitch, you'd do it again."

I didn't feel like crying anymore, though I felt sadder than I had before.

"You don't have to answer my original question," he said. "I know you don't wake up like that."

"Stop it, Carter," I said.

Some trucks were revving up outside; no sooner would one roar away than another would be coming from the other direction. Carter and I never talked like this. It was dark and harsh, and I didn't know what he might say next. I only knew I didn't want to hear it.

I walked up to Carter. "So *serious*," I said. I knew right where to strike. He lurched away from me when I pinched him under his arms, where he was most deadly ticklish.

"Come on," he said.

"Whatever you say, Mr. Serious," I said, and dove for his armpits again.

He held up his hands. "You're right," he said. "This *is* serious."

He lunged at me and started tickling hard, no-nonsense, moving to the most vulnerable spots on my thighs, on my stomach, under my arms. I shrieked, buckled, kicked, punched. Retaliation tickling never worked when Carter had his mind set on letting me have it. I snatched up the towel I'd been crying into, dropped it in the dishwater and whacked him with it, which finally made him back away. I chased him into the living room, around the couch, over it, up the stairs. He shut the bedroom door behind him, tried leaning against it to keep me out. I took a sailing leap at the door, bashed it open and sent Carter flying.

"Truce!" he yelled. He held up his hands, panting.

I held the wet towel at two corners and rolled it into a tight whip.

"Peace!" he screamed. "Absolution! Amnesty!"

"I have my conditions," I said.

Carter dropped to his knees and crawled to my feet. He popped open the snap of my jeans with his teeth, was pulling down the zipper by its tongue when a horn downstairs brought his eyes to the open window.

* * *

I'd never put up streamers before, but I wanted them to look just like Jotta's had. I taped the end of one of the green rolls over the doorway to the kitchen, stretched a strip to Poppa Dad's poster and taped it over his head. It looked like toilet paper stuck on the wall. How had Jotta gotten it to look so pretty?

"For me? You shouldn't have." Tom pushed open the screen door and walked in.

"Good of you to make yourself at home," I said.

He walked to the crepe paper I'd taped up. "Is that the way you want it to look?"

I yanked the streamer and it floated to the floor. Tom shook his finger at me.

"Temper, temper," he said. He picked up the end and taped it back over the doorway. He started at the top, twisting the streamer till he'd worked his way to the roll I was holding. He nodded at the roll. "May I?"

"What do you want, Tom?"

He pointed at the crepe paper in my hands.

"You know what I mean," I said.

He tore the twisted section from the rest of my roll, pulled the second piece of tape from where I'd stuck it to hang the first strip. He fixed the new end to the wall, closer to the other end so the streamer draped in the middle.

"Pretty classy, huh?" he said.

"It looks better."

He picked up a roll of the pink from the couch, where I'd laid out everything I was using to fix up the room.

"I may just take up interior decorating," he said. He took the Scotch tape from me and stood on the couch.

"I've seen some interior decorating of yours," I said. "You did wonders with Jotta's place a time or two."

He stuck the end of the roll to the ceiling. "I've never claimed to be proud of how I've handled things." He stepped off the couch and started twisting the roll. "Now have I, Orphan Annie?"

"I wish you'd stop calling me that."

111

He crossed the room with the roll and stood on the reclining chair. "You used to like me when you were a kitten. Remember our rides?"

I remembered. Chinatown. Fisherman's Wharf. Jotta would always make me promise not to tell Marie.

"You used to beg me to take you down Lombard Street—Zigzag Street you called it."

I had loved that. I'd bury my face in his jacket and squeal from the scary fun of it. Hard left, accelerate, hard right, speed into the about-face you always knew was coming. What would Carter have said? He'd say I was too young to understand being afraid.

"I told you once," he said, "that we were ducks in a shooting gallery, that we had to go as fast as we could or the bullets would get us."

"I remember. I ran to Jotta, crying."

He was on the last corner of the room, twisting the roll. "And you ran to me the next time you saw me," he said, "begging to do it again."

I walked to the couch, stared down at the pile of paper and ribbons.

"We could use some of that green to cut all this pink," he said. "Ambience is getting a little girlish."

I started to unroll the green paper I'd been holding. "I need the tape."

Tom stood next to me. "Hold out your arm," he said. He tore a dozen or so strips of tape from the roll and stuck them on my forearm. I watched him, wondering if it would hurt to pull them off.

"We oughtta start getting creative here," he said. He tied a new pink streamer to the leg of the reclining chair, circled it once, twice, headed for the window.

"I'll have to clean this up, you know," I said.

"So tell me about this bearded fellow you came all this way to see," Tom said. He wound a strand carefully around a lamp hanging by the door.

112

"Carter," I said. "He was my teacher."

Tom turned and looked me up and down. "I'll bet there wasn't much to teach you that you didn't already know."

I lifted a piece of the tape from my arm, stuck the end of the green roll as high as I could over the chair by the kitchen door. He hadn't looked away. I twisted the roll in my hands, the way he had, and walked to the farthest corner of the room from him.

"Get creative, Orphan Annie," he said. He raised the roll above his head, uncoiled it slowly as he turned in a small circle. The streamer wrapped itself around him like the stripe on a candy cane. "Won't the old boy be tickled when I come leaping out of the cake?"

"You look ridiculous," I said.

Tom paused, looked me in the eye, gentle and calm through all the pink. His arm shot from between the streamers and the tape dispenser hit the wall with a solid crack. The plastic shattered into so many pieces that it seemed to hang in the air for a second before it drifted down. "That was an inappropriate thing to say to me," Tom said quietly. "I was making rather merry till you said that inappropriate thing. Maybe we could start all over. Do you think we could, Orphan Annie?"

I wanted to tell him again not to call me that.

"Do you?" he said.

I nodded.

"Very nice. I turn like this, and I stop like this, and I say, 'Won't the old boy be tickled when I come leaping out of the cake?' And you say what?"

I looked at my hands, realized I'd squeezed the roll of crepe paper into a tight figure eight. "There isn't any cake."

"That's sad," he said. He took small steps to the couch so he wouldn't tear the paper wrapped around him. The streamer connecting him to the lamp pulled taut when he walked. He looked down at everything laid out on the couch. "What did you get him?" he said.

"It's upstairs," I said. "It's chokecherry wine."

"Nice choice," he said. "They're pretty things growing wild, much too bitter to eat straight up. I'll bet that wine is black as ink."

"I've never had it," I said.

"My merry mood is waning," he said. "But there's no sense in wasting paper. Come help unroll me."

I stood next to him, and he handed me the roll.

"Remember what you used to say, when you'd beg me to take you down Zigzag Street?"

I shook my head no. "What do you want me to do with this paper?"

" 'Let's go play shooting gallery,' " he said.

I tried to remember if that's what I'd say. Through the front window I saw Poppa Dad's car pull up. "Tom, you gotta go now."

"Here's my hat, what's my hurry?"

"No kidding, Tom. Come on." I ran through the kitchen to the back door. I twisted the knob, couldn't force the door open. There was a sliding latch high up; it stuck, gave way. The door swung onto a couple acres of weeds and a concrete lot where semi trucks were revving up and driving in and out. "Wyoming Farms Transport," it said on the trucks. The wilderness paradise. Carter's dairy.

Tom wasn't behind me. I heard the screen door open. From the kitchen I watched Carter freeze in the doorway, the other men mounting the porch behind him. Tom hadn't moved from the center of the room, where he stood wrapped in pink crepe like Baby New Year.

"Surprise," he said.

Carter didn't move. The long-haired guy from the other night was craning his neck, trying to see around him. I heard Poppa Dad say "What the hell." Carter stepped aside and Poppa Dad walked in, a grocery sack in his arms. First he stared up at Tom like a tourist at the grizzly bear cage. Then he looked at all the crepe paper strung around the room, a single pink trail starting over the kitchen doorway and ending at Tom's feet.

"Annie..." he said.

"Tom Cleaver," Tom said, and extended his hand. Poppa Dad looked down at it.

"Tom was just leaving," I said.

Tom turned to look at me. "Inappropriate," he said. He reached up and tore the streamer that connected him to the lamp. He fluttered his arms, and the paper drifted to the floor.

"It's just that you really ought to go," I said.

Tom smiled. He walked to me, bent down, and kissed me on the cheek, a gentle, deliberate act. "See you at the shooting gallery," he whispered. When he turned to go, the air smelled sweet, like whiskey.

"Ten to one he won't be back," Max said after Tom was out of earshot.

"I wouldn't touch those odds," Poppa Dad said, and carried his grocery sack into the kitchen.

In the next fifteen minutes nobody said a word about the decor. Max cleared the paper and ribbons off the couch so he and one of the curly-headed twins could sit down. The long-haired guy sat on the floor next to the bald guy with the red tufts over his ears. The longhair had picked up one of the strips of crepe paper from the floor, was tying it into a string of knots while he talked. Carter was outside with the other twin. He'd headed straight for the porch as soon as Tom left.

I found Poppa Dad in the kitchen, loading the refrigerator with bottles of beer.

"He's outside," I said. "On the porch."

Poppa Dad screwed the cap off one of the bottles and handed it to me. "Guess he doesn't know which way to China."

I touched the spot on my cheek where Tom had kissed me. "Why wouldn't Carter say anything to him?"

Poppa Dad looked over his shoulder at me. "Your n'anderthal buddy?"

"He's not my buddy." I held the bottle to my lips, drank as much as I could in one long pull.

"Go ask him," he said, and shut the refrigerator door.

* * *

I brought two bottles of beer out to the porch. Carter and the twin were leaning on the railing, staring in different directions. I handed a bottle to each of them. Carter took it but didn't look at me. The twin smiled.

"Cathy?" he said.

"Annie," I said. "You got the *ee* part."

"Max's friend, right?"

I shrugged. "Sure."

The twin went back to staring.

"Could I talk to you, Carter?" I said.

He didn't answer, just took a slug from his beer. The twin looked at him, looked at me, said, "Think I hear my brother calling" and went inside.

I sat on the couch, but Carter didn't move, just leaned with his elbows on the banister like he was the only living soul in the state of Wyoming. I fixed my eyes on him shamelessly, stared him down from behind his back. The denim of his jeans was soft and faded, the stitching frayed over a back pocket. His shirt was in its usual state of being tucked in but not quite, making him seem both younger and older than he was. I knew that I'd go on to meet a lot more people in my life, but I just couldn't get over the way his shirt stretched tight across his shoulders, or how his pants hung low on his hips, how he moved like nobody else.

"Happy birthday, Carter," I said.

He shook his head. "What gets into you I'll never understand."

I waited for him to go on, but he didn't. "It's nice," I said, "how you're never clear about anything, except that nothing could ever be right."

"I'll try to make clear to you precisely what's not right. A Hell's Angel in pink ribbons is not right."

"He's not a monster, you know. You can talk to him and everything."

116

Carter nodded. "Good afternoon, Mr. Psycho-biker. What's new in the brutality business?"

"Are you going to turn and face me?" I said.

He wheeled around, without moving closer. "Take a look at that guy," he said. "He's bad news. He's *it*."

"It?"

"Everything," he said. "The reason there's disease and people everywhere starving. Why I don't blow party horns, why I'll never have babies. Why Judy left me. Why I'm here."

I crossed my arms in front of me. "Gosh," I said. "Sounds like Tom's been busy."

Carter lowered himself into a crouch, looked me in the eye. "I want to make you understand this," he said. "You don't even talk to men like him, Annie."

"He's not proud of what he's done," I said. "God knows he's not alone in that."

Carter stood and walked to the farthest corner of the porch, then leaned his elbows on the railing again. I felt different than I had since I'd come to Homer: it was time to give up on something, but I wasn't exactly sure why. Carter started whistling, slow and dreamy, like he wanted it clear that he was in another world in case I had any illusions about trying to reach him. I couldn't match the words to the tune at first. Then I remembered Bear Willie White's voice from one of Carter's old recordings. It was "Lost Woman Blues," the story of a man whose wife had just died of TB. The voice in the recording had given me chills; it was pure and lovely and full of grief. I heard the words in my head as Carter whistled: "Cool, dark earth ain't nothin', woman, but great lone quiet ground; I feel the cold earth under me, an' pray it's where I'm bound."

I leaped to my feet. "You've got no right."

Carter turned to me.

"All your singing the blues," I said. "All your moaning and whining and running away. It's too damn bad you don't know how to love somebody. Just make sure you stick to singing about what you know."

117

Upstairs, collecting stray shirts and socks to stuff in my backpack, I couldn't reconstruct that walk from the porch to the bedroom. But I knew that it would be a long time before I could think of Carter without remembering him whistling on the porch, and how there was suddenly no possibility of staying.

I dragged Poppa Dad into the kitchen and told him good-bye.

"You're loco," he said. "You know that."

"Day after tomorrow, tonight, what's the difference?" I said. "I've got to get out of here. Tonight. That's the most important thing."

He shook his head, which I'd already gotten used to him doing around me. "You don't leave at sundown for a cross-country drive."

"I can't stay another night, Poppa Dad." My voice didn't quiver, and I didn't shed a tear.

He put his hands on my shoulders. "There's always heading back, you know. Put on your jammies and watch television, bacon and French toast for breakfast. Dinner dates with nice-lookin' boys your own age. No shame in just going home."

I had to stop two beats to fix on where it was he meant. "San Francisco," I said. "Frazelli's Bail Bond."

"Come again?"

"I have to go finish packing," I said. I turned to head upstairs.

"Hold it," he said.

I stopped, waited.

"You're leaving tonight, aren't you?"

I nodded.

"You're eighteen years old, and you don't know where you're going."

"That's right." A shiver ran up my neck.

Poppa Dad put his hands in his pockets and let out a long sigh. "You ever get the urge to see New Hampshire?"

I knew what he was getting at, and I wanted to kiss him for it. But after what I'd been through with Carter, I was scared to seem to want anything very much.

"Look," he said. "I got a good old friend, name of Rose— she lives in the mountains out there. We take your car, and I spare my darlin' Oldsmobile another humiliating Illinois breakdown. You'd like Rose, Annie." He paused, shifted his weight. "You got to get yourself away from here."

I looked at the floor, held my elbows.

"Well?" he said.

I threw my arms around his neck, shrieked his wonderful name, kissed his lovely bald head until he blushed from ear to ear.

— 6 —

I woke with my cheek pressed against the passenger window.

"Where are we?" I said.

"Halfway to Laramie."

"How far is that?"

"Not far."

I sat up straight, switched the vent on.

"You hangin' in there?" Poppa Dad said.

"I'm just glad we left." I angled the vent so the air blew into my face.

"You go ahead if you feel like talking," he said.

I tried to decide if I wanted to talk. The next step would be what to say. I could think only in questions, ones I knew were too hard to answer. Forget the big ones, I thought, start small, immediate. Who was this man driving my car? I knew the answer to that one: He's a man I never met until yesterday at dawn, when I fed him water under a juniper bush in Homer, Wyoming.

"I feel like talking," Poppa Dad said.

"Talk then."

"All right," he said. "What'd you think of Homer?"

A semi truck passed us on the right. I looked to see if it

was Wyoming Farms Transport. Move It With Allied.

"I guess I don't feel like talking," I said.

It was an hour before Poppa Dad spoke again. "How you fixed for cash?" he said.

"Okay," I said. "Why?"

"We're fifty miles outside of Laramie. We could get a motel room. We could park in a campsite and sleep in the car. Or we could drive."

Another car passed us at a good fast clip. Our speedometer hadn't gone past forty-five since we started. "I don't want to be locked up in a strange room right now or sleep in a cold car either. Could we drive a little faster?"

Poppa Dad stared ahead. The speedometer needle didn't budge. "Why don't you tell me how you're doing," he said.

I rolled my window down far enough to hang my fingers outside and feel the cool air whip through them. "When I was little, there was this building on Sixth Street that somebody had torched. It looked normal from the outside, but if you looked in a window you could see there was nothing there, only a few rafters and everything black. Whenever something would happen that I couldn't stand, I'd pretend I was that building, and there was nothing inside me to wreck."

"Sounds fine," he said, "till something good comes along. A nice sofa maybe. You need someplace to put it."

We were quiet for another few minutes.

"If I start to talk, I might cry," I said. "And if I start crying, I don't know when I'd stop."

Poppa Dad slowed and pulled off the road. When we came to a stop, he cut the engine. "I normally wouldn't suggest this remedy for someone of your tender age. But this is a special circumstance, and we got driving to do." He popped the rearview mirror out of its socket and rested it between his knees. "Ever do this stuff before?" He unbuttoned his shirt pocket and pulled out a tobacco pouch.

"I never did like to smoke," I said.

He looked at me like he didn't think he heard me right. Then he laughed. "Won't make you smoke it, darlin', though I've seen it done." He shook the pouch till a square of magazine paper fell onto the mirror.

"A little homemade envelope," I said.

Poppa Dad opened the flap with his thumb. He unfolded the envelope till it was just a square folded in half, held one of the corners over the mirror and sprinkled a mound of white powder onto it.

"Poppa Dad," I said.

He fished a razor blade from the pouch and started pushing the powder around on the mirror.

"Cocaine?" I said.

He stopped chopping and looked up at me.

"You just seem," I said, "I don't know. Fatherly. The name and all."

He reached out to touch my cheek but I pulled away. He stroked my hair once lightly, rested his hand on my shoulder. When I still didn't look at him, he took it back.

"I guess I'm just scared," I said.

"Scared?" he said. "You, with your hobbies? Riding around with wife-beating bikers? Inviting them in when you're home alone?" He turned to the dashboard. "I had to get you away from there before you ended up in sixteen different shoeboxes under Sweetwater River."

I touched his arm. "I'm sorry."

He was nodding slowly, looking ahead. "Scared to sit in a car with me," he said.

A truck sped past us. The car rocked, stopped.

"I don't know you from the devil," I said.

" 'Bout time you learned the difference."

I watched the speedometer as Poppa Dad pulled us back onto the highway. Forty, fifty, sixty-five, seventy.

"Now I really feel like talking," I said.

I told Poppa Dad about Marie and Jotta and San Francisco.

I told him about Gloria and B.R. finally marrying and about Mr. Hoops dying of distemper. I gave him a lecture on the bail bond business and the short-sighted liberals who want the government to take over.

"Driving is so great," I said.

I rolled down my window all the way, had to yell to be heard above the roar of the wind. "You know Springsteen?" I said.

Poppa Dad shook his head.

"He's got this song, one whole song about rolling down the window. I can't remember what words it's got, but I have to sing for you—it's like, 'Hey, hey, baby, what else is there, baby, but rolling down the window of this car.' "

"Couldn't hear a word, Annie."

"The great part about that song," I yelled, "the amazing part about that song, is the 'what else.' Rolling down the window is such a 'what else' thing to do."

Springsteen. How long had it been since I'd thought about those kinds of songs? Hadn't I had enough of the dirty, low-down, hang-your-head blues? I needed songs about getting on with it, songs about riding fast and holding on tight—*highway songs*.

> . . . *Nat'ral born, easin' on the road again* . . .
> . . . *Freight train for my pillow, blanket me with starry sky* . . .
> . . . *Across the Rio Gran-dee-o, across the lazy river* . .

So many songs about riding, about *riders. My rider left on a midnight flyer . . . I know you rider, gonna miss me . . . She is a noted rider, tell me where my easy rider gone.* I'd always wondered what the rider lines meant, but it was all so clear. It was me in the songs, born to ride the highways: the songs, they *knew*.

Poppa Dad said something.

"What?"

"I'm cold," he shouted.

I rolled up the window, and my hair drifted down over my

face. I could hear my heart beating fast in my ears.

"It's too quiet in here," I said.

I turned on the radio, twisted the dial, could only get pops and sputters. I snapped it off. Was I still happy? Or was I about to wail? There seemed to be such a slight difference.

"Does it stay like this?" I said.

"Talk to me some more," Poppa Dad said.

"What about?" I said. "I told you about everything, almost."

"Almost."

So we were back to that again. "I wouldn't be able to say his name without sobbing all over myself."

"Try," he said.

I shut my eyes. "Carter." I imagined my eyelids were a movie screen and put different shots of him on it: his face, his body, in my favorite shirt, then naked. "I don't feel anything," I said. "My heart's beating too fast to feel."

"I knew it'd be good for you," he said. "Just for when things get rough."

"It's like instant burned-out building," I said. "Only it works."

I thought Carter, he's gone. Carter, never again. So what's ahead of me? What am I driving to now?

"I hardly know you, and you've done so much for me," I said. "Now I want to cry."

"You're a good kid," he said. "Carter's a good guitar player. He's not for you."

Yes, it was true, it had all been wrong: the wrong man, the wrong place, the wrong songs. Now I was out in the world with a whole different kind of man, one who thought enough of me to take me on his road trip, introduce me to his friends. I felt like crying again. I had to roll the window down just a third of the way.

"Did you mean what you said?" I asked him. "That you'd wanted to get me away from there, so I'd be safe?"

"Course I did," he said. "You're too pretty to get chain saw massacred."

I had to take a deep breath just to be calm about this great man, who'd taken me away from where I shouldn't be and given me something to help me understand that it was best. And now he was telling me I was pretty.

"You're"—I had to pause to make sure I used the best words—"a truly wonderful man."

Poppa Dad nodded and took the car up to seventy-five.

We stood in the lobby for ten minutes, waiting for the woman behind the desk to get off the phone. When we first walked in, she'd seemed my age or younger. But it sounded like she was arguing with her kid, and it was old enough to be giving her some serious lip.

Poppa Dad was slumped in an armchair he'd turned toward the window so he could keep an eye on the car. I was too exhausted to care whether somebody drove off with it, though I couldn't stop pacing the lobby, turning the postcard rack, flipping through pamphlets of recreational opportunities in La Salle, Illinois.

"I'm so sorry," she said to us after she'd slammed down the phone. "No lunch break today, plus baby-sitter can't drive, equals no swimming lesson. Period."

"Sounds reasonable," Poppa Dad said. His eyes were bloodshot and swollen, and I could hear the effort in every syllable. We walked to the desk and rested our arms on the counter.

"A room. Any room," Poppa Dad said.

"You're not serious," the woman said.

Poppa Dad and I looked at each other.

The woman pointed at the clock without taking her eyes from him. "Three o'clock, the Fourth of July. Do I look like I can do miracles?"

"Fourth of July," I said.

"Swimming lessons, rooms on a holiday," she said. "People slay me."

We stood in the parking lot and stared at the car.

126

"There's got to be somewhere," I said.

Poppa Dad pulled a quarter from his pants pocket. "Heads I ride, tails you drive."

I nodded. He flipped the quarter, caught it, slapped it onto the back of his hand. "Tails." He let himself in the passenger door and tossed me the keys.

Three hours and thirteen motel lobbies later, I pulled onto Highway 7 toward Joliet.

"It's gotta have something," I said. "I've heard of it and everything."

We turned onto Jefferson Street toward the airport, figuring that'd get us to a cluster of motels. After passing a few SORRY signs, Poppa Dad spotted our first neon green WELCOME. I pulled into the arch outside the lobby and parked underneath the outdoor chandelier.

"I don't care how much it is," I said. "If it's a motel, I'm gonna sleep in it."

"*Ho*tel," Poppa Dad said. "But I hear you can sleep in 'em just as easy."

I drove the car to the back lot and parked in the stall marked "311."

"Three flights of stairs and we're home free," I said.

I dragged my backpack out of the back seat and slung it over my shoulder. "Race you," I said.

"Throw me the keys," Poppa Dad said.

"Your bag's right there, behind the seat."

"We got to unload the trunk," he said.

"Nobody cares about your old guitars." I started toward the stairs.

"Annie," he said, in a tone he'd never used with me. He'd said my name like Marie always used to when I was to quit my fussing and hop to.

"Yes sir, ach*tung* sir." I threw the keys on the hood and marched up the stairs.

127

* * *

" *'Cheerleaders' Beach Party,'* " I read. " 'Nineteen seventy-seven. Four promiscuous cheerleaders use their charms on the rival team in an effort to save their own football team.' "

"Next," Poppa Dad said.

" *'Dream Wife.* Nineteen fifty-three. A handsome young bachelor must choose between—' "

"Next."

" *'The Divine Nymph.* Nineteen—' "

"Next."

I put down the listing. "You're sure in a persnickety mood for someone with no brain cells left firing."

He lifted the washcloth from his eyes and rolled onto his side. "Don't we get cable?"

I held up the booklet. "That was the cream of cable." I lobbed it onto his bed.

"We need a good old movie with some shootin' in it," he said. He thumbed through the pages. "Wednesday, Thursday, Independence Day."

It was still light out, though the sun must have set. I could hear firecrackers in the distance, going off in clusters. I pictured Carter sitting on his porch alone with his feet propped up on the banister. Or maybe he was having a party. With women. An Independence Day party with women and pink crepe paper streamers.

" *'Sundown on the Alamo,'* " Poppa Dad said. He got up and flipped the TV on.

"Dandy," I said. I walked over to the closet where Poppa Dad had set his guitar and two mandolins.

"Looking for something?" he said.

I pulled one of the cases toward me. "You mind if I play your guitar?"

He paused and watched me for an uncomfortable second. "The guitar, okay."

I hadn't considered that he might actually care. All three of the cases looked like they'd been through worse than an amateur fumbling with them. One of the mandolin cases had padlocks on all four of its snaps.

"Never mind," I said.

I heaved my backpack onto the bed and started foraging through it for something to wear to bed, the one thing I had never thought to pack. I could feel three switches along the bathroom wall. The first one turned the room red and hot. The second started a fan. The last one made the room so bright I had to shade my eyes.

My shampoo was the same as Carter's; I'd been using it for months to remind me of the smell of his hair. I shaved my legs as usual and not my underarms, because he'd said once he thought armpit hair was sexy. The T-shirt I'd brought to change into was from Antonio's Nuthouse, Carter's favorite bar south of San Francisco. I turned out the light and flipped the switch that lit the room red.

I sat on the toilet and let my muscles go limp, felt the rising sweat mix with the water dripping from my hair. Even now, in Joliet, Illinois, I thought of Carter when I smelled, looked at, listened to, tasted and touched the world around me. The highway songs promised freedom and no used-to-be's, just mile upon mile and anything possible. I wondered how many of those miles you had to go before those highway promises came true.

— 7 —

"So is Rose your sweetheart or what?" I said.

"You keep your concentration on the highway," Poppa Dad said.

"Coy doesn't suit you," I said. "Out with it."

Poppa Dad opened the glove compartment and started poking through the maps, like that was something he'd always been meaning to do. I had to smile.

"Sweet old thing," I said. "You're *shy*."

"Don't know which of those three-letter words I dislike more," he said.

A Mercedes zipped by doing a cool eighty. I'd gotten used to being passed since Poppa Dad was set on us going not a mile over fifty-five. It was twelve hours since we'd left Joliet. After our first night on the road, neither of us had said a word about the cocaine, or going seventy-five miles an hour, or driving all night, or Carter John.

"Rose is good," he said. "She'll make you laugh."

"Any woman'd be with you has got to have some wild sense of humor."

We were gaining fast on a Mack truck going thirty in our lane.

131

"Didn't think it was possible," I said, "somebody slower than us."

I put on my left blinker and checked the mirror. It was there, in the distance, again.

"Look behind us," I said. "Third time I've seen it."

Poppa Dad turned in his seat to look out the back window. I glided off the road into the emergency lane.

"What the hell you doing?" Poppa Dad said.

"Let's just see. If it passes us, we'll know for sure it's not him."

When we came to a stop, I put out the lights. I started counting to thirty like Jotta had taught me when I was little— one Mississippi, two Mississippi—to meter out full seconds. Nobody passed us.

I turned on the lights and eased back onto the road. "We'll get off the next exit and phone the cops," I said.

We were quiet until a sign for a rest stop came into view.

"There's no call for police," he said.

"Poppa Dad," I said, "you and Carter have spent a lot of breath convincing me I ought to learn to be scared of things. There might be a dangerous man following us. That's enough to be scared of."

"Look," he said, "your Hell's Angel buddy's on the road after his ex-wife. No reason he'd care a damn about me or you."

The last thing he said startled me. But it was true after all. Tom had only been using me—I had to remember that. And what would there be to tell police?

The speedometer had climbed to sixty-five. I tapped the brake and watched the needle move back to fifty.

"I'm sorry," I said. "I'm trying to learn. I'm going overboard, is all."

Poppa Dad brushed my hair back behind my shoulder. "You know I'll look after you. I wouldn't've left with you otherwise."

I looked in the rearview mirror again. Nothing behind us but night.

* * *

My first instinct when I woke in the back seat was to look at my watch. It was so dark I had to stare hard to focus on the face. Five after two. The car was bouncing and gyrating so much that I'd dreamed we were driving onto sidewalks and into buildings, up staircases that led to more sidewalks and buildings. But out the windows in waking life, nothing led to anything— no lights or billboards, no headlights, no signs.

"Where are we?" I said.

"Well, well," Poppa Dad said. "You been out cold since Albany."

"We driving over bowling balls?" I said.

"Been after her for years to get this paved. Throw gravel over it at least."

"We're going to Rose's?" I said. "Two A.M.?"

"She'll be just hitting the sack," he said. "Or just getting up. One of the two."

I fumbled in my backpack and pulled out my comb; I hated having to meet Rose looking and feeling so raggedy. While trying to tease the rats out of my hair, I strained my eyes to fix on something, anything, outside.

"Forest, swamp, or desert?" I said.

"Mountain, mostly. Trees, ponds, snow in the winter and mud in the spring."

The car angled steeply up, over, and down. We pulled in next to a long flat building with a row of a dozen lighted round windows.

"Unusual design," I said.

"Used to be a veal farm."

"And now?"

"Now," he said, "it's not."

Poppa Dad ran up to one of the windows, leaving the passenger door hanging open. After I slammed mine shut I had to stop and listen to what sounded like ten more car doors slamming, one after another, in what I guessed were the mountains surrounding us.

"Rosie!" he yelled, and ten more Poppa Dads called after him. He motioned for me to follow. We stopped at a door in

133

the middle of the long building, then Poppa Dad almost tripped as he reached for the knob. He bent down and shook the muzzle of an enormous dog sprawled against the door. It lifted its head, opened its eyes halfway.

"Rise 'n' shine, lunchbox head." Poppa Dad rapped the dog's skull with his knuckles.

"You're early," called a voice from somewhere inside the building.

"Couldn't wait another day," Poppa Dad said, and winked at me. He nudged the dog with his foot, but it had already fallen back asleep. I could hear footsteps inside, and rustling sounds. Uh-oh, I thought. I shifted my weight from foot to foot, unfastened my watchband and fastened it again. Poppa Dad's Rosie cheating on him? I didn't relish the idea of being around when the sparks started to fly.

"Sure wish you'd've called her," I said.

He frowned at me.

"To tell her I was coming," I said.

The door opened and the dog rolled inside. Rosie stood somewhere under five feet, with boot-black hair hanging in a low bun at the back of her neck. She held a three-foot-long kid under one arm. He was wearing only a pajama top, and he was about as alert as old lunchbox head.

Rose leaned over the dog and kissed Poppa Dad, then me.

"I have to get the bottoms on him," she said.

Poppa Dad and I stepped over the dog and stood alone in the lights of the long hallway.

I pointed after her. "Hers?" I said.

Poppa Dad laughed. "Rosie's ten years free of the moon." He lowered his voice. "That one's her daughter's. Her Kimberly ain't quite right."

I wandered a few feet down the hall, which amounted to no more than a long runway with a series of doors on either side.

"Reminds me of my grammar school," I said.

"Rosie bought it ten years ago and we fixed it up. Did all

the doors and windows myself." He turned to the front door, and we both looked at it.

"I can't figure exactly what," I said, "but there's something out of the ordinary about that door."

He ran a finger along an edge of the giant wooden X that spanned it. "A door's supposed to be held together by a Z," he said. "Got my letters confused."

Rose reappeared in the hall. She looked happy to see Poppa Dad, but her step was anything but hurried. Her bright purple robe lagged behind her on the floor, and her slippers shuffled as she walked. When she got to Poppa Dad, she leaned against him. He curled an arm around her waist and they both looked at me. There seemed to be a shortage of small talk in this mountain household.

"I'm Annie," I said.

Rose smiled.

"Poppa Dad was sure you wouldn't mind."

"I'm fifty-seven years old," she said. "I'm not about to start minding now."

When the sun first hit my eyes, I didn't know where I was. I sat up in bed and gripped the sides of the mattress, scanning the room for something familiar. The wallpaper was white, with a pattern of delicate blue ivy. The bed was covered with a faded heavy quilt. Some clothes were hanging in a tall wooden box instead of a closet built into the wall. The clothes were white and starched stiff, all made for a toddler or a midget. I remembered the kid slumped over Rose's arm. Then the dog, Rose, Poppa Dad: You know I'll look after you. Okay.

I stood and looked down at the nightgown I was wearing. It was high-necked and long-sleeved, made from starched white linen like the clothes in the wooden closet. I got a whiff of strong coffee when I opened the door and followed its smell down the hall.

When I got to the kitchen doorway, a young woman and

a red-headed teenage boy looked up at me from the table. The dog at the woman's feet turned its glance to me without taking trouble to raise its hollow head.

"Is Peter coming?" the young woman asked me.

"I came with Poppa Dad," I said.

"Peter Pan," she said.

The boy rolled his eyes. "I guess she thinks you're Wendy," he said. "She's got a thing about that story."

"I don't want to grow up either," the woman said.

"Cut it out, Kim," the boy said.

"Rose gave me this to wear," I said. It wasn't my fault this fruit loop thought I walked out of a fairy tale.

"You want some coffee?" the boy asked me.

I nodded, and he got up from the table. Before I sat down, I pulled the chair to the far end of the table from the woman. That didn't stop her from locking a nervy stare on my face. The darkness of her hair, her eyebrows and eyes gave the stare a creepy force.

"I'm Annie," I said.

The boy set a mug of coffee and a spoon in front of me. He sat down, took the woman's face in his hands, and swiveled it toward him.

"It's not polite to stare, Kimberly," he said. She seemed just as happy to look at him, and he must have been used to it enough to go about his business.

"Kimberly had a dose too many a few years back," he said.

"Dose of what?" I said.

"Orange Sunshine, I hear," he said. He poured some milk into his coffee and passed the carton to me. "Who did you say you were?" he said.

"Annie," I said. "Poppa Dad's friend."

"Cool," he said. He pulled the sugar bowl toward him and dumped three heaping spoonfuls in his cup. His skin wasn't freckled like most redheads I'd seen. It was pure, untainted white, like it had never seen a ray of sun.

"Sometimes she's okay," he said. "She comes and goes."

136

Kimberly pulled the sugar bowl toward her and lowered her face to within an inch of it. I nodded and stirred my coffee. I thought I'd seen it all at the bail bond office. But by the time the nut cases got to Marie, they'd usually progressed from sugar bowl staring to snatching invisible things out of their hair.

"What's the dog's name?" I said.

"That's Zeke," he said. "Zeke's older than God. He's our father figure when Poppa Dad's away."

We both looked at sleeping Zeke, still as a rock, his trunk and limbs spanning a quarter of the floor space in the room.

"I'm up for the summer," the boy said. "I'm Kevin."

"Kimberly's brother?"

"He is not," Kimberly said to the sugar.

"I know her brother George from school in New York," he said.

"Kimberly's brother George," she said. "Uncle George." This sent her into a peal of giggles. Tears started streaming down her face as she laughed. Kevin handed her his napkin and she pressed it to her eyes.

"I think I better get my stuff out of the car," I said.

I found Rose and Poppa Dad outside, talking to a young guy in a pickup truck. They both smiled when I walked up to them. The guy in the truck looked down, pulled his cap a little lower on his head.

"The dead awoke and appeared to many," Poppa Dad said.

"You sleep okay?" Rose said.

"This one could sleep through a fire bombing," Poppa Dad said.

Rose turned to the man in the truck. "Duane, this is Annie," she said.

Duane lifted his cap without looking up. "Ma'am," he said by way of a greeting. His cap read PARKING LOT across the front.

Rose leaned and whispered in my ear, "I think it's the nightgown embarrassing him."

"I'm covered from neck to ankle," I said.

"Duane came up to invite us to a whoop-de-doo at his ranch tonight," Poppa Dad said. "Live musicians and everything." He winked at me.

"Some boys from down't the high school," Duane said. "Muriel's expecting me." He started the engine. I headed for my car.

Poppa Dad took the pack from me as I was dragging it from the back seat.

"They sure grow 'em shy around here," I said.

"They get less bashful as they get older," he said. "Duane's not twenty. Father of three, though."

He hoisted the pack on his shoulder and headed for the house. When I slammed the car door, the echo jolted me into an awareness of the place. The whole area was made out of half-bare trees and mountain. The land behind the house rose to a dirt trail two-thirds of the way up the slope. On the other side, the ground slanted gradually from where we parked the car to a creek barely close enough to be seen. Rose's place had the look of a weather-beaten railroad train that had been stranded, by accident or by will, as far off any track as nature would allow.

I changed clothes, made the bed, and headed out the front door on an exploratory hike. I'd stopped outside the house to choose my direction when I first heard the roar of a car engine heading toward us on the road. Since the land banked up behind my Mustang, I couldn't see but ten feet of the road in back of it. The car seemed to be coming at us at ungovernable speed, given the terrain it was covering. Should I climb the grade and warn the driver that I'm parked just over the hill? Next I knew, the nose of the broadest car I'd ever seen was sailing over the top of the bank and angling down toward my rear bumper. Then there was an unearthly long screech, dirt flying, silence. I listened while scattered bits of gravel rained down on my trunk, which was not six inches from the front grille of the mountain-side dragster.

Poppa Dad stood at the front door with his arms crossed over his chest. The pale black-haired boy in the driver's seat looked at his steering wheel. That trail on the high road seemed mighty appealing to me. I was out of earshot before a car door opened.

It took the better part of an hour to get to the top. Rose's mountain was the tallest thing around, though there were peaks in the distance that made a dwarf of it. Sitting in the sun at the top of that cliff, looking down on the jagged hillsides and the valleys they made, I closed my eyes and tried to feel the power of being in that place. But all I could summon was drowsiness and a half dozen sneezes from the dry, dusty air.

I could hear Poppa Dad shouting before the veal farm even came into view. Once I got to the front door, I stood there for a few minutes, wondering whether to go in. Things seemed to have quieted down, so I took the chance.

I found Poppa Dad and Rose sitting at the kitchen table. Rose was reading a paperback. Poppa Dad was just staring, his hands wrapped around a coffee mug. He looked troubled, but I could tell it wasn't Rose he'd been fighting with. Neither of them looked up when I walked in, so I set about getting myself some ice water with all due respectful quiet.

"It's like I always told you," Poppa Dad said.

Rose didn't lift her attention from the print.

"That boy," he said. "He'd steal your face right off your head, and you'd find a way to keep reading your book."

Rose turned a page. "I expect Annie's hungry," she said.

"It's not like it's the first time," he said.

"Uh-huh," Rose said. "She's probably been hungry before."

"He is your boy," Poppa Dad said. "But the business is half mine. I'm not out of line in kicking up dirt about this."

I was having a hard time keeping myself busy enough to justify knocking around the kitchen. Once I had my ice water drunk, I took the near-full ice tray back out to run water in it. Who'd been stealing, and stealing what? What business did Rose and Poppa Dad own together?

"I told him just now," he said, "if I catch him a mile radius within your money again, I tear him asshole to appetite."

I started to pull a loaf of bread from the fridge.

"We're leaving for Duane's soon enough," Poppa Dad said, "so don't you be filling up."

I let go of the bread and went back outside.

When I spotted Kevin, Kimberly, and the black-haired boy sitting by the creek, I fought off the temptation to sneak up and listen. I didn't like how I was feeling like a spy in that house.

Everybody turned and looked at me when I walked up behind Kevin. I waved, like a foreigner or a little kid.

"*There's* Wendy," Kimberly said.

"*Ann*ie," I said. "People have trouble with that first syllable."

Nobody said anything. The black-haired boy picked up a stone and threw it sidearm at the surface of the water. It dropped with a hearty plunk.

"Now watch this time, George," Kevin said. He flung a stone at the water and it skipped along the surface, bouncing four times before it disappeared. "You've got to give it spin."

George found another stone and sent it flying just like Kevin had. But it sank at first contact with the water.

"Fuck it," George said. He reached in his back pocket and pulled out a joint.

"Mama said tonight we would dance," Kimberly said to me.

"I guess," I said. "Mr. Personality came by and invited us."

"Mr. Parking Lot," Kimberly said.

"How come it says that on his hat?" I said.

" 'Cause that's all that's under it," George said. He took a long drag from the joint and passed it to Kimberly. She may

140

have talked, acted, and thought like a little girl, but she was all pro when it came to making the most of that joint.

"I believe I nearly met you earlier," I said to George.

"Kiss my ass," he said, and continued staring at the creek.

"George has had a rough day," Kevin said.

"Another Mr. Personality," I said.

Kevin took the joint from Kimberly. "It's probably best to lay off him," he said.

"Just trying to pass the time of day with a kid who almost totaled my car," I said.

Kevin held the joint up to where I was standing.

"I've got an important engagement," I said. "With grown-ups." I turned and headed back toward the house. I tried to ignore the footsteps behind me. Soon I felt a hand on my shoulder.

"Wait up," Kimberly said. She bent over, panting.

"You okay?"

She was still, then held her sides and started to cough. She couldn't seem to get air.

"Should I get somebody?" I said.

She stopped coughing, started drawing her breath, slow and deep. When she seemed back to normal, she stood up and smiled.

"Eggs-her-shun-all-as-ma," she said.

I shook my head. She repeated what she'd said. I listened hard, thought for a minute.

"Some kind of asthma?" I said.

"George is mean," she said.

We were quiet walking back up the slope to the house. I didn't know whether I should talk to her. I couldn't figure out how much she understood.

"What was all the fighting about earlier?" I said.

Kimberly laughed. A few minutes later she started singing a song as we walked, to a tune something like "Mary Had a Little Lamb."

> *The cow and the tick and the three blind mice,*
> *Three blind mice,*
> *Three blind mice,*

The cow and the tick and the three blind mice,
Sat on the blacktop shooting dice.

"That's a good song," I said.
"You sing the next verse," she said.
I never was very good at improvising lyrics, but I decided to give it a whirl.

The cow he rolled the snake eyes twice,
Snake eyes twice,
Snake eyes twice,
The cow he rolled the snake eyes twice,
His tears drowned the tick and the three blind mice.

Kimberly didn't say anything when I finished. At first I was scared that my verse was too violent—God knew what kinds of things upset her. When we got to the house, she stopped, took my hand in hers and squeezed it.

"That was good," she said, and walked inside alone.

"Your mother and father both redheads?" I asked Kevin.
"So I've heard," he said. "I can't say firsthand."
Whoops. I'd been trying during the whole drive to get Kevin to talk, just so he'd know it wasn't him I'd been mad at down by the creek. The four of us were stuffed in the back seat of the car George had been tearing up the mountain with. I was pressed between Kevin and the window. Kevin had the pleasure of being wedged between me and Kimberly. George had refused to sit anywhere but the window seat. Poppa Dad was driving, and Rose was in the front seat with Kimberly's little boy in her lap. As far as I could tell, Kimberly never made a move toward the kid or even acted like she knew him. Rose was bouncing him on her knee and humming a tune in his ear.

"Somehow, though," Kevin said, "I got these from Poppa Dad." He leaned his face close to mine and pulled down the skin under his bloodshot eyes.

142

"What's he saying?" Poppa Dad said.

"Not a word," I said.

"Could've sworn I heard some little flyspeck besmirching my good name."

Kevin started making a buzzing noise up behind Poppa Dad's ear. Poppa Dad reached back and swatted at him.

"You're gonna look funny, all rolled up in a ball," Poppa Dad said. He swatted at Kevin again and again, but Kevin always ducked just in time, came up buzzing all the louder. Kimberly was rocking back and forth, giggling.

"Rolled up in a ball," Poppa Dad continued as he swatted, "looking all around for a friend to help you, and all you can see is hemorrhoids."

Sometime, while Kevin buzzed and Poppa Dad swatted, while Kimberly was hugging her knees and laughing, I caught a glimpse of brother George, staring me down. He had Kimberly's dark hair, eyebrows, and eyes, and his skin being many shades whiter made his face look a whole lot fiercer than hers. But there was something that had nothing to do with hair or skin that made me know what was behind brother George's stare. Somehow I'd made an enemy, and there wouldn't be a thing on earth I could do to change it.

– 8 –

I leaned in Kevin's ear and whispered, "Tell me that's not made of what I think it's made of."

Kevin lowered his face toward the serving dish, turned a mound of casserole over with his spoon. He looked up at me and winced.

I mouthed the words: "Casserole out of potato chips?"

He nodded, sadly. It was the second time we'd both gone through the buffet line. We'd hoped we had missed something edible on the first round.

Kevin pointed to another dish.

"Peas in Miracle Whip," I said.

"You're making that up," he said.

"I asked a lady first time through," I said. "She said it was good, but she didn't take any."

Kevin shuddered. "I'm checking out the dessert table."

"Wait," I said. "There's chicken."

"Take a good look."

I put a drumstick on my plate. "So?"

"That's Rice Krispies it's coated in," he said. "Chicken and breakfast cereal together isn't right."

He cut out of line and headed for the desserts. I was hun-

145

gry enough to eat chicken in any company. I speared the biggest breast on the platter.

Once Kevin had loaded his plate with desserts, I followed him to the picnic table where our group was sitting. Rose was happily working her way through a heaping plate of processed-food casseroles. Kimberly was devouring a plastic bowlful of green Jell-O with marshmallows. Kevin sat down next to her and started scooping his chocolate pudding on top of his cake. George had Kimberly's kid on his lap. He was holding a spoon of applesauce to the little boy's lips and inching it just out of reach every time he'd try to take a bite.

I put my plate on the table and tapped George on the shoulder. "You got the kid on Weight Watchers?"

George jerked around to look up at me, like the bully caught torturing the neighborhood cat. His eyes were so red that I'd've thought he'd been sobbing all day if I hadn't known better. Kimberly was oblivious, as always, and Kevin had set about shoveling cake into his mouth. Rose was eating with unnecessary concentration; it was hard work, ignoring the evil in George.

"Benny ain't family to you," he said, "so fuck off."

The spoon went flying out of George's hand when I grabbed Benny under his arms and lifted him onto my hip. His stare stayed locked on George's plate while I carried him away.

"We'll get you your own damn applesauce," I said.

There were a half dozen people milling around the dessert table. The whole town of Lesh, New Hampshire must have been in attendance at that party. Duane's lawn circled his house, a quarter mile in each direction. There were three other clusters of food tables scattered around, but I didn't have much hope for the cuisine anywhere in the state.

Once I found the bowl of applesauce, I was faced with the task of loading a plate with one hand. I'd never held a little kid before—we didn't get a lot of two-year-old traffic at the bail bond office. My arms were already aching. Can you put a kid that age down in a strange place? Babies of every size and shape were crawling, climbing, tumbling, and falling just about everywhere on the property I looked. I lowered Benny to the lawn, propped him against a leg of the table.

"Hang loose," I said. "I just need a minute to get you a plate ready."

Benny hugged the table leg and stared up at me with his mother's eyes.

"Your first?" someone said.

I looked from the table to see a round-faced woman in a pantsuit, beaming at me.

"I haven't eaten yet," I said. "I'm getting some for the kid."

The lady frowned, then laughed. "I meant, your first little one," she said. "I could tell by how careful you been watching him."

I picked up a paper plate and spoon, tried to make myself look too busy to talk. I scooped some of the runny applesauce onto the plate. The angel cake looked pretty harmless, so I cut him a wedge of that. I spooned some fruit cocktail beside it, added a little whipped cream.

"You Dawson kin?" she said.

I looked up at her in mid-scoop.

"Who's your people?" she said.

"Oh," I said. "I'm stepsister-in-law, once removed, to Great-aunt Muriel's third cousin Phoebe."

The woman nodded and smiled warmly. I hoisted Benny in one arm without spilling a drop.

I sat us on the grass next to where Poppa Dad was playing horseshoes with Duane and two other young men. One of them sent the horseshoe spinning toward the pole with all his might. It clanged so loud when it hit that Benny jumped and fell against me, screwed up his face in preparation for tears.

"Check this out," I said, and held a spoon of applesauce up to him.

He looked hard at the spoon without unscrewing his face.

"Mmm," I said, and took a bite. I filled another spoon and held it to his lips. "Benny's," I said.

He wrapped his fist around the handle and forced the spoon into his mouth. I wondered if all babies smelled like him—a combination of clean laundry and sour milk.

"Ain't that precious." George almost tipped over trying to sit cross-legged on the grass.

"Must be some weed you kids got," I said. "Not half a brain left between you."

He gave me another hard stare with his black and red eyes.

"You really think you're something special, don't you," he said. "You showed up here thinking you knew it all."

I balanced a bite of cake and some fruit cocktail on Benny's spoon. "I know some things," I said. "I know Poppa Dad's a man of his word. If he says he's going to tear you inside out, you may as well go ahead and notify your tailor."

Poppa Dad stepped up for his turn. He measured the distance with his eye, tossed the horseshoe in a gentle, slow arc. It fell on the grass, bounced, and tapped the pole.

"You don't know shit about Poppa Dad," George said. "You don't have the guts to hear the truth."

The men playing with Poppa Dad were all patting him on the back and smiling. Duane took off his Parking Lot hat and put it on Poppa Dad's head.

"You're one of those chicks," he said, "acts really smart and tough. You're one of those who's really just scared and don't know shit."

"You're high," I said.

George uncrossed his legs, rolled onto his feet and stood up. "If we went back home before the rest tonight," he said, "I could prove he's not what you think he is."

"I have no interest in your little-boy lies," I said.

"Whatever," he said. He started wandering backwards, away from me. "You say no, and I'll always know you were scared."

He turned, walking aimlessly.

"You'll know it too," he called over his shoulder.

Benny was slapping the whipped cream with both hands. I shook most of it off them, wiped his fingers on the grass. Poppa Dad was making raspberry noises while Duane was taking aim.

"Some things," I said to Benny, "you can't let people get away with saying."

I told Poppa Dad everything George told me to say so we could get the keys to the car.

"You sure you're okay?" Poppa Dad said.

"I'll be fine," I said. "I just need to lie down by myself."

He handed me the keys. "Just don't let George behind the wheel. You drive home, make Kevin drive back."

I nodded. It seemed better than lying with words.

He kissed my cheek. "Sweet dreams," he said.

George and I didn't say a word to each other while we sneaked out to the car. I let myself in the driver's seat and pulled up the passenger lock from inside. George slid in and slammed the door.

"Sure you're not too sick to drive?" he said with a grin.

"If you say one more word to me before we get to the house, I'll smack you till your eyeballs turn white again."

George didn't lose that grin during the whole drive to the veal farm. I tried to remember if I'd ever hated somebody so much or if I'd ever participated in anything that made me so ashamed of myself. I kept trying to tell myself it'd be worth it, to stop his talk for once and for all. But there was a hard truth underneath my going back: If there was something secret and ugly about Poppa Dad, whatever it was, I wanted to know.

I eased the car slowly up and over the hill behind my Mustang. The little punk got out before I'd shut the engine off, strutted inside the house and turned on the lights. When I got to the doorway, he was standing in the hall with his arms crossed in front of him.

"This way, please," he said, and motioned me to follow him down the hall. He walked ever so slowly, started talking without turning around.

"So I guess you noticed," he said, "we're losers, us kids. Kimberly's an acid casualty. I steal, smoke, deal—when I can get my hands on something to deal."

"I don't want to hear it," I said.

"There's nice, sweet Kevin," he said, "who you like so much. Next time you see him, ask him to show you his track marks. There's a fresh one from this morning behind his knee."

"You're a liar," I told him, knowing all the while that what he said was probably true. The skin, the eyes, all that sugar in the coffee. I'd seen enough junkies in the bail bond office to wonder why I hadn't suspected Kevin before.

George opened the door to the room where Rose and Poppa Dad slept.

"This is stupid," I said. I thought of the haunted house downtown where Jotta took me every Halloween when I was little. I always knew it was only kids wearing sheets who'd jump out at us in the dark. But there was always that fear that something would catch me off-balance, something I hadn't seen in the shadows. The thing about Kevin had been no fake. George turned on the light.

"We've got no business being in here," I said. I put my hands in my pocket so he wouldn't see them shaking.

He patted the bed. "Make yourself comfortable," he said.

I pulled the chair from the old oak desk and sat down. George crawled halfway under the bed and pulled out Poppa Dad's mandolin case.

"He doesn't like people messing with his instruments," I said.

George lifted the mandolin case to the bed. He went to the dresser, opened the middle drawer and started looking under the sweaters.

"Poor Poppa Dad," he said. "All these years he's tried to straighten out us loser kids. He's tried money, and threats, and fancy schools." He held up an inch-long key and shut the dresser drawer.

"It's not his fault if it didn't work," I said. "I can't judge him. He's been too good to me."

George sat on the bed and started unlocking the padlocks. "He should've been," he said, "after how good you've been to him."

"I haven't done a thing for him."

He unhooked the last padlock, flipped up all four snaps and lifted the lid. The case was stuffed neck to belly with plastic bags full of white powder.

"You gave him cover," he said. "A beaten-up yellow Mustang and a stupid girl on a cross-country trip."

I walked to the bed and stared down at the case.

"You been used, lady," he said. "By my sort-of daddy, who always set us such a good example."

I picked up one of the bags and held it. It was soft, light; you could squeeze it together like flour, only there were little white rocks in places. I'd wanted to be able to laugh off George and all his melodrama, but something kept my blood pulsing fast. It wasn't the cocaine that mattered—how could I get high-and-mighty after filling my nose with it that night on the road? But all this time, through all that had happened, he'd never told me we were moving this stuff. It all came back in a rush: the speed limit driving, his watching over my old Mustang like it was worth something, his shooing me away from the mandolin case. Was I just one of his wards, like George or Kevin or Kimberly?

"I better go back," George was saying. I heard it about a minute after he said it. When I looked up, I saw that his grin was gone. He was standing in the middle of the room, looking sadly at the floor. He left, and I heard the car start up. It backed over the hill, turned around; then slowly, meekly, the sound faded away.

I unsealed the bag, wet my finger and touched the powder to my tongue. The taste brought back that first night on the

151

MICHELLE CARTER

highway, the bitter saliva at the back of my throat. Carter had made me feel scared and helpless, but Poppa Dad invited me to New Hampshire and made me feel strong and important. He had to get me out of Wyoming, he said. To keep me safe. Was that what he told the others too? Rose's Kimberly ain't quite right, that's what he thought of her. He didn't think enough of George to trust him behind the wheel of a car or around his own mother's money. How was it he'd spoken of Carter? Too selfish to feel: a child. All these chances taken, all these miles down the road, I could as well have stayed in Marie's back room.

I found a straw in the kitchen and cut off a short piece with a carving knife. In the bedroom I stuck the straw in the bag, held one nostril shut and breathed in a lungful. I breathed out through my mouth, in again through the bag. First came a searing pain, all the way to my eyes. I let the air out slow, waited for the euphoria that had wiped away Carter that long, empty night. My heart sped up, and I could feel the blood rush. It wasn't wiping the unwelcome thoughts away. It was making them clear and orderly, giving them size and shape and power.

I took a blank sheet of music paper and a pen from the desk. They'd given Carter his song in Homer, his bear-wrassling song that made his lies into legend. Now it was my turn.

I drew a tall treble clef along the left side, sprinkled sharps and flats on the page like stars. Along the top I wrote my title: "THE REAL-LIFE LEGEND OF A MAN CALLED DAD." So many words were thundering to be put onto paper.

> 'Neath the bushes, passed out cold,
> Without a shirt and lookin' old:
> He's Everyone's Dad, or so I learned
> (Once the great man's strength returned).

> Whose Mustang was it anyway,
> Driven slow to keep the cops away?
> Who held his hand, who took the wheel
> When tiredness made his eyeballs reel?

152

> *But little girls do what they're told—*
> *Otherwise they'd act too bold;*
> *They don't ride motorcycles, don't do junk,*
> *Don't get told what's in the trunk*

I was writing fast and could have pushed on and on till they all came home, but I wasn't about to be found sitting at an oak desk writing verse. Poppa Dad didn't know what a natural I was with danger, how as a kid I'd printed names on the folders at the bail bond office, the names of thieves and murderers and rapists, still on file and written in my hand. But there wasn't time to put all that in the song. I stopped to think of some closing lines, something to tell Poppa Dad I was nobody's child, that my time was coming any day, don't worry 'bout me, no.

> *I'm hot as a pistol but cool inside—*
> *Bound for hell in a bucket, and loving the ride.*

I took the bag of powder and left the paper on top of the mandolin case for Poppa Dad and the world to see.

The dark it was getting was the deep empty dark of no signs and no buildings. I got good at holding the bag and the straw so I could breathe in whenever I wanted to without stopping from driving. There went a signful of letters meaning nothing—OMPOMPANOOSUC—and then RIVER, which had a meaning. If fifty-five was halfway between danger and safe, then seventy was closer to danger but without being all the way there.

Massachusetts and Jotta were south, and when I got south, I'd figure out how to get to her. Jotta was trying to learn to live safe, which I could never do so there was nothing to risk. There was a day Jotta spilled boiling pudding on my bare thigh when I was still in kindergarten. I was crawling under her feet and she tripped with the pan, and it felt like lava eating through my leg. She took me to the doctor and I watched him pulling the dead skin off with a tweezers. The doctor said, you'll have the greatest scar, Annie, it will form the shape of a letter *A*. I watched him pull off the dead skin and saw the *A*, while Jotta stood beside me and couldn't look, could only cry. I'll get to her before Tom and warn her and save her from crying and from not being safe. I can do that because I can watch things burn without ever having to look away.

Then a sign with meaning: WELCOME TO MASSACHUSETTS. Thank you. Then more signs. Highway 91 to Springfield? To 202 east? She's near water, that's east. Thank you sign, thank you 202.

When the red light and the siren came and I looked down, the needle said eighty, too far toward danger. I stuffed the bag in the glove compartment, slammed it, it wouldn't shut, I was making the car weave. He made me stand outside and he looked right where it was and found it. When he was putting handcuffs on me and reciting something his breath smelled like coffee and I asked for some. I'm sorry, he said, and I could tell he was, and when I said I might be sick, he put me in his front seat and told me to fix my eyes on the lines in the road, not to either side and not ahead.

There was a woman at a desk, questions, black ink on my fingers and a flash picture. Another woman took my clothes, and she wasn't sorry like the policeman had been. When I asked her why she had to stick her finger up me she said Drugs, and I said Why the hell would I keep them in there? but she didn't answer. In a toilet in a cage with a woman asleep in a high bunk, I threw up cake and chicken and probably Rice Krispies too. Curled up in a low bed with my face to the wall, I knew the flames had finally spread throughout me, that there was too much black and dryness for tears. But the muscles of my face and chest and stomach squeezed tight like they were sobbing, pulsing with sobs so I could hardly breathe. It was everything from inside that caused the pain, so that what came in from outside only soothed the sting from the fire and the ache of the dryness. The sound of footsteps were rhythm—the tick of a clock, a song. The jingle of keys was music too, and the whine of hinges. A woman's voice saying my name, the touch of a hand on my shoulder. The voice calling from the door down the hall. "Wake up," it said. "Wake up, Orphan Annie."

– 9 –

"Does she want more coffee or not?" I heard the waitress say.

Tom smiled up at her. "Old 'Nam injury," he said. "She can't hear too well."

When the waitress left, he took my hand. I pulled it away. "What kind of a joke was that?" I said.

He reached across the table and took my hand again. When I tried to pull it away this time, he held it so it wouldn't budge.

"You're still a little dopey, my dear," he said. "You're not processing information as efficiently as you otherwise might."

I tried again to pull away, but he squeezed my hand harder, too hard. I knew it wasn't going to stop, so I relaxed the muscles, the bone, the skin, till it didn't hurt so bad.

"And I also think," he said, "we can safely say you'd be better off not resisting me." He held my hand harder.

"Tom, stop," I said, "or easier anyway."

"Don't you think we can safely say that?"

I nodded. A tear fell down my cheek. He let go of my hand. The fingers seemed to crack when I tried to make them bend.

"I thought you were sorry about having always been rough," I said.

He looked away. I rubbed my knuckles, but it wasn't helping the ache. Tom was right about me being dopey still. But that didn't mean I'd let anybody hurt me. I repeated that to myself since it was getting to seem important.

"I am sorry," he said.

Another tear fell, and I couldn't say why. "I'm just so tired," I said.

It was getting light outside the window that looked onto the parking lot. My watch said almost five. "I don't know what town this is," I said.

Tom started to take my hand, then stopped. "I want you not to worry," he said.

"That's a thing," I said, "I been hearing lately."

I stopped at the cigarette machine on the way to the bathroom. I remembered how when I was a tiny kid, Jotta used to lift me up to the slot so I could put her money in. I thought how nice it would be now to drop in the coins, pull a lever and hear a pack thud into the tray. I'd go back to the booth and light one up like Jotta would, lose myself in the rhythm of drawing a puff, blowing it out. But I'd never smoked before, and I didn't have any change. Was my backpack in the car? Was there still two grand stuffed in the side pocket?

I couldn't believe what greeted me in the bathroom mirror. My face was puffy, and my eyes glistened—red, glazed, slick from tears. Okay, so I had trusted two people, loved them even, and they didn't treat me like I wanted them to. So shove an ounce of cocaine up my nose and get thrown in jail? Get myself messed up so bad that Tom Cleaver starts taking charge? I let cold water run onto my hand until I couldn't feel the soreness. It was time, past time, for pulling myself together.

"I need the keys," I told Tom. "I need something from the car."

A wide smile spread across his face. "Sit down," he said. "You're in no shape to drive."

I let out a long sigh and sat at the edge of the booth seat. "I'm in no shape to trump up lies," I said. "Give me the keys."

"We have matters to discuss, you and I." He pulled some papers from his back pocket. "We've got arraignment forms here—a notice to appear, a statement and charges slip. It seems I signed the dotted line a time or two to get you sprung—not to mention the little matter of you know what money."

The waitress came and poured me more coffee without asking. There was a run behind her knee, tearing its way to her ankle. I took a deep breath.

"Thank you, really, for posting bail," I said. "I want those papers and the keys to the car."

He shrugged, pulled the keys from his pocket in a slow motion, put them on the papers and pushed them across the table.

"However and wherever you want to play it," he said.

He touched my elbow as I turned to go.

"Farley, Massachusetts," he said.

I stared back at him. He smiled.

"That's where you are," he said.

My car seemed different from before. The dawn rays shone cold and white, lighting up every fingerprint, every scuff on the dash. The cops had pulled everything out of the glove compartment and left it in a heap on the passenger floor. One look at the backpack told me that everything had been taken out and stuffed back in however it would fit. I checked the side pockets till I found the envelope of twenties.

I started to shove everything they'd thrown on the floor into the glove compartment, then stopped to tidy the stacks as I went. Once some kind of order was restored, I pulled out the U.S. map. Step one would be to plot a course.

Farley was on 202. I'd been heading east, I vaguely remembered. To Jotta—I had fixed on her, I'd wanted to save her from

Tom forever. Now I just downright needed her, like I'd never needed anybody.

When I started the engine, the needle barely lifted over *E*. At the station I could get directions to 202. I pulled out of the parking lot as Tom headed for the door. Let him go to her one more time. I was going to get there first.

− 10 −

I was in no shape to drive. After a half hour I stopped at a Howard Johnson's for a breakfast roll and two coffees to go. The farther east I got, the more cars jammed the highway.

The names of Massachusetts towns sounded like nothing in the West. Road signs offered to take me south to Belchertown, Old Furnace or New Braintree. I could go north to Athol or Ashburnham. As I approached Leominster, a billboard bragged: THE PIONEER PLASTIC CITY.

The coffee kept me rolling down 495. I passed Boxborough, Marlborough, North-, South-, and Westborough. Winnecunnet. Ninnenicket. Snipatuit. Assawompsett. By the time I got to the Cape, Buzzards Bay sounded like a sensible name.

I pulled up to a phone booth and sat with the engine idling. It had been almost a year since I'd seen her. It was right after she'd moved to Santa Barbara, right before she married Sam. They'd been talking even then about moving to Cape Cod, where he'd spent time as a boy. I couldn't remember the name of the town, but they'd spoken about it like it was Oz.

A warm wind whipped through the booth while I paged through the phone book for a list of towns. I finally found a map of rates and prefixes. I remembered they'd said it wasn't far from Provincetown, which was way to the end of the hook of land. Nothing sounded familiar at first, not Orleans, not Truro. But I knew it as soon as I spotted it. Terrapin, just south of Wellfleet.

The operator gave me Jotta's number without pausing a beat, like she'd been waiting for me to call and ask for it. I looked at the number, scrawled on the cover of the phone book. So there it was. It was simple as that.

I was just about to give up when I heard someone lift the receiver. The voice sounded like it was under water.

"Jotta?" I said.

She paused. "Who's this?"

I almost hung up out of nervousness. "Did I wake you?"

"Annie?" she said. "Where the hell are you?" A greeting I hadn't expected.

"I take it you've talked to Marie," I said.

"You're in Wyoming aren't you, with your Roman Polanski friend."

Though I'd declared Carter officially out of my life, remarks like that still made me hot.

"Are you?" she repeated.

"If this is going to be your attitude," I said, "I just may not tell you where I am."

"We're issuing phone threats are we?" she said. "Oh aren't we grown up."

"The royal 'we' is a nice touch," I said. "They print your face on stamps in Massachusetts?"

We both went quiet at the same time. At least we still shared the same sense of when things were getting out of hand.

"Are you somewhere safe?" she said.

"Jotta, I hope so."

Jotta was sitting on her front lawn when I drove up. The first thing that struck me was that she'd cut her hair short. Without all that frizzy hair for her to hide in, her face seemed bold, fearless.

We hugged before we said a word. Jotta made me nervous when she drew away. She stood and looked me up and down, like she was hoping to find a clue as to what had made me so pale and dirty.

"I like your haircut," I said.

She nodded.

"Okay, so I look like hell," I said.

She looked away. I must have looked even worse than I'd thought.

"You got food in this house?" I said.

She turned without answering, and I followed her inside.

Jotta tried to talk me into an omelet, but I needed something heavy and bland. We sat at the kitchen table while my hamburger cooked.

"I'm not going to pump you," she said. "But if you feel like it, you can tell me. Anything."

"Thanks," I said. "I don't think I'm ready yet. Especially not for the anything part."

She got up and flipped my hamburger over.

"How're you and Sam?" I said.

"Good," she said. She smiled and said it again. "Good." She washed her hands and sat back down. "You take care of that from here on in," she said. "Patting the grease and all that." She shuddered.

"Since when are you so squeamish about hamburger grease?" I said.

"Oh," she said, "since about three months ago."

I waited for her to go on, but she just looked at me. When I didn't say anything, she rolled her eyes.

"I quit smoking then too. Enough clues?"

"You? Quit smoking?" I couldn't think of why she'd do such a thing.

"Three months," she repeated, and patted her stomach. "Get it?"

Her belly was a little full, but that wasn't unusual for her. "You're kidding," I said.

Jotta frowned. "I'm thirty-eight, that's what I am," she said.

I got up and turned the burner off. I stood and watched the coil fade from red to black.

"But you hate kids," I said.

She shrugged. "None of them's ever been mine before."

I pulled some paper towels from a roll and laid the hamburger on it.

"At thirty-eight," I said, "isn't it dangerous?"

"That's a relative word, Annie," she said.

After I ate, cleaned up, and slept a few hours, Jotta took me on a walk around where she lived. The main street downtown was packed with tourists, she said. But the places we walked were woody and lush. The houses were old and several stories tall. Most of them had porches with rocking chairs, and houseplants hanging everywhere. We'd pass ponds around one bend and sand dunes around another. The road ended right on a beach, where sea gulls floated on the water like ducks.

"Don't they have waves here?" I said. "Or cliffs? Or wind?"

"You can go up to Maine for all those," she said.

On the way back I took a good look at Jotta's belly. She didn't look any different from when she put on a few pounds. We passed a yard where a woman was hanging clothes on a line. A little blond boy was running a truck over her feet. Jotta smiled at the kid, then she and the woman exchanged a knowing, loving nod.

"I remember," I said, "more than once, you saying there was nothing uglier than a clothesline or kid's toys scattered around a room. You'd leave a restaurant if there was a baby somewhere in it 'cause you couldn't relax with it screeching in your ear. You wouldn't eat from a salad bar since you were sure some kid had been picking at it."

Jotta was nodding. "You're right," she said.

I waited, but she didn't add anything.

"So?" I said.

"So what?"

"So you're pregnant!" I said. "So what happened?"

Jotta crossed her arms in front of her. She seemed to be giving it serious thought.

"I just feel different now," she said.

We walked awhile longer without saying anything. Next I knew we were back at the house.

"Let me give you a tour of the place," she said.

I followed Jotta through two stories of woody rooms. They all had fireplaces and low-to-the-ground furniture strewn with colored pillows. In the attic we sat on a trunk by a narrow window that was round on top, like windows in church. We looked out on grass, and dunes, and the dirt road leading down to that calm, sleepy ocean.

"Just look," Jotta said. "This is part of why it's different now."

"It's pretty," I said.

"It's not just that," she said. She crossed her legs and rested her chin in her hand.

"I don't mean to be aggravating," I said.

She shook her head. "I just can't find words for what I want to explain."

She unlatched the window and pushed it open a foot. "Look straight down," she said.

I stuck my head outside and looked down on a strip of close-cropped greens surrounding the house.

"That's my garden," Jotta said.

"Looks nice."

"It does more than look nice," she said. "Sam taught me how to do it. He knows all about weather, and the seasons, and planting by the stars. Remember how I used to get depressed about things, and crazy?"

"You always kept it under wraps."

"Oh, yeah," she said. "I had shrinks, and therapy groups, and diets. Regulated, of course, by whatever Tom had in mind for me. And if I ever did start to get better and pull away, he'd drag me back down so fast I'd get a nosebleed."

Tom. I'd hoped he wouldn't come up quite so soon.

"Then I'd be back at booze and pills," she said. "And then he could beat me for being back at booze and pills. So then I'd be more messed up and need more booze and pills. That was me under wraps."

The breeze was whistling through the open window. The latch squeaked when I slid it shut.

"Now," she said, "if I feel a little lost, a little crazy, I take a spade out to the garden. Now, out of all my frenzied digging, I get carrots, lettuce, onions, beets." She was pointing out the window. "Jasmine in the spring. Sweet potatoes in the fall."

"That's great," I said, but I was thinking about Tom.

Jotta folded her hands over her belly. "Tell me what happened to you," she said.

I shook my head. How could I ever tell her about his following me to get to her?

"Annie," she said. "This isn't Marie you're talking to."

She was right after all. This was Jotta, my Jotta, and my keeping quiet was only hurting her. I started with Carter and at dumpy Oakland bar. After Wyoming was New Hampshire, George opening the mandolin case, me grabbing the bag and skidding straight into jail.

"I can't get over," Jotta said, "how they sprung you so fast."

I stopped, slid up the latch and pushed the window open again. "And on my own recognizance yet," I said. "Lucky thing, what with nobody to put up bail. I ate breakfast alone in this horrible diner. In Farley, I think it was. Farley, Massachusetts."

* * *

166

I was sprawled on colored pillows and flipping through a gardening book when Sam walked in the front door. He smiled when he saw me lying there. I realized I'd never seen him look surprised about anything.

He knelt next to me and buried a furry kiss on my cheek. I grabbed his neck and held him down so I could rub my face against all those blond, fleecy whiskers.

"Somebody should make a sweater out of you," I said.

"Booties," he said, and raised his eyebrows. "Hear the news?"

I nodded. "I'm happy for you."

"Guess who dropped by," Jotta said coming down the stairs.

Sam clapped his hands together. "Great timing," he said. "The horseradish should be coming of age today."

The floor shook under me as he stomped from the room toward the kitchen.

"It's a rare man," I said, "that gets excited for horseradish."

By suppertime I was starting to feel like a person again. I'd spent most of the day lying around and sleeping. I'd taken two showers, eaten pears from Jotta's garden and half a loaf of Sam's homemade bread. Around sundown Jotta and I sat at the dining room table, where they'd laid a lacy white tablecloth, thick clay plates and heavy silverware.

Sam carried in a steaming kettle and rested it on a potholder.

"Stew," I said. "My favorite."

Sam shook his head. "Specialty of the house," he said, "in honor of your visit. New England boiled dinner."

I nodded. "Boiled," I said.

He took my plate and lifted hunks of pale food onto it with a strainer. He set the plate back in front of me, slapped a scoop of something white onto it, then a scoop of something yellow and chunky. He served Jotta, then himself, and the two of them started cutting up their food.

"No offense," I said. "But what's on my plate?"

Jotta frowned. "Will you ever outgrow that fussiness?" she said.

I was summoning a reply till I felt Sam scoot his chair next to me.

"This"—he pointed with his knife—"is beef. This is some of Jotta's cabbage, her carrots and sweet potatoes." He cut a piece of the beef and a piece of the cabbage and stuffed them onto my fork. "This is how it's done." He dipped the fork into the white stuff, then the yellow stuff. "Open," he said.

I opened my mouth, and he fed me the bite. That mouthful of pale food shocked my taste buds with all kinds of different flavors at once—salty, sweet, then fiery hot. I blinked hard, then opened my eyes wide.

"The horseradish," Sam said, "has officially come of age."

"What's that?" I pointed to a spindly plant with heavy green buds.

"Okra," Sam said.

"Oh," I said. "What do you do with it?"

"In civilized nations we eat the pods," he said.

We continued our tour of Jotta's garden, lit up by the moon and the lights from the house. When we walked to the far end of the biggest patch, I realized the light was coming less from the house than from the sky.

"It's bright out here," I said.

Sam pointed to the sky. "See Venus?" he said. "Rises first and shines the best. Next brightest, there, Polaris lights up the handle of the Little Dipper"—he sketched it with his finger—"in Ursa Minor, the Little Bear."

"You write lots of books about the stars?"

"Just that one," he said. "I have an agent who tells me what some publisher or other wants written. You can stretch a very little bit of knowledge into an awful lot of print."

We started to walk back to the house. Sam stopped at a tree by the back door and took my elbow. "Look." He pointed to a cluster of matted twigs and straw in the crotch of the tree. "See how low the squirrels are building their nests."

"Are they afraid of falling?" I said.

"It tells you there's a bad winter coming," he said. "There've been signs already. Sweet potatoes are growing a tougher skin; carrots have been reaching deeper in the earth. The bark's thicker on the trees. Screech owls sound like women crying."

"Owls," I said, not thinking about owls. I was thinking about Tom coming and how I had no choice but to start preparing us all for it.

"Did Jotta ever tell you much about people in San Francisco?" I said.

Sam was leaning closer to the nest, being careful not to touch it.

"There's someone," I said, "you probably ought to know about."

Sam backed away and turned toward the house.

"Squirrels," he said, "or maybe just jays. Not worth stirring things up to find out."

Sam and Jotta looked at me as I was coming down the stairs. Sam was stacking wood in the fireplace and Jotta was crumpling newspaper.

"Up front with it," Jotta said. "What're you hiding behind your back?"

"Not so fast," I said. I stopped at the bottom stair. "Elegant glassware, please," I said.

Sam returned from the kitchen with three long-stemmed crystal goblets.

"Now," I said. "More than just a nightcap."

I held out the fancy white bottle of chokecherry wine.

"Sweet wine out of bitter fruit," I said.

I filled our glasses while Sam touched a match to the fire. The newspaper lit up white and blue under the logs as we lifted our glasses. Sam started to say something.

"Let me do the toast," I said.

Everything was quiet for a minute, except for a sizzling from the logs catching fire.

"I can't tell," I said, "if it's an end or beginning. Either way, everything is different now."

"Don't get maudlin on us before you even take a sip," Sam said.

I couldn't think of how to say what I'd wanted to. My words were about as clear as my understanding of things.

"To us," Sam said.

"All of us," Jotta said, and rested her hand on her belly.

I counted my twenties upstairs in the room they'd given me. There was $1,540 left, plus some ones and the change in my pocket. Rents were probably no joke on the Cape. There'd be first and last months, plus deposit. I had to start getting more money together. But Sam seemed to go off somewhere during the day to write; how could I go look for work and leave Jotta all alone in the house? I had to tell her, and soon, that Tom was coming, was probably already here. It felt like the hardest thing I'd ever had to do.

Downstairs Jotta was sitting with Sam's head resting on her lap. He was stretched the length of the couch with his legs draped over the arm. When I sat at her feet, I could hear him quietly snoring.

"Used to be," she said, "I couldn't sleep with his snoring, as mild as it is. The faintest sound wakes me up sometimes—a dog barking somewhere, a faucet dripping. Him, he can sleep through anything."

"Evidently," I said.

She brushed the hair from his forehead. "Look at that sweet, hairy face," she said.

"He's a beauty," I said.

"Not so long ago," she said, "I wouldn't have thought so. I'd have said he wasn't my type. Him, the house, the garden, the works."

"Jotta," I said, "he's on his way here."

She stopped stroking Sam's hair, then started again. "What **are** you talking about?" she said.

"I saw Tom on the road."

"On the road doesn't mean he's coming here."

"He is," I said. "I know."

Jotta looked hard at me. "Okay," she said. "I want to hear everything you know and how you know it."

I turned toward the fireplace. Some of the wood still held its shape, though now it was only powder and ash.

"I'm going to look for work tomorrow," I said. "I only told you about Tom so you wouldn't stay home alone." I stood and walked to the stairs.

"You have no right to be cryptic, Annie," she said. "You have to tell me."

I knew that it wasn't fair, that she deserved to know everything. He followed me here, I imagined myself saying. You were safe here, and happy, but I needed you. I came here knowing he would follow behind.

"It's two A.M.," I said, and leaned toward her to kiss her good night. She pulled away.

"Tomorrow, Jotta," I said. "I promise."

I turned and climbed the stairs, without another try at a kiss. I couldn't risk her pulling away again.

— 11 —

"The owner knows you're here," she said. "He should be right with you."

I watched the woman's blond ponytail bob while she walked away. It was tied over her right ear, so that it looked like she'd sprung a leak in the side of her head. My fanciest dress didn't look very elegant in this place, with its antique ships in glass cases and its velvet walls. It was the eleventh restaurant in Provincetown I'd applied to that day. July, they had all said, was not the time to be looking for work in a tourist town.

"This way," she said from over my shoulder. She flashed me her million-dollar smile again. Walking behind her, I wondered how her white silk dress could hug all the curves in her butt and thighs without showing lines from underwear or stockings. I'd worn my dress without the sash, so none of the fabric would cling to my bony hips. If they wanted women who looked like her, I hoped they'd spare me the interview.

She motioned me to sit at a table in the last dining room, where a young curly-haired man in golf shorts was bent over a heap of papers. He didn't look up for a few minutes, though he must have known I was there. This room, the third we'd walked through, was split-level and crowded with vines and plants of every size and every shade of green. The wall opposite us was made entirely of glass, showing the ocean gently rolling onto clean white sand.

"Nice place," I said.

The man kept writing. "Right with you," he said.

After a few more minutes of writing, he shot out his hand. "Steve," he said. "A pleasure."

I shook the hand. "You know who I am?"

He pulled my application from the top of a stack of papers. "Got it all right here," he said.

He scanned the application, moving his finger over the lines as he read them. The finger didn't move any too rapidly.

"Lots of restaurant experience," he said. "B.R.'s Place, Marie's, Poppa Dad's Bull Room, Carter's Beef. All in the West, though. What kinds of places?"

"Good places," I said. "Busy, you know."

He slid a heavy leather menu across the table. THE CHATEAU ROUGE was printed on the cover in loopy gold script.

"You know about all the cuisines in there?"

The writing was so flowery it was hard to read. I made out a few items—Cape Cod Scrod, Pilgrim's Prime Rib.

"These words don't look French," I said.

He snorted. "So?"

"I just thought from the name," I said. "Chateau Rouge and all."

"You're new around here," he said. "We're the most renowned establishment on the Cape. We got customers coming up every year from Connecticut and New York. We do colonial cuisine. Whatever they want."

He slapped the application onto the stack farthest from him.

"I'm leveling with you," he said. He looked down at his hand, twisted a ring that sparkled from gold and diamonds. "We've been hit with a manpower shortage this week." He lowered his voice. "We got a lot of faggots working here. Prima donnas, the lot of 'em."

He stopped while a short, near-spherical waiter passed with a tray of candles. When he crossed behind Steve, he opened his eyes wide and stuck out his tongue.

"So," Steve said. "You're on at five."

"Tonight?" I looked at my watch. "An hour from now?"

He picked up his pencil. "Gigi will show you the rear entrance," he said, and bent back over the papers again.

"I told you, I don't know what time," I said.

Jotta was silent on the other end of the line.

"Sam's not going out tonight, is he?" I said.

"I refuse to start taking on baby-sitters," she said.

When I stepped outside the phone booth, I almost collided with a pack of teenage boys in leather pants. I jumped back in the booth again. Only four-fifteen, still forty-five minutes before I was due at the restaurant. Jotta's place was twenty minutes away, so I was doomed to pass some time on this carnival of a street.

I tried to dawdle to look in shopwindows, but the press of people on the sidewalk wouldn't allow it. The street was dense with opposites: teenagers with rainbow hair, chubby middle-aged couples toting bags from gift shops, sweet-faced short-haired men in packs, brazen-faced spike-collared men in packs. They all had a kind of energy in common. This was no snail-paced resort town. Everybody seemed on the move after something.

A couple of blocks later I started casing the storefronts for a refuge. Gift stores, T-shirt shops, Cock-Robbin Leather. I finally peered through a window to see records hanging from the ceiling. GROG'S, announced the sign beside the door. A placard of a human-size cat gripping a frothy beer mug pointed the way inside.

The store was empty except for the tall, skinny guy in a ripped T-shirt standing behind the counter. His eyes were closed, and he was rocking back and forth to the reggae music blaring from all around the tiny store. I stood waiting to be greeted, but he only rocked. His nose curved down over his mouth, so he looked like a flamingo pecking to the beat. I opened the door again and slammed it behind me. He opened his eyes halfway.

"Hi," I said.

He shut his eyes again. I checked my watch. Four-twenty.

I flipped through the half dozen records filed under "Bluegrass," which included a secondhand copy of Grandpa Jones's Easy Banjo Method. Behind the bluegrass section, another dozen records were divided into "Wimmins's Music" and "Blooze." To the right, "Reggae, Rock & Soul" stretched the length of three walls. The song that had been blasting faded out; the amplified needle scraped against the label.

"Requests?" The guy from behind the counter was facing me, waiting.

"A respectable bluegrass collection," I said.

He walked up beside me and pushed the stack open to the six bluegrass records.

"Here," he said.

I pulled out the banjo instruction record.

"The latest in progressive bluegrass," I said.

He snatched the record out of my hand. I watched him walk to the counter, then push through the American flag draped over a doorway behind it. I heard him lift the tone arm. Seconds later the needle started popping and sputtering on tired, old vinyl.

The skinny guy took his place behind the counter and closed his eyes. Over the speakers, in full volume, a lone banjo started slowly plunking the melody line to "Little Brown Jug."

"Welcome," said a cheerful male voice, "to the wonderful world of banjo music."

The guy behind the counter started rocking to the tune.

"Catchy stuff," he said, and looked at me through half-open eyes.

"The banjo," said the voice, "is a fretted string instrument, probably invented right here in the good old U. S. of A."

The counter guy saluted.

"Very educational," I said, "but I think I'll pass."

When I turned the front doorknob, a burst of barks and growls seemed to hurtle toward me from out of nowhere. Then the skinny guy was cursing and lunging over the counter, and a mass of eyes and teeth and black fur pushed me down by the shoulders and threw me onto my satin-lined butt.

"Damn it, Marley," the guy screamed. The dog was licking my face, then the guy was on top of him and seemed to throw him across the room by the collar. The dog cringed against a record rack.

". . . a hollow circular body with a stretched diaphragm of vellum," the record was saying.

The skinny guy knelt beside me, leaned in close to my face, then pulled back.

"Marley's not mean," he said. He turned to the dog and yelled, "He's too stupid to be mean."

The dog cringed again.

"It's okay," I said, and touched my face. When I pulled my hand away, it was covered with saliva.

The counter guy reached out and tried to wipe the dog spit off my face.

"Don't worry about it," I said. "I'll just wipe it on my only good dress."

I reached up for the doorknob and pulled myself to my feet, then patted a dusty pawprint from the front of my skirt. The counter guy looked up at me through his slightly crossed black eyes.

"No whiplash?" he said.

I reached my hand out to him. He took it and I pulled him up.

"Not me," I said. "Can't speak for Marley, though."

When he heard his name, Marley started to whine. The counter guy raised his hand like he was going to swat him. Marley slunk behind the counter and through the flag.

"I'm due at work," I said.

177

"Hey," he said, "let me make it up to you. I'll buy you a drink tonight."

I shrugged. "I don't know when I get off," I said. "It's my first night."

"Where?"

"The Chateau Rouge."

He slapped a limp-wristed hand to his face.

"Something wrong with that?" I said.

"You'll be off by eleven," he said. "I'll be in the bar."

I opened the door and started out.

"E, G, B, D, F," said the banjo record.

"Hey," the skinny guy said.

I turned.

"Ask them the secret to their homemade bisque," he said.

The woman yanked a brown paisley skirt off its clothespins and held it up to me.

"Perfect," she said, and draped it over my shoulder.

I held it out, put it to my waist.

"Is it supposed to be this long?" I said.

She was flipping through the rack of white peasant blouses below the skirts. She pulled one off a hanger and tossed it to me. When she slid open a drawer and leaned over it, her body seemed to have two thicknesses—one from shoulder to butt, another from thigh to ankle. She turned and handed me something that looked like a white shower cap.

"Let's see the shoes," she said.

We both looked down at my leather sandals. She pointed to them.

"You're not serious," she said.

"Mrs. Reeba," I said, "your son hired me an hour ago. He didn't—"

She waved my answer away. Under the rack of blouses, she burrowed through a pile of dusty black flats till she found two that matched. She held them next to my feet.

"You're set," she said, and flounced out of the room.

* * *

There was nobody in sight when I stuck my head out the dressing room. Around the corner, waiters and waitresses were chopping things and talking, all out of view. I wanted to get a look at one of the women, since I wasn't sure how to fix my cap. I'd shoved all my hair up under it and pulled it down over my ears, but since there was no mirror in the room, I couldn't tell how it looked. The chubby, bald waiter I'd seen before rounded the corner, threw up his hands and shrieked.

"I can't figure out . . ." I started to say.

He lifted one arm and pretended to be scrubbing under it. "Ohhh sohhh-lahhh-meee-ohhh," he sang.

Another waiter and a waitress peered around the corner, then laughed when they saw me. The woman's cap was pinned on top of her hair, tilted back on her head. I reached up and snatched mine off.

The other waiter lifted his arm and started scrubbing and singing along, "Ohhh sohhh-lahhh-meee—"

I pulled myself back inside and slammed the door. How was I supposed to know what to do with the damn thing? I threw the cap on the floor and kicked off the shoes so they flew against the wall.

The door opened and the waitress leaned in.

"I'm Kate," she said. "Want a little help with your monkey suit?"

"I don't need this crummy job," I said.

The woman walked in and shut the door behind her. She picked my cap up off the floor. "You wouldn't think so," she said, "but these things have a lot of practical uses."

"Besides humiliation?" I said.

"That's an important function," she said. "You can also smuggle weapons out to the floor."

"Handy," I said.

She drew it tight across her mouth. "Or perform emergency surgery."

I had to stop and look at this woman, no stockier than I

179

was and shorter by half a foot. She struck me as being sturdy somehow, with her strong cheeks and chin and her shiny hair that hung to her shoulders in thick brown curls. Such a good-hearted soul she seemed, yucking it up to lift the spirits of a stranger, that I couldn't stand there and pout. I took the cap and wrapped it around my neck.

"Or you could be Father O'Malley and give last rites," I said.

"Only if they order the special," she said. "But watch. This is the best." Kate took the cap from me and pulled a pen from her pocket. She pointed to a pencil-drawn line on the linoleum floor, and we both stood behind it. "Hold one end," she said.

I took an end of the cap, and we stretched it taut. She clicked the pen so the point was out, then nestled the top in the elastic band and pulled it back like a bowstring.

"Ready," she said, "aim," and sent the pen flying. It arched up, then sailed down, point pricking the wall. We walked over to where it hit, in the outermost circle of a bull's-eye drawn lightly on the plaster.

"Five points," she said. "We usually play to five hundred."

I pointed to the area outside the circle, where most of the blue, red, and black ink dots were concentrated.

"With this crowd," I said, "game must be slow as Christmas."

Kate looked at me. "Are you from the South?"

"South of Market Street," I said.

"Don't know it," she said. "Is that in Nebraska or something?"

"I had these friends," I said. "From Wyoming. Shouldn't we be chopping vegetables?"

"This is the specials board," Kate said. "Only they're not specials, they're 'additions to this evening's fare.' You check them before you go out on the floor."

"Where do you write them down?" I said.

She laughed. "No cue cards at the Chateau," she said.

I counted the items of the blackboard: eight, plus two soups, two appetizers, and three desserts. Most of the dinner items were some kind of fish with fancy butter. I read the first few out loud.

"Salmon with tarragon butter. Yellowfin tuna with garlic butter. Bay scallops with capers and parsley butter, poached with wine and shitake mushrooms."

"Did your Wyoming friends teach you pronunciation?" Kate said.

My face burned for the second time since I'd been there. "We don't get a lot of shit-take mushrooms in the West."

"Shi-tawk-ee," she said. "But we'll come back to this later."

Kate took me on a tour of the kitchen, pointing out an order-writing station, a salad-making station, a dessert station, and schedule postings. The other waiters and waitresses washed lettuce, poured cans of things into mixing bowls, chopped carrots, sliced bread, keeping up a constant flow of chatter. It was a beehive with everybody humming, and me the odd drone out.

"You take a prep chore when you come in," Kate said. "Depending on what needs to be done. Say you check the salad station"—she slid open the door to a glass-walled refrigerator—"and the dressings are low." She pointed to some plastic tubs. "They're not," she said, "but just say they are."

We walked through the kitchen area to a storeroom in the back with three walls lined with different-size cans.

"Bottom shelf, right," she said, "our four homemade dressings: Florentine, Parisienne, South Sea Island, and Californian."

The labels on the cans read: Italian, French, Thousand Island, Blue Cheese. They all said "Restaurant Package, Not for Retail Distribution."

"You restock whatever kind is low," she said. "Then check the other stations."

"Restock," I said.

"As in—fill." She looked at me slant-eyed. "Is that what they called it at all those places you worked in Wyoming?" She winked at me.

"You must have some Wyoming in your blood," I said.

* * *

She introduced me to a dozen people in the next five minutes. There was a Robert, a William, a beautiful, shy Maya, plus brown-eyed Mark with the beefy shoulders. The bald, round waiter who had teased me about the cap was named Alex. He didn't even nod when Kate said "This is Annie," just rushed on by us like he was late for a train.

Kate took me through the four dining rooms and showed me how the tables were numbered. I tried to remember how the number system worked, but the order always slipped away the minute she stopped explaining it. The back room with the plants was the Green Room, the one next to it was the Map Room, then the Surf Room, the Arboretum, and the bar.

"Phillip," she said to the bartender, "this is Annie, from out in wild Wyomin'."

Phillip looked up from the sink and smiled. He had deep brown eyes and straight brown hair cut square around his face. I wanted to ask him if people always told him he looked like Ringo Starr but decided they probably did and stopped myself.

"A ramblin' gal in Chateau corral," he sang, his eyebrows high, "ramblin' ramblin' ramblin', amblin' and a'gamblin'."

Alex pushed between me and Kate and slammed a tray on the bar. "Setups for M room," he said. "If you can spare the time."

Phillip bowed, but Alex would have none of his silliness. He stared in the distance and drummed his fingers on the bar until Phillip finished loading wineglasses onto his tray. Alex strutted away without so much as a thank-you.

"I declare." Phillip rolled his eyes and drawled like Scarlett O'Hara, "Miss Alice, she got her knickers all in a twist today."

"He's just moody that way," Kate said. "Take him with a grain of salt."

Gigi beamed when we passed the front desk. "Isn't that outfit precious on you?" she said. She rocked her head a bit when she spoke, so her ponytail bounced over her ear.

"It's all in the cap," Kate said. She pulled a menu off the desk, took my hand and tugged me away.

We scanned the menu at the waiters' station where the schedules were posted.

"Don't sweat it," she said, and pointed to the menu tacked to the bulletin board. "You can look up the prices till you learn them."

I took a deep breath. Everything was under control. There was a map on the board showing the dining rooms and table numbers. They didn't expect you to know the prices right away, so I'd just write down the orders and look them up later. I still couldn't read the script on the menu, but as long as the customers could, what did I care? My eye caught the loopy *B* on the first appetizer.

"Does that say 'bisque'?" I said.

Kate nodded. "They're crazy for it."

"I've heard," I said, "there's a famous secret."

"It's highly confidential," she said. "We're not allowed to tell."

I crossed my heart.

Kate led me to a row of steaming metal kettles. We knelt down to the rack underneath, and she pulled out an industrial-size can of Pantry Fresh Concentrated Bisque.

"They beg you for the secret," she said. "Waiters take the fifth."

"Out with it, Kate," I said.

She pointed to the instructions, to where it said, "Add two cans water for every can of concentrate."

"We don't," she said.

Alex bustled over and lifted the lid to one of the other vats of soup. "Which is this?" he demanded of no one in particular.

"Bean with bacon and basil," Kate said.

He leaned in closer to the soup. "Basil, are you in there?"

I laughed, loud enough so I knew he'd hear. He slammed the lid and scurried to the waiters' station.

"Let's get you some checks," Kate said.

Kate pulled a pad from a drawer in the desk at the waiters' station. Alex was writing his name on the stubs at the bottom of his checks. I stood next to him, leaned over the desk and started doing the same on mine.

"Who'll be responsible?" chimed a voice I vaguely recognized. I turned to see Mrs. Reeba, Ma Chateau Rouge who'd issued my uniform, standing hands on hips, glaring at a puddle on the floor.

"Who'll be responsible," she said, "when someone falls and breaks a collarbone?" She looked at Kate, who opened a closet and pulled out a mop. Mrs. Reeba stormed out of the kitchen.

"And a good day to you, Buffalo Snatch," Alex called after her.

I watched the doorway to see if she'd heard him. Seconds later the image hit me.

"Buffalo Snatch," I said. "That's great."

Alex looked up at me. I started to sing:

> *Buffalo Snatch, won't you come out tonight?*
> *Come out tonight?*
> *Come out tonight?*

Alex shrieked "Of course!" He grabbed a pant leg with each hand, pulled them out like a skirt and curtsied. We did a two-step while we finished the song.

> *Buffalo Snatch, won't you come out tonight*
> *And dance by the light of the moon?*

Gigi came in and wrote something on one of the charts. "Ladies and gentlemen, deuce on M sixteen." She shot me and Alex a schoolmarmish look and bobbed away.

I whispered to Kate, "Deuce on M sixteen? We supposed to play blackjack or clean our rifles?"

She pointed to the diagram of the Map Room. "M Room, table sixteen. Deuce is a party of two, then it's three-top, quartet, five-spot, et cetera."

"Et cetera?"

Kate checked the posting Gigi had written on. "I'm up," she said, and left the kitchen.

My name was fifth in the row along the top of the chart. Below each of our names was a column of empty boxes. "M16–4" was written in Kate's topmost box.

Once I finished writing my name on my checks, I took another tour through each of the rooms. At the bar, Phillip looked up from the limes he was slicing.

"Gonna be a wild night, Wyomin' gal," he said. "Three hundred ressies."

Résumés? Residents? Resignations?

"What kind of corkscrew you use?" he said. "Ah-so or Italian?"

"Actually," I said, "I haven't had time to go home, so I don't have mine on me."

"I'll spot you one," he said. "Which do you favor?"

"Either one," I said. "I lean a little toward Italian."

Phillip slapped something on the bar that looked like a Swiss army knife.

"Need a crumber?" he said.

"You bet," I said.

He passed me a concave gold strip the size of a ballpoint pen. It even had a clip so you could fasten it to your pocket.

Gigi leaned over a barstool and whispered, "You're up, honey."

When I passed through the waiting area, it was crowded with well-dressed diners. In the chart at the waiters' station, the first box under my name said "G4–2." The Green Room. I checked the map. Far corner by the window. Let me at 'em.

"How's it going?" I said to G4.

They both looked up from their menus, a little startled.

"Just fine, thank you," the man said.

They were fifty or so, both dressed in tweed, both growing a sweet crop of gray in their reddish hair.

"I don't guess you're ready," I said.

The woman shook her head and smiled. I hummed all the way back to the kitchen.

Alex took my arm at the waiters' station.

"G four's gonna want to know all about the monument," he said. "I can always call 'em."

"Monument?" I said.

"The *Pilgrim* Monument," he said. "That tower in the middle of town. They'll want to know what year it was erected, how, why, and out of what."

"Shit," I said, "I'd be dead."

"We'd all be," he said, "if we had to know the answers. Just wing it. They're happy, you're happy."

Alex stuffed his book of checks in his pocket and headed for the Map Room. How could I wing it? For me, Cape Cod was at the end of a road from Homer, Wyoming. I knew less about it than any tourist in town.

I paused at the doorway to see if I could look all the way to G4. The couple was hidden behind a palm tree, but I decided to give them another minute. Alex's table was against the wall six feet down from me.

"Is the chowder New England or Manhattan?" I heard an old lady ask him.

Alex propped one hand on his hip, pointed out the window with the other. "Honey," he said, "does that look like the East River to you?"

"What do you recommend for a first-course dish?" the lady at G4 asked.

"Oh," I said, "it's hard to pick. I can't tell you the secret to the bisque, is all I know."

She nodded. "Well, then, I'll just have shrimp cocktail, then the sirloin tips, medium rare."

186

I knew waitresses always abbreviated. I wrote "shrimp cock, sir tips mr."

The man threw his menu down. "Sounds lovely. Make it two," he said.

They both smiled up at me as I took the menus. I felt happy about having such a job, where just giving people what they want could bring them so much pleasure.

"Tell me," the woman said, and pointed out the window. "The Cape is so terribly disorienting. What direction are we currently facing?"

"Now?" I said. "Currently?"

They both looked at me.

"West," I said, "right now. That's west out there."

The man clasped his hands together. "Wonderful," he said. "This is our last night on Cape Cod, and we've yet to see your sunset."

"We've heard so much about it," the woman said, and looked up at me. "Thank you so much."

I clipped the check to the wheel, like everybody else had been doing.

"I'm Annie," I said.

The cook looked up at me over his wire-rimmed glasses. He was young and his features were small and perfect, but he was working up a scowl that overwhelmed the baby face. He pulled the check off the wheel with a pair of tongs.

"This supposed to be cute?" he said.

I shrugged. "That's what they ordered."

"Shrimp cock?"

I felt myself blush, an unnatural reaction for me. Kate slid a big tray up to the counter.

"I don't think she meant anything personal," she said.

"Calm down, Greg," Alex called from the salad station. "Annie can't have heard those rumors yet."

I heard scattered laughter from all around the kitchen. The

cook dropped the check by the tongs into the garbage barrel.

"Somebody show her how to write an order," he said.

I stood at the entryway to the Green Room, watching G4 eat their shrimp with tiny forks. The place was filling up pretty steadily; the hum of the voices was starting to overpower the piped-in classical music. That cook Greg would be a problem. Kate said he was family, so you couldn't give him lip. But I wasn't going to let old Shrimp Cock get me down. This job would free me up to use my cash for a place to live, something nice. Maybe I'd get a cottage by the ocean, where I could sit at my own window and watch the sea gulls land on the surface of the water.

"You checked the chart lately?" Kate said. She was straining to hold a tray of dinners up over her shoulder.

"I've got G four," I said.

"And?"

I just looked at her.

"You better get your butt in the kitchen," she said.

M11–4 was written in the second box under my name. Kate already had three boxes filled in, and I would be up again in a couple of tables. I scanned the Map Room diagram and almost collided with dark-eyed Maya on my way out the door.

"What'll it be?" I said to M11.

All four of them looked up suddenly like I'd just belched. They were middle-aged, all dressed-up classy. The woman on my right had her head in a turban, and the man on my left had sunglasses sitting on top of his head.

"Welcome to Burger King," he said under his breath. The woman next to him giggled. I noticed that his place setting wasn't right and thought maybe that was why they were acting out of sorts.

"Sorry about that," I said, and moved the spoon from where it lay, longways above his plate.

The woman in the turban snickered under her hand. The

man with the sunglasses looked smugly at each of the other three.

"Aren't we Continental?" he said, and moved the spoon back over the plate.

"That's the way they set tables in France," Kate whispered in the kitchen. "That's also why he wanted the salad after the entrée."

"Well, this ain't France," I said. "It ain't sunny in here either, and I'm telling him so."

When I turned to go, Kate grabbed my arm. "If it's worth getting the ax, then go ahead and do it."

I took a deep breath, thought about my cottage and my sea gulls. If only Carter had been what I'd wanted him to be.

Kate let go of my arm and left the kitchen. Gigi wrote another number under my name.

It was eight-thirty before I got a chance to look at my watch. Streaks of salad dressing, meat juice, and God knows what ran from my elbow down to my black old-lady shoes. I had forgotten to serve salads and I'd lost checks. I'd also taken out the wrong food, dropped glasses, and pushed corks down the neck and into the wine. In the course of three hours I'd gotten every class of person in the restaurant, cook to customer to waiter, leaping, spitting, teeth-grinding mad at me.

Gigi tapped my shoulder while I was staring at the white space on the dining room map. Even she couldn't fake a smile for my benefit.

"Can't you do something about G four?" she said.

"Like what?"

"Like get them to go home. They've been here for three hours."

She tried her best to smile, but it came out more like a wince. While she bounced back to the front desk, I tried to gather my courage to go back into the dining rooms. It was hard enough being the most hated person in the building without having to pitch my only nice customers into the street.

One of the busboys in the Green Room was lighting the candles on all the tables. G4 was empty. Their coffee cups were pushed to the center of the table, their napkins folded at their places. At least those two nice people got everything they wanted that night—shrimp, steak, and two hours of sipping coffee. I started to clear the table. Napkins, cups, salt and pepper, sugar. There was a pamphlet folded in two in the ashtray, showing photos of Cape Cod harbors, the Pilgrim Monument, fishermen casting nets. Through the window I saw the tide had gone out. Where the waves had tumbled and broken on the shore, the sand stretched out slick and gray to a darkening sky where no sun had set.

— 12 —

I couldn't fake any enthusiasm about seeing him at the bar. It had been only a few hours, but it seemed like days ago—the store, the how-to banjo record, the dog. I hadn't thought he'd show up. I hadn't thought about it at all.

"Don't look so happy to see me," he said. "I might get ideas."

He looked different now, in the dark Chateau bar, though he hadn't changed out of his T-shirt with the holes you could sail a Frisbee through. The light from the candles softened the sharp angles of his features and cast a goldness on his skin. He looked clean and sincere, but like nobody I'd ever been with before.

"No offense," I said. "I had a lousy night."

"They serve bisque for employee dinner?"

"Dinner," I said. "I guess I forgot about that."

On cue my stomach grumbled. He pushed me a bowl of fish-shaped crackers and pointed to the stool next to him.

"I don't think I'm off yet," I said.

In the opposite corner of the bar, Phillip the Ringo-Starr bartender was showing off in front of a dozen young men with

191

too-short hair. He was mixing drinks, slicing limes, loading the dishwasher, carrying on a stand-up routine all the while.

"Miss Alice," he said, "she waited on a pair of newlyweds tonight. They took her aside and told her they'd heard"—he lowered his voice to a whisper—"that all the waiters here were gay."

"No!" shouted the men at the bar.

"No lie," he said. "Only one thing confused them. They weren't sure about the bartender."

Phillip's end of the bar exploded into laughter. He stood erect and put his hands on his hips.

"Happens all the time," he said.

His audience whooped louder, shook their heads.

"It's true!" Phillip said. "They just assume I'm a woman."

I felt like a tourist in a foreign country, listening in while the locals joked. The guy from the record store was dipping a cracker-fish into the whipped cheese dip, ignoring the goings-on at the end of the bar. I'd seen plenty of gays at the bail bond office, but they were usually all business in their dealings with us. Here, at the bar, was a different business-as-usual—men calling each other "she" and laughing about being girlish.

"You got a name?" I said to him.

"Hunter. No relation, just a coincidental resemblance."

I looked at him, blank. "To what?"

He lifted his chin, turned to show his profile. "Tab," he said. "Of course."

My last party of two passed through the bar on their way out. Hunter balanced a cracker on the summit of his sturdy, upturned nose. "Hunter's best as a first name anyway," he said.

"Looks like I've got a table to bus," I said.

"Go for it," he said.

Part of me recognized the faces coming at me from the front door of the restaurant. Yet I was so dead sure that Marie and Gloria were far away that I watched them with no expression at first. When the two of them plus Jotta stopped a foot from me, I had to sit on the stool next to Hunter.

"Surprise," Jotta said. She forced a guilty smile.

"Jotta," I said. "You told."

She looked away. It's all right, I said to myself. She probably just called and let them know I was here. Jotta wouldn't have told them everything.

Gloria was beaming, so I broke down and gave her a hug. It seemed strange that she'd come out to Jotta's territory—she and B.R. had always had their doubts about Jotta. I remembered the day they bribed me with cupcakes so I'd go home and forget about whatever present Jotta had promised me. Holding Gloria now, I tried to fix on what Jotta's present had been, or if I'd ever even gotten it. But I was lost in Gloria's magic smell: new cars. It made me want to hug her a long time.

When I leaned toward Marie, she didn't move. I went through with hugging her anyway, waited for her to soften. She didn't even lift her arms.

"The last thing I need," I said, "is somebody else mad at me today."

Her face was pale and her hair was out of place, like she hadn't been curling it in the mornings. Her eyes were red.

"You have no idea," she said, "do you."

Gigi appeared behind Marie and shot me a dirty look. I nodded, yes, I'd be there in a minute.

There was a burst of applause at Phillip's end of the bar. He bowed low from the waist, then jumped up on a milk crate.

"Elect me governor!" he shouted. "Me, Miss Phyllis. I could be His Honor and the First Lady all at once."

Jotta couldn't take her eyes off Phillip. Marie was still glaring at me.

"I know," I said to her. "I should have called."

"Called," Marie said. "Yes, you should have called."

She took a breath to go on, then stopped herself.

"Say," Hunter said, "do I get introduced or what?"

Marie, Gloria, and Jotta all turned to Hunter, who held out his hand to the group.

"I've got to bus a table," I said.

* * *

"No," I said. "She's my aunt."

"Oh." Kate went back to sweeping. "I just figured that one of them would be your mother. The one woman looked too young, and the other one looked too black. Process of elimination."

I was adding up my food and bar totals for the night, the last thing you had to do before you could go home. I couldn't get either of my figures to match the ones Gigi had done at the desk.

"Is that guy your boyfriend?" Kate said.

I decided she meant Hunter, though the word still made me think of Carter. It was a word Carter would have hated—with good reason, since he was neither a boy nor much of a friend.

"I don't have those," I said. "They're against my new religion."

"New as of when?" she said.

"Just new," I said. "Since Independence Day."

I heard the sweeping stop. Kate put the broom in the closet and left the kitchen. I got the same total as before for food, a different one for wine. Both were still way off what Gigi had written. One more time, I told myself. Then I was turning in my checks and hitting the road.

Soon Kate was back and looking over my shoulder.

"What happens if I turn it in wrong?" I said.

"Your punishment," she said, "would be to go for a drink with me tonight."

"Thanks," I said, "but these friends just got into town."

When I looked up, I saw she'd changed into her regular clothes. She had on a lavender shirt and shimmering gold pants tucked into short tiger-striped boots.

"My dancing togs," she said. "We've got a couple of great discos in town. You work tomorrow night?"

She was tapping her foot in a jittery way, putting her hands in her pockets only to take them out again. There was a nervous edge to her voice now, like a guy gets when he's had to work up his courage to ask a woman out.

"I haven't checked my schedule," I said. "I think I better go do that."

Gigi gave me a slip of paper with my hours for the week and told me to hand in my checks at the bar. My next shift was lunch, eleven to four. I could tell Kate that I wouldn't be around tomorrow night. Everything felt different with her now.

Phillip smiled when I walked up to the bar with my checks.

"I'll be right with you, Wyomin' gal," he said.

He reached under the bar and pulled open the door to the dishwasher. Clouds of white steam swelled up around him.

"Mr. Wizard!" yelled one of his friends. "Help me, Mr. Wizard!"

Phillip opened his eyes wide and chanted, "Razzle frazzle dazzle drone, time for this one to go home."

The three of us stood in the middle of Jotta's living room while she and Sam shuttled suitcases upstairs. Gloria settled into the most comfortable chair in the room and kicked off her shoes.

"Take a load off, Marie," she said.

Marie showed no sign of having heard her. She just stood with her hands in the pockets of her coat, staring somewhere into the dark dining room.

"So what brings you guys here?" I said.

Gloria let out a "Ha!" and tried, too late, to swallow it back.

"Cocaine," Marie said. "Honestly, Annie, that's a bit passé these days, don't you think?"

Jotta stopped on her way down the stairs, and we all froze for a minute while I felt my heart beat in my throat. Even when they came in the bar, even with Marie so mad, I hadn't thought

Jotta would have told them about the cocaine. That explained why Gloria had come—nobody kept Marie cool like she did. I turned to Jotta with a look that must have been fiercer than anything I could have said.

"Annie," Jotta said, then didn't seem able to finish.

"So this is the new Jotta," I said. "Happy and fertile and loyal as a snake. You must've lunged for the phone soon as I kissed you good night."

Jotta stomped down the stairs so fast I thought she might slap me. She stopped herself just short of it. They were all standing now, all looking hard at me.

"It scares me," she said, "you acting so stupid."

I stormed through the dark dining room and kitchen and slammed the back door behind me.

I sat cross-legged in a chair in the garden, waiting for them to come challenge me. I summoned everything in me, set myself square against their anger. What right had they to judge me? Who were they anyway? An aunt, an ex-pill-junkie, and an old black lady who'd rented out cars all her life. They didn't know anything about why I did what I did. They didn't know anything about me at all. Jotta was supposed to know, used to know. Now all she knew was horseradish and colored pillows, and closing up the shutters tight to keep the breeze from tempting her away.

An hour or so later one of the bedroom lights went out upstairs. Maybe Sam, I thought. But his and Jotta's room was on the other side of the house. I hadn't heard any voices for a while. Marie must have hit the sack so she could be fresh to jump on me in the morning.

The moon lit up the neat rows of Jotta's vegetables surrounding the house. A collection of tools—a hoe, a rake, several sizes of claws and spades—were leaning against a tree near where I sat. It looked like Jotta had done a lot in the garden that day. Some greens had been pulled up, some cut back; the trees seemed to have been shaped, pampered. I heard a low moan from somewhere far away. What had Sam said about

196

screech owls? They cried, he'd said, the season before an early winter. Like women, he'd said. I shivered and held my arms.

I jumped when I saw something move as I turned to climb the stairs.

"Just me," Jotta said.

I had to squint to see the shape of her in the dark. She was curled up in the corner of the couch, her knees pulled tight against her chest.

"I thought everybody went to bed," I said.

She didn't answer. I walked to the couch and sat opposite her, pulled off my sandals so I could put my legs on the cushions. I leaned against the arm, rested my bare feet on hers. She jerked them away.

"So you're still mad," I said.

"Your feet are icebergs," she said.

She rubbed the tops of my feet fast with her hands, warming them with the friction.

"Now I can take it," she said. She laid her feet on top of mine.

We sat for a long time, staring at what was left of the fire. Sam must have built one while I was outside. The flames had burned out, but the embers seemed to glow hot enough to ignite again. Jotta's warmth spread from my feet up through the rest of me, made me realize how cold I'd been.

"So you told Marie everything," I said.

Jotta kept staring at the fireplace. She leaned over to the coffee table, lifted a cigarette to her mouth and struck a match.

"Jotta," I said. "You quit."

She lit the cigarette, shook the match out.

"I know," she said. She took a few long drags.

"This is not the easiest time for me," she said after a while.

I wasn't sure at first what she meant. Then it hit me that somehow I'd forgotten about Tom, what with the Chateau job and Marie coming. I couldn't think of what to say to comfort her, especially since I was scared she'd ask more about the coke thing and want to know how I'd run into him. But I had to make her know how much I cared, and how much I wanted to help her be free of him.

"Tom can't hurt you anymore," I said. "Not with the baby coming and everything."

She laughed, got up, and flicked her ashes into the fireplace.

"Oh, Annie," she said. "Don't you see? It never mattered before, and now it does."

"Just wait a minute," I said. "He's only one creepy, crummy guy. We get one look at him, Marie'll get the cops in motion. We'll put him away again, for good this time." But we both knew better than that, after all these years. Whatever was most dangerous and threatening to us about Tom was neither plainly visible nor plainly illegal.

Jotta was crouched next to the fireplace now, just staring and staring.

"Marie never understood," she said. "She never knew why I stayed with him."

"Marie and the rest of the world," I said. "Anybody that ever knew the both of you. You all smart and likable, Tom a card-carrying psychotic criminal."

I went on some more, but I knew neither of us was listening. Jotta was looking into the fire and thinking God knows what. I was remembering the feel of Tom's face against mine when he kissed me good-bye in Homer. The sweet, leathery smell of him when he turned to go.

After I finally finished talking, we were quiet a long time, and we didn't move.

"She doesn't know," Jotta said. "Marie doesn't know the magic."

"Of what?" I said, with as much belligerence as I could muster, though I wanted to say: I know. It's like running a red light and not looking to either side.

"It was a comfort, really," she went on. "I'd do a certain thing, knowing that he'd hit me, and how hard. I knew where the bad was coming from, what it would look like and how it would feel."

Her answer was different from what I'd expected. It wasn't that part about Tom that I ever imagined; it was the risk and the freedom, and anything being possible.

"I'm working lunch tomorrow," I said, and stood to go upstairs.

Jotta stood and walked next to me, took both of my hands in hers.

"You're still frozen," she said. She crossed her arms in front of her and pulled the sweater she was wearing up over her head.

"I'm okay," I said.

She handed it to me. "For tomorrow, then," she said. "I want you to have it."

I could barely see it in the dim light, but when I took it in my hands it was heavy, woven thick and soft. I looked up at Jotta and she nodded.

"You made this," I said. "I can't believe it."

"It took me forever," she said. "I started it when I met Sam, before I had the garden. It's no pro job, but you put it on and it makes you warm."

I couldn't remember Jotta ever making anything, except waffles once, and pudding from a box. Now there was a beautiful knitted sweater, vegetables to eat, and someday soon a baby. I hugged her around the neck.

"It's great," I whispered.

Halfway up the stairs I stopped and turned back.

"I understand," I said. "You calling Marie."

I thought I could see her nod. Her cigarette glowed brighter in the dark.

– *13* –

When I came downstairs, Gloria was lying on the couch in a pink quilted housecoat, the morning paper propped up on her stomach.

"You sleep well?" I said.

"Like a queen," she said. "Jotta's running a class act these days. Felt like I was sleeping in Hansel and Gretel's castle."

She lowered the paper and stuffed some more pillows under her back.

"Did Hansel and Gretel have a castle?" I said.

"They should've," she said. "Everybody should."

I decided I'd thought enough about Hansel and Gretel for one morning and turned toward the kitchen.

"Bobby wanted to come along, you know," she said.

That stopped me cold. I imagined B.R. standing in front of me now, looking sad and hurt and disapproving—that would have done me in for sure.

"It's just as well," I said. "What with his health and all."

"He would've tried to take you over his knee. Probably would've broke his back."

I looked away. "Plus," I said, "I don't need another person

older than I am, acting like it's me making all the mistakes on this earth."

She lifted her newspaper. "He sends his love," she said.

I found Jotta on her knees in the garden, throwing greens over her shoulder onto a knee-high pile.

"Morning," I said.

She turned to me, blew a dangling strand of hair up out of her eyes.

"Why don't you try getting Marie in for some breakfast," she said.

I waited for her to notice me standing in the hot sun, wearing the sweater she gave me. But once she turned back to her weeding, there was no getting her attention.

"Get Marie in from where?" I finally said.

"The front lawn," she said. "She thinks she's Pocahontas guarding the fort."

Walking up the path along the side of the house, I wondered why everyone had their fables mixed up. But when I saw Marie sitting Indian-style in the middle of the lawn, there seemed to be enough truth in Jotta's description that the wrongness didn't matter.

"Breakfast?" I said.

She shook her head. I plopped down next to her.

"Can't think of when I last saw you in jeans," I said. I thought of the picture under the glass in the bail bond office, one corner torn loose from when I'd tried to pull it free.

She stretched out her legs. "I've worn plenty of jeans in my day," she said.

I smiled. Tell me about those days, Marie, I wanted to say. But asking about other days only seemed to jar her into silence, into thinking up ways to keep some part of her farther from me.

A frowzy blue bird landed near Marie. We watched him hop, take an occasional peck at the lawn.

"When's your arraignment?" she said.

"Next week."

"Where?"

I gripped a handful of grass, ripped it out by the roots. The last thing I needed was some of Marie's meddling—a phone call to this bondsman, that judge, till someone happened to mention that one Tom Cleaver posted the bail.

"West of here," I said. I lobbed the grass toward the bird. He eyed it, unimpressed. Marie nodded, she'd accepted what I'd said.

"So whatever happened with the teacher?" she said.

Though she still couldn't bring herself to say Carter's name, she managed to speak the question honestly and without meanness. She deserved a straight answer. I took a long, slow breath.

"I left him," I said.

Once I spoke those words, I felt giddy at the truth of them. She'd asked the question simply, and the answer had been short and just. After all my sadness and hurt feelings, it was me that picked up and left because things weren't right.

"That felt good to say," I said. "I've never said it before."

She looked at me and smiled. "I knew you'd get out of it eventually."

I turned toward her on the lawn. "How did you know that?"

Marie looked ahead of her for long enough that I was eager for the answer.

"I knew it wouldn't work," she said, "that he couldn't give you what you really want."

The bird skittered a few feet from us, then flew away. I wanted to ask her what she meant, but I could tell her mind wasn't really on me or what I wanted. Her face was tense and distracted, like something was about to blow and she'd taken it on herself to be ready.

"That son of a bitch," she said, and I knew she didn't mean Carter. Marie's acting this angry always made me feel like a kid again. I wanted to say something that was calming yet showed I understood the importance of things.

"Jotta's got her life together now," I said. "Tom's just a deadbeat. He can't hurt her anymore."

203

Marie shook her head, like I'd done an arithmetic problem wrong. "He'll always make a wreck out of her," she said. "It's like your teacher, only so much worse. It's the same damn, stupid mess. For years I've watched it with the two of you."

So we were a mess, and damned and stupid to boot. Jotta had been right last night. Marie didn't understand anything.

"Good of you to come three thousand miles to set me and Jotta straight," I said.

Now she was yanking up handfuls of grass. "Jotta's seen it coming over and over, and when it comes this time, she'll take it again. And you, you grow up watching it, which teaches you what? To jump in a car at eighteen and stir up some fires all your own."

"I see." I looked ahead, nodding. "So what we both should do, Jotta and me, is get ourselves some nice little skirts and a nice little business—set up across the Hall of Justice so we can feel like there's something exciting about it."

My face flashed hot saying these words, but Marie didn't shift her weight or turn away. I wanted to knock her flat with something, show her she had no right to judge us. "I hope it hasn't been too unpleasant coming out here to sit on Jotta's lawn. You probably haven't seen a resort beach since my three grand disappeared."

I felt a jolt of shame at having gone too far. But I'd been wondering about the money for weeks, and the question needed answering. If Marie was so different from us, she could do some explaining of her own. I added nothing to soften what I'd said.

"I saw that you cleared the account," she said. She crossed her arms, struggling not to look shaken.

"I just want to know," I said. "I've got a right to know what happened to the rest of my money."

Marie closed her eyes. When she opened them, they were looking at the sky.

"The back room," she said. "There was no place for you, all those years. I thought if I had a room built, if you had some privacy—"

"—then I wouldn't leave."

Marie stretched out her arms, rested her hands on her knees.

"Take a look at Jotta," she said, "who you've spent your life adoring. She's three months pregnant and trying to make a home, but she can't let go and just be happy. She doesn't know how."

"Come on, Marie," I said. "Have you seen that garden? They made me a whole dinner out of it. And look at this." I held out the front of Jotta's sweater. "You can be on your own in the world and do things. Make things."

Marie shook her head in a way that meant she didn't want to talk anymore about it. That awful room, I thought. That awful room with a single bed where the door to the outside used to be.

"She hasn't slept, knowing," Marie said.

"What?"

"Since you told her Tom was coming. She smokes all night and waits."

I stood and brushed the grass off my jeans. "Tom's probably bored with the idea by now. I sure am." I turned to go.

"Annie," she said. I stopped and put my hands in my pockets, stared ahead at the house without looking back to her.

"I want you to remember some things," she said, her voice even and soft. "When you think of riding fast and living on the streets, you remember that things are different for us."

"Different for you," I said.

"Us," she said. "You, me, Jotta, Gloria, your girlfriends from school, the hookers on Sixth Street. You want to live on that dark side you've read about in books and heard about in songs. But what I'm telling you to remember is that it's not there for us—sleeping in bus stations, hitching rides with truck drivers, sharing stories shoulder to shoulder, living dime to dime. The streets are all about power, Annie, and the closest we can get is the back of a motorcycle and what they offer us in exchange for spreading our legs."

I heard noises that seemed sudden but were only sounds

205

of the day—water running in the garden, the wind in the leaves. "I've never heard you talk like this," I said. "I've never heard you say there was anything we couldn't do."

Marie walked to the edge of the lawn and stood looking sadly out at the street. I shut the screen behind me, then turned and watched her, wondering what she'd do next. After a long time, she spread her arms and held them stiff like she was balancing, twirled once, twice, again and again, like a little girl, like there was no one watching.

- 14 -

When I walked in the employees' door, I knew I'd have no use for Jotta's sweater that day. Alex was standing in front of one of the refrigerators with his shirt unbuttoned, fanning the cool air onto his plump chest with the glass door. I didn't recognize any of the other half dozen waiters and waitresses doing chores around the kitchen. I walked over to Alex, struggled for something to say.

"Guess it's going to be a scorcher," I said.

"Hotter than Satan's nipple rings." He waved some more cold air onto his chest with his open shirt. It might have been his joke that made me notice his nipples. A tiny gold hoop hung from each, pierced through the tender skin. A shiver ran up my body, despite the heat in the kitchen. Walking to the dressing room, I crossed my arms in front of me, pressed them hard against my chest.

My first table was in the Map Room, in the darkest, most tomblike corner of the restaurant. Alex said the old couple came for lunch every Tuesday and sat at the same table, blizzard or heat wave. I had to yell for them to hear anything I said.

The place filled up between noon and one. The table numbers got added under my name faster than I could keep track, and people were usually mad by the time I got to them. But somehow it didn't seem as urgent as it had the night before. All of us were way behind on our tables, but nobody acted too tense over it.

The first lull came about two-thirty. Alex and I leaned in the doorway of the kitchen, watching our customers clean their plates and drink their iced tea.

"I'll bet it gets hotter than this in Wyoming," Alex said. He pulled a handkerchief from his back pocket and dabbed at his forehead, his neck.

"I never worked in a kitchen in Wyoming," I said.

A waitress with short black hair walked between us and sat down with two others by an open refrigerator. She reached in the front pocket of her skirt and pulled out a cigarette.

"How come things are so different today?"

Alex looked back into the kitchen. "Different how?"

"Different from last night." I pointed to the group of waitresses.

"Girl, you haven't noticed?"

I shrugged.

Alex took me by the hand and pulled me to the Green Room, where only two tables were still full. He walked me to the picture window, pointed outside.

"The royal family," he said.

Down the shore from the restaurant, a yacht with a rainbow-striped sail bobbed in the water. I could see Steve, the man who hired me, pulling on a rope that hung from the sail. Buffalo Snatch leaned back in the other end of the ship, her feet propped up on the side. On the beach, not thirty feet from the window, Shrimp Cock shared a towel with Gigi, who still had her hair pulled over to one side. She was squirting mist on his back with a spray bottle. Maybe the streets were all about power, like Marie said. But the Chateau Rouge was as far as you could get from the dark side, and there was Gigi, making her own bargains.

"They wouldn't be caught dead in here on a day like this," Alex said. "So we peons are *laissez aller*."

Greg turned over on his towel. Gigi sprayed his chest, his stomach.

"Gigi says the Reeba boys tell jokes," Alex said, "about getting AIDS from fag sweat."

Alex held out his collar, swabbed under it with his handkerchief.

"Gigi tells you those things," I said, "then keeps hanging out with them?"

He slipped the handkerchief back in his pocket. "Honey," he said, "it's the fastest lane in town."

Alex left to check on his last table. I watched Gigi chase Greg with the squirt bottle, till he finally jumped in the water and swam to his brother's boat. Once he'd pulled himself up and climbed aboard, she sat in the center of the towel, stretched out her arms and legs to cover it.

I nodded when Alex asked me if I was headed downtown. My car was parked in the Chateau lot, but I was in no hurry to go back and sit on the front lawn with Marie.

Alex looked at home walking down Commercial Street in his faded jeans and black T-shirt. He walked with his hands in his pockets, whistling a tune I couldn't place. I tried for a while to drum up things to talk about, but soon I felt comfortable enough just walking with him.

The mile or so between the Chateau and downtown was lined with prim, old-style houses, mostly white with their trims painted different colors. Some of them were hotels and boardinghouses, but lots of them seemed to be private homes with well-kept gardens and cats on the lawn. Several in a row had blue plaques mounted over the front door, hanging from a roof, underneath a gable window. Once I started looking for them, I saw the plaques on lots of the houses. I stopped to look closer at one of them. It showed a little white house, resting on water.

"That has something to do," Alex said, "with them having been floated over."

"Over from where?"

"From wherever they were. Somewhere out there." He waved in the general direction of the ocean. "They used to be on some hunk of land that started to sink."

He turned to walk on.

"So what happened?" I said.

"So," he said, "they floated their houses over. A long, long, long, long time ago."

"How'd they do that?"

Alex tensed his mouth. "Do I look like a one-queer tourist information bureau?"

I turned and walked on ahead. Hell with him if he was so damn moody. I heard his steps behind me, but I kept walking.

"I just remembered how they did it," he said.

I still didn't turn around. He put his mouth up close to my ear.

"They took the biggest, roundest, fattest, most floatable faggot," he said, and the next I knew, his back was under my knees, hoisting me off my feet and onto his shoulders.

"And they strapped everything onto him"—he started running—"and gave him a big, hard, mighty *push*."

Alex ran me down another block of houses to where the shops and bars and crowds began. He weaved us through the tourists, with me shrieking and him yelling "blub, blub, blub." He slowed at the first bench, dropped to his knees while I climbed off. He flung his arms onto the bench and panted, doubled over. I collapsed next to him, waiting for my heartbeat to slow to normal.

"I'll never, ever," I said, "put us through another history lesson again."

After he got his breath back, Alex heaved himself up onto the bench. Since all the mess with the coke arrest, he was the first person I'd felt like opening up to. He was funny and warm and from a different world. I watched him lean back on the bench and close his eyes, letting his pale, chubby arms fall to his sides. All those years in the bail bond office I'd seen hundreds of them on the other side of the counter—bi, trans, and homosexuals, mostly young and very young men who came to San Francisco for a new life. I thought how Alex would probably laugh if I told him: You were the ones who always seemed to belong. I knew things were hard for you in the world, but I'd watch you from my desk at the back of the office, all of you putting down your names and your money, taking care of each other. I'd think, They've got something, these people; me, I got to go change Mr. Hoops's papers.

I'd made only twelve dollars at lunch, but I still had forty from the night before. I would sweep Alex off to a grand, festive, celebratory dinner, in honor of this new place and my brand-new way of belonging. He could show me how to break open a lobster and eat it without messing up my shirt. We'd suck the sweet juice from its tenderest parts, and I'd tell Alex about everything and how it all was changing now.

Alex opened his eyes, clapped once, and stood up. "Dearie, I'm late for the ball," he said.

I stood up too. "Where you headed?"

"The Cent-annual Midsummer Tea Dance." He pointed to a sprawling hotel down the street. He leaned toward me and kissed me on the lips. It was a nice kiss, but a good-bye kiss, and I knew I wasn't welcome to go along.

I sat back down, then scooted over a foot to be under the shade. The bench faced a store with ice cream cones painted on the signs and windows. A pack of teenage girls pushed through the narrow doorway, wandered out a minute later stuffing slices of pizza into their mouths. One of them ran to the first in a row of phone booths that lined the front wall. I watched her balance pizza, purse, and shopping bags, somehow pulling out a quarter. It was the same booth I'd called Jotta from the day before, to tell her I wouldn't be home till late. I thought of starting for home, but no. Now she had Marie Frazelli's Lawn-Sitting Vigilante Corps. I looked over my shoulder to where Alex had pointed; he'd already disappeared into the crowd outside the hotel. I turned my back on the hotel and the wall of phones, headed off with no purpose except to be free of all of it.

* * *

Within half a block I had to cut around the crowd to keep a walking pace. The one-way traffic came at me head-on, but since parking wasn't allowed on Commercial, it was easy to keep clear of the cars. I heard an engine rumbling behind me. I looked over my shoulder quick, couldn't see much through the crowd trailing me in the street. The sound didn't fade as I walked—it was a motorcycle for sure, going against the one-way traffic. Tom must have gotten all the information he needed from me; why would he be tailing me now? I walked faster, knowing it wouldn't do any good, not if he wanted something. I took a deep breath, stopped walking, turned around. A young couple almost plowed into me, had to let go of each other's hands to go around. As the bike engine grew louder, I braced myself for the blast of his siren. Some kids passed me, two young men, then I was standing, face to helmet, with a motor-cycle cop.

"Sorry," I said, and hopped aside. He eyed me for a long minute, revved his engine, and rolled on along with the crowd.

"Christ," I said out loud. How long was I going to spook myself? I needed a friendly face to shake me loose of the ghosts.

– 15 –

Hunter didn't even let on that he recognized me when I opened the door to his record shop. I stood halfway in the room, my hand on the knob. He just rocked back and forth to the reggae music, like he had the day before.

"Remember me?" I said.

He kept his eyes narrow. "Maybe."

I frowned.

"Oh, sure," he said. "You're the lady whose parents I'm not good enough to get introduced to."

"They weren't my parents," I said.

He closed his eyes, rocked a few beats. "Black lady was nice. Other lady a tad chilly."

"My aunt, Marie," I said. "I didn't come to talk about her."

"Uh-huh. And you came why?"

I shrugged, stepped inside, and closed the door behind me. A gust of cape wind sucked it shut, hard and loud. I heard the thunder of excited paw steps from behind the American flag in the counter doorway.

"Shit," I said, but Hunter was way ahead of me. When Marley came sailing through the flag, Hunter hugged him around the belly in midair and both of them dropped to the floor. Marley rolled over on his side, panting like a puppy. Hunter collapsed on top of him.

"You should do something about that dog," I said.

"I should shoot him and put both of us out of our misery," Hunter said through the fur.

I walked over and held out my hand. He smiled, took it, let me help pull him to his feet. I wasn't accustomed to having to look up so high to see a person, female or male. He reached down and pushed my hair behind my shoulders, like Poppa Dad used to do. It seemed like too warm a thing for anyone to do right then. I moved back a step.

"You sleep in that shirt, or you got a drawerful of them?" I said.

He looked down at it.

"I like the air-conditioning," he said, and punched a fist through one of the holes.

I turned and walked to the window. The motorcycle cop had turned around, was following the crowd on the other side of the street.

"Since nobody comes in here to buy records," Hunter said, "I'm guessing you came to give me another chance."

I watched the cop till he disappeared in the crowd.

"Why not?" I said, and we both tried our hardest to smile.

While Hunter was closing up shop, I waited in front of the post office. It was an old building, with a dozen concrete stairs stretching the width of it. I sat on one of the middle steps, spread my arms and leaned back, letting the sun warm my face, draw sweat to the pores. The heat felt so good that I didn't even take off Jotta's sweater. I never had spent much time in the sun, since little of it ever pierced the fog back home. That was something I could do a lot of in this new place, this new time in my life. Bake the old body, heat the new blood.

"Where to?"

I sat up, shielded my eyes to see him.

"You're the local," I said, and stood up.

"First," he said, "got a present for you."

He bent down and pinned a button the size of a Kennedy dollar on Jotta's sweater. I twisted it up to see it. He'd made a button out of a picture of me lying on the steps with my face in the sun.

"How'd you do this?" I said.

"Shucks," he said. "Part of the business."

He pulled another button from his pocket and pinned it above one of the holes in the middle of his T-shirt.

"I try to put these to better uses," he said, "than slogans and rock stars."

Hunter's button showed him in cutoffs and mirrored shades, lying under a stereo speaker like he was sunbathing in its rays. He tapped the button with an index finger.

"Not a big seller in the shop," he said. "But then, what is."

"Now that you mention it," I said, "your store's been empty every time I've walked in. How do you guys stay in business?"

"Charisma," he said. "And generous mommies. Let's hit Carla's and grab some chow."

The red vinyl booths and teapot wallpaper gave Carla's a coffee shop look, but the smell of a tangy spice promised something other than pigs in a blanket. I looked at my watch.

"Six o'clock," I said, "and nobody here."

"Carla doesn't care," he said, and nodded toward the booth closest to the kitchen.

No sooner had we slid into our seats than I heard a woman yelling something that sounded like B.R.'s Spanish. I turned to see her young dark-skinned face watching us from over a tall counter. The order wheel hung over her head like a crown in the margarine commercials.

"*Que é isso, rapaz?*" she said. It sounded like when B.R. said "What's up" in Spanish, plus the strange word *rapaz*. "*Mais uma

215

das suas amiguinas?" That was close enough to Spanish that I knew she was asking about his friend.

"Nada de isso mulher!" Hunter spoke like a native, but a native what? *"Essa aqui é gente boa."*

"What's that you're talking?" I said.

Hunter laughed. "I guess you don't hang out with a lot of Portagee fishermen."

I shrugged. "Only been here a few days."

He smiled in a way I didn't like. "I bet you had a fight with your daddy," he said, "over that B-plus you got in English class. You stormed out of the dormitory and drove to Sin City, just to make him sweat."

I wasn't hungry enough to sit and listen to some kid sound off. I stood up.

"Seems to be a lot," I said, "you don't know in the world."

"Hey, lady." He held up his hands. "No offense intended."

The woman from the kitchen stood next to me, pad and pencil in hand. "He make you sick at the stomach, before you even eat?" she said.

I looked her straight on, right into her collarbone. Her dark face glared down at me. She tapped the pencil on her pad.

"Whatever country you all hail from," I said, "you sure got tall genes."

The woman looked down at her pants.

"Danny," Hunter said. "Meet Annie. You guys rhyme, like a poem." He tried to laugh.

Danny looked from her pants to me. I held out my hand.

"I thought maybe you were Carla," I said.

Danny looked down at my hand.

"Danny's my sister," Hunter said. "She works here."

I shot him an oh-really look. He frowned.

"Menina," he said to her, "we're hungry like dogs. Annie, park it, wouldya?"

Danny sniffed and looked back at me. "My brother with the holes in his clothes," she said. The floor trembled while she stomped back into the kitchen.

"Thought you were gonna give me another chance," he said.

"I did," I said, and turned to go.

"Annie," he said.

I looked back.

"Third time's the charm," he said, smiling.

I leaned over the booth, rested my palms on the table. "Number one," I said, "I don't go to any college. Number two, I don't see so much sin in this city as I do lonely old gays and T-shirt shops. Number three, I don't have a daddy. Have I made myself clear?"

He smiled, rested his hands on mine. "There are girls," he said, "who wouldn't take those things like insults." He looked back toward the kitchen.

The last man who'd taken my hand was Tom. I remembered trying to pull away, feeling him grip even tighter. I looked down at Hunter's thick knuckles and gangly fingers, more touching my hands than holding them. He was right, after all. It was a privilege to say no to college, then drive a car across the country on a whim. But it was more than a whim; it had to be. It was looking for a place to live a life. I turned my hands palms up, gave his fingers a squeeze.

"Why don't you do the ordering," I said.

"I already did."

By the time we were finishing our second beer, Danny came charging from the kitchen, her arms loaded up with eight steaming plates.

"Professionally speaking," I said, "I'm impressed."

I expected her to announce the dishes as she sat them down, like on Grant Street in Chinatown. But she just left us to puzzle them out.

I pointed to a sea creature whose head stared through thick red sauce.

"Now that's fish," I said. "Right?"

Hunter dove in like he knew his business, spooning a little

bit of each kind of food onto two empty plates. I remembered how Jotta always snapped at me when I'd demanded to know what I was eating. I put some of the fish sauce on a pile of rice and took a spoonful.

"Wow." I sucked cool air into my mouth.

Hunter looked up. "Too hot?"

I drenched the walls of my mouth with beer.

"Great stuff," I said, and waited till he wasn't looking to scrape the sauce off the rice. I had to get the conversation away from the food.

"So you're Portuguese," I said, "and I didn't even notice you had an accent."

"I don't," he said, and shoveled a heaping forkful into his mouth. A bell tinkled as the front door opened. An old man with a thick head of white hair sat in the booth by the window and stared into the kitchen.

"Funny how this place does so little business," I said. "What with the streets so crowded."

Hunter chewed his mouthful, swallowed. "Those streets are crowded with gays and Dorchester weekenders," he said. "None of 'em got a taste for braised octopus."

"Crying shame," I said.

"Or reggae music either," he said. He loaded his fork again. "Guess all of us are in the wrong business. All but the trawlers."

"The guys that sell souvenirs?"

Hunter looked at me a second, then let loose a hearty laugh.

"I think I like how you're too damn stubborn to correct," he said.

"You better like it," I said. I loaded my mouth with rice and fiery sauces, chewed it slow, and let it burn.

The fisherman they called Tail didn't even nod in reply.

"And this is August," Hunter said.

"Charmed," the old man said, but I didn't believe it. None of Hunter's three fisherman buddies would look at me square, though I could feel them eyeing me when I turned away. The only lights in the bar came from the pinball machines, but I'd seen plenty of their type, Portuguese or no. There was August, the bearded old buffalo in the tweed coat who'd bowed when I'd walked in. Young, curly-haired Noosebaum had glared up at me with his black eyes, then bent back over the table and made his shot. The one they called Tail had the longest ponytail I'd ever seen, on woman or man. He'd nodded once, barely, then turned away. I stood for a couple of rounds, watching them shoot pool in silence. I turned to Hunter.

"Your friends are a scream," I said, "but I believe I'll go make conversation elsewhere."

Hunter pushed his way up next to me at the crowded bar. "They don't mean any harm," he said.

"How do they act if they do?"

The bartender asked "What'll it be?" and I ordered beer. We watched him take the bottle from the cooler, pop the cap.

"They're my friends," he said. "I had a coupla bad go-rounds with girls the past few years."

I pushed two dollars toward the bartender. He slid one of the dollars back to me.

"I get it," I said. "Chicks are all the same."

"My friends, they see their buddy hurt," he said. "What do they know. They're not big on reggae either."

I took a long pull from the bottle.

"So what made it so bad?" I said.

"It?"

"With the girlfriends," I said.

Hunter signaled the bartender, drew a dollar from his wallet. "Depends on who you ask," he said.

"Okay. What if I asked, say, Noosebaum."

Hunter stood up straight and sucked in his belly, made his hands into fists and flexed the muscles in his arms. "Hunter my friend," he said with a husky accent, "you run after them like puppy. They like to look up tall to see a man." He beat his chest.

"I know the type," I said. "How about Tail?"

He relaxed his back and shoulders, slumped against the bar and closed his eyes. He pinched thumb to forefinger, pressed them against his lips and took a long drag from a phantom joint. "Hear me out, man," he said groggily, "here's what you do. It's like, the world is really this really big shoebox, except instead of shoes inside are all these thousands and thousands of girls. I mean, *thousands*." He took another long drag, exhaled slowly and stared off into space.

"And?" I said.

"And then he stumbles out the door," he said, "and wanders back ten minutes later with an armload of doughnuts."

"Fattening advice," I said. "So that leaves old August."

Hunter reached across the bar and pulled a cigarette from somebody's pack. He dangled it from his lips, took a puff, coughed. "I know the problem. I seen it happening for years," he said. "They don't wear skirts in the summer no more." He shook his head sadly, started coughing again.

The bartender delivered Hunter's beer and waved the dollar away. Hunter lifted the bottle as a toast to him.

"What if," I said, "I asked you—why it hurt so much."

Hunter took a sip, looked back at his friends. Tail was leaning over the table, lining up a shot.

"I don't know," he said. "Girls never stay."

I heard the crack of one ball against another, then there was cheering and a burst of applause.

"I had a girl for a few years once," Hunter said. "Maxie. She hated her name. I thought it was kinda great." He set his bottle on the bar, looked down at it while he talked. "Me and Maxie were really happy for a while. She even married me and everything."

"Wow," I said. "You've been *married*?" I turned away out of embarrassment at the gawking amazement in my voice.

He smiled. "Yeah," he said. "I was somebody's husband once. I can't say I ever much looked the part. But I took out the garbage and kept the garage pretty neat. I don't think I was so bad at it."

220

We both were staring at Hunter's beer. I thought of putting my hand on his, but it didn't seem right to act like I had any power to soften a real-life hurt.

"What happened?" I said.

He picked up his beer and turned to face the pool table. He talked softly, like he wasn't angry at all. "All of a sudden she wanted out. Nothing to do with me, she kept on saying, she just needed her freedom, and real, real bad. All this came out on this one day, a Tuesday, eleven o'clock in the middle of the morning." He lifted the bottle to his lips, but he didn't seem to take a drink or swallow.

"Did you hear much from her again?" I said.

"Oh, sure," he said. "I got letters from Boston, the happiest, healthiest letters you ever saw in your life. She got a job in some company out there, they do stuff for lawyers. Maxie hates lawyers and she can't type either, but they kept saying all kinds of nice things about the good work she did. I didn't hear from her for a few more months, then I was leaving the shop to mail something and there she was coming out of the post office."

"Here?" I said. "She came back?"

Hunter nodded. "Boy did she—with about eight months' worth of some other guy's baby riding out in front of her. We talked for a couple of minutes, just chatter, nothing real. Then I walked right up to her, and I put my hand on her belly. I did it without thinking, and I thought she'd probably push me away. It was so hard there, Annie; it felt so ... *full.* We'd been apart too long for it to have been mine, but I let my hand rest there on her, I just wanted to so bad. And frisky ol' Maxie, you know, she just let me."

There was another cheer from the pool table. Old August looked over at us, and I smiled. He nodded shyly, then turned back to the game.

"Twins," Hunter said. "I saw her pushing them down the street two months later, in a double-width carriage with clowns' heads printed all the hell over it. 'I got the perfect names for 'em, Max,' I felt like telling her. 'You can call one of 'em Free, and the other one Dum.'" He shook his head slowly for what

221

seemed like a long time. "Here's to your freedom, baby," he finally said, and lifted his bottle in the air to no one.

August was lining up a shot now. "Sink it, guy," Hunter yelled to him.

"You seem pretty calm," I said. "About Maxie."

Hunter shrugged. "She's back in Boston now I hear, living with some guy who works for the city. Nobody comes to this town for keeps. Part of the deal, I guess." He tipped back his head and drank.

"I got myself a job," I said. "Soon as I get a little ahead, I'll be renting myself a cottage."

He set the bottle on the bar and looked at me.

"I mean," I said, "there are people who are willing to give it a shot. Staying around, I mean."

Hunter smiled. He looked down at the button of him lying under the stereo speaker, unpinned it from his shirt and stuck it on my sweater.

"Wait," I said. "Too many buttons for one skinny person."

I pulled off the button of me in the sun, pinned it over the hole in his shirt where his button had been. We smiled at each other, no bull this time. I took his arm, and we walked back to watch some pool.

"Stop," Hunter said. "Gloria. Now she's the black lady who got married last month."

I nodded. Tail missed a close bank shot, stared at the ball long after it had stopped rolling.

"You was robbed," Hunter yelled to him.

Tail looked up and his mouth slid into a smile.

Hunter turned back to me. "You say Gloria came out here to keep your aunt from killing you?"

"Something like that." He'd asked for my "story," and I'd opened my mouth and let the words tumble out. Hunter was a small-town boy—how much did I really want to let on? About the only thing I'd left out was the cocaine arrest.

222

I drained my beer. "You dry?" I said.

He held up his bottle. "Backwash."

I got up and Hunter reached for his wallet.

"My turn," I said.

Noosebaum looked from the bottles of beer in my hands, to me, to the beer.

"Not your brand?" I said.

"Brand?" he said. "Noosebaum, choosy?" He looked like a different man when he smiled so sweet; buying a round seemed like a significant gesture in this world. Old August was leaning over the cue ball, pulling back his arm to make a shot. Noosebaum rapped the table with his stick.

"Hey hey," he said. "*Menina* buys your beer, you make her stand holding it?"

August dropped his cue, and he and Tail sprinted to take the bottles off my hands. "Such a darling!" August called to Hunter.

"As long as you don't mention her daddy," Hunter said.

Tail leaned over and kissed me on the forehead. "Much obliged," he said.

"Hunter," I said back at my stool, "I've never seen such hoopla over a round of Buds."

He took a long drink from the fresh beer. "It doesn't sound like your old boyfriend's buddies were so appreciative."

"It doesn't sound like you need to know much before you pipe up about something." I wedged my thumbnail under a corner of the label, started nudging the paper off the glass. Hunter took my chin in his hands, turned my head to face him.

"How come you keep fighting me?" he said.

I pulled his hands from my face but held them in my lap. Hunter's buddies cheered at August's shot. Noosebaum and Tail were patting him on the back, and August was waving his cue in the air.

"I don't know how come," I said.

"You missed my shot!" August yelled to us. When neither of us answered, he looked back to his game.

"I think"—Hunter squeezed my hands—"there's a reason people act how they do. A person acts like you, they usually been kicked around a little."

"Nobody kicks me around," I said. "I been doing fine since long before I laid eyes on you."

He squeezed my hands again.

"Okay," I said. "I'll try to be better." That was something that Carter had said. One of so many days when he wasn't able to love me.

Hunter reached around my neck and pulled me toward him with one arm. I felt his lips touch mine, move lightly in a slow circle around my mouth. Here was a good, dependable, likable man, kinder than the highway, worlds richer than the Reebas. He stopped, waiting, I knew, for me to move closer. I didn't pull away, but I couldn't kiss him back.

"Hunter," I said, "I have to take care of something first."

I stood up, spotted a phone booth across the street. "Five minutes," I said.

When I walked away, he watched with sad eyes, mouth held firm, like someone used to being left behind. I knew he didn't expect me back. I hoped so much that I could prove him wrong.

"I was sure you'd be awake," I said. "I'm really sorry."

Ten forty-five—quarter to nine his time, yet I was ready with the sorries. Five seconds on the telephone had me back at my old habits.

"Just give me a second to rouse myself," Carter said.

I listened to the muffled rustling of sheets, imagined Carter shaking his head roughly, combing his hair out of his face with his fingers. He'd be sitting up by now, stuffing pillows under his back. I hated knowing the look of the room, the angle of the ceiling, the smell of the dry Wyoming air drifting in through the window I knew would be open.

"You okay?" he said.

"Don't act like I only call when I need something from you," I said.

I listened to the hum of the wires. I heard him blow his nose.

"Carter," I said, "I need something from you."

He didn't answer at first. "Rumor has it," he finally said, "you been practicing your disappearing act coast to coast."

He must've talked to Poppa Dad. Why did everybody everywhere seem to keep tabs on me?

"So he told you I left," I said. "Did he mention his little secret cargo?"

"I suppose you consider your good self used," he said. "Poor little mississiness."

"What?"

He took a loud breath. "Miss In-no-cence," he said.

I gripped the receiver tighter. "If innocence means not passing out before nine o'clock, then I guess I qualify," I said.

He breathed a few more loud puffs. " 'Cept for the odd stolen ounce bag. From what I hear."

"Everybody's heard everything," I said. "Just one thing I want to hear from you."

We both waited to see what I'd come out with next. I knew what I wanted and had no idea how to ask for it. Though Carter and I hadn't spoken since I left Homer, not a thing between us had changed. Phoning long distance, sharing a beer or sharing a bed, we were two people who'd never learned how to talk to each other.

"I don't really mind anything that's happened," I said.

There was faint static on the line, like water running. A souped-up car full of teenagers roared by.

"Okay," Carter said.

"I guess what I want is to understand better," I said. "Before I go on with things."

He heaved a long sigh. "You want to know why it wasn't magic," he said. "Why good didn't triumph over evil, why love didn't conquer all, why truth and beauty didn't prevail . . ."

I stopped listening to Carter's words, heard only the familiar, drunken rhythm of the sounds. They were lulling me into a plain, flat-footed truth. All the questions I'd rehearsed would tell me nothing: Why didn't you love me, Carter? Wasn't I good enough, smart enough, pretty enough? No. There was only one question, and it wasn't Carter who held the answer.

"Carter," I said.

He stopped.

"The day you're qualified to talk about love'll be the day I get elected pope."

He was quiet for a moment. "You used to hold different opinions. You used to think I made pretty good love."

"It's got nothing to do with making love, Carter. It has to do with why I fixed on a man who would never be able to love anybody."

"Lo-o-o-ve . . ." bellowed a voice behind me. Tom sat at the curb, perched on his bike, one hand over his heart and the other reaching to the sky. ". . . is a ma-n-n-n-y splen-n-n-n-dored thi-i-i-ing," he sang.

Carter was saying something I couldn't hear. I tried to slam the door of the booth, but it stuck halfway.

"It's noisy here," I said into the phone.

"I said," Carter yelled, "that you seem to have gone on fine, whatever wrongs you think I did you."

I looked over my shoulder at Tom. He was swaying on his bike, playing a pretend violin. I kicked at the door of the booth again, jarring it more off track.

"You know what they say," Tom said.

I covered my free ear. Tom sang along with his violin, "You can't close the door once the walls cave in."

"Just be happy," Carter was saying. Tom switched to trombone, was tooting a melody as he played.

"You hear me?" Carter said.

I felt ridiculous suddenly for having called him. Whatever it was that needed figuring out, it had nothing to do with Carter anymore. Nothing.

"Can you hear me?" he said. I hung up.

"Awwwww," Tom cooed. "Unhappy ending."

I forced the door open, walked up next to him. "I was wondering when you'd show up," I said.

"Magical, wonderful *l'amour*," he said, "mysterious *l'amour*, Louis L'Amour."

"Tom," I said, "whatever you've got planned for Jotta, you may as well forget it."

"From looking at a man like me," he said, "the average ignorant person might not think I know as much as I do about love."

I looked at him leaning back in his seat, his arms crossed in front of him, the leather stretched tight across his shoulders.

"Love sort of sneaks up on you," he said, "like freezing to death."

I held my sides, felt the warmth of the sweater Jotta had made and given me. Tom cocked his head, nodded at the button Hunter had pinned on me.

"Fetching," he said. "Making friends?"

"Listen," I said. "You'll never even get in to see her. There's people living with her, protecting her."

Tom sat up and scooted forward on his seat. "Hop on," he said. "We have lots to talk about."

Through the window of the bar I could see Hunter at the pool table, rubbing chalk onto the end of a cue, watching us.

"I'm not letting you worm anything more out of me," I said. "Leave Jotta alone, that's all I've got to say to you."

He started the engine. "Annie," he said. "I made room for you. Hop on."

The leather on the seat behind Tom looked well worn, soft. He'd only use me for information again.

"She's married, Tom," I said. "She's got a husband and a garden, and soon she'll have a kid. You've got no power anymore."

I started to cross the street, but he backed up and cut me off. Hunter and Noosebaum crossed the doorway to the sidewalk, Tail and August a few feet behind.

"What's the deal here?" Hunter said.

227

Tom leaned back, smiled. I thought how he moved the slowest when everything else was going fast. "Last fair deal in the country," he said. "Just offering an old friend a ride."

Tail walked up next to Noosebaum and Hunter, cutting off Tom's path. There was something different about how they looked at Tom, like these fishermen had seen more bikes and more leather than the men on Poppa Dad's porch ever had.

"You need a ride somewhere, Annie?" Hunter said.

Everybody turned to me, waiting for an answer. I looked at the space behind Tom on the seat. The streets are all about power, Marie had said; the closest we can get is the back of a motorcycle. It's me with the power now, Marie, I imagined myself telling her—they're having their showdown, muscle against muscle, but it's me in the middle, I'm the stakes in their wager. Then Marie's face turned to Max's, he was winking at me from the doorway at Poppa Dad's house. Stakes? he was answering, just like that first night in Homer. Darlin', he said, that's the least of what matters.

"Annie," Tom said without a smile, let alone a wink.

"I don't need any ride," I said.

Tom did smile now, still looking at me, then he turned back to the three men in his way. "If you would excuse me, gentlemen," he said. He sat up higher in his seat, revved the engine loud and long. Old August walked up and stood behind Hunter, Tail, and Noosebaum. Other than that, nobody moved.

Tom rolled back a few feet to where I stood. I'd never seen him coast his bike quietly, on his own power. He reached out and touched my cheek with the back of his hand, a touch so light could hardly feel it.

"Just remember," he said, "where you learned about love. If you forget"—he lifted a finger to my face, shook it—"I can't be responsible for what becomes of you."

He roared off without a blast of his siren, teetering as he weaved his way against the flow of the crowd on the one-way street. I watched till his taillight turned out of sight.

"Annie." Hunter hadn't moved, though his friends were

heading back inside. I noticed for the first time he was still holding his pool cue.

"I'll be right there," I said, and went back to the phone booth. I couldn't go back to Jotta's; I didn't want to talk to them about anything that had happened today. Jotta had Sam, Marie, and Gloria with her. Did they need me running home? I'd come all the way out to the end of Cape Cod to warn her about Tom. It was time for me to figure out what I wanted, to get on with my new life.

"I have two messages," I said when Gloria answered.

"Marie thought you'd be home for supper," she said. "She made us wait till quarter past eight. That Sam, he turned Jotta into some cook."

"Yeah," I said. "Listen. First message is, I won't be coming back tonight. Second—"

"Oh boy," Gloria said.

I heard her put down the phone and yell for Marie. I called out for her to come back, but it was Marie who picked up the receiver.

"We waited two hours for dinner," she said.

"I know," I said. "I'm sorry."

"You leaving work now?"

I took a deep breath. "Two things," I said. "One, Tom's here. He might even be showing up there tonight."

"Oh God," she said. "You saw him?"

"I saw him," I said. "Second thing is, I won't be coming back tonight. So I wanted to make sure you knew, about Tom being around."

"Number one," Marie said, "climb right in that car and point it straight at this house. Number two—"

Walking back to the bar, I felt a little giddy from all the hanging up I'd been doing. No more talk, I told myself. No more excuses, sorries, or lies.

August was lining up a shot when I walked up to the table.

Noosebaum set upon me, his dark eyes angry.

"Those men," he said. "Those are up to no good for girls. You see one coming, you turn and run."

I felt embarrassed and ashamed, like a kid caught trying to dash in front of a speeding car. Hunter put his arm around me. "It's okay," he said. "It's over with."

There was only so much helplessness I could stand feeling in one day. Hunter had taken action for me, which seemed like more than I had a right to expect from anybody. It was time to take some action of my own.

Hunter handed me his pool cue. "Want to take my shot?"

I leaned it against the table, took his hand and pulled him out the door.

— 16 —

No sooner had we shut the door behind us than Marley was leaping over the counter. Hunter dropped to one knee and held the dog to his chest. "Cool out, boy," he chanted while he stroked his fur.

"The both of you live here?" I said.

Though Hunter tried to hold Marley still, his whole body seemed to be wagging along with his tail.

"The landlady would pitch us if she knew," he said. "Two thou a month for this rathole store. There's never been enough profits to rent us an apartment."

Hunter went behind the flag, and soon music was coming out of the stereo speakers.

"I'm getting to like this reggae stuff," I said.

He reappeared, closed his eyes, drummed the counter softly with the heels of his hands.

"Some people complain," he said, "that you can't understand the words."

"Right now," I said, "I consider that a virtue in a song."

Hunter opened his eyes and walked up next to me. "Another virtue," he said, "is how you can dance to it."

He put his arms around my waist and pulled me close. His

shoulder was too high for me to rest my chin on. When I put my head to his chest, I felt bone, not muscle. I thought how I'd never danced with Carter. Through the front window I could see young men wandering up and down the sidewalks, mostly alone. Carter's not dancing seemed to go along with his not loving. I could hear Hunter's heart beating faster than mine.

"Annie," he said, "you sure you didn't know that biker?"

I hooked my hands around his neck. "Why would I know some gorilla on a bike in Massachusetts?"

Hunter shrugged, and I could tell he believed me. We danced in silence for a minute, then he tilted my chin to his face. "You know," he said, "you could be more careful once in a while."

I closed my eyes and pulled him tighter against me. "It's my new motto," I said. "Dare to be careful."

We tried to walk upstairs with our hands linked, but the steps were so steep I had to clutch both rails. Marley trotted past me at the top landing. There was no light on at first. Hunter's steps creaked across the room, then a bare bulb flickered on, swinging from the ceiling.

The wall to my right was heaped with open boxes of shoes—dainty white sandals, work boots, size twelve loafers.

"My landlady charges people to store their shit," he said. "Those come from Cape Footwear." He pointed to a corner stacked with piles of linen. "Tablecloths from Christy's Café—great food, but they don't store any of that here."

Hunter went around the room, listing off the contents of T-shirt boxes, gallons of latex house paint, rolls of fiberglass insulation. Marley was working his way from one end of the attic to the other, maniacally sniffing.

"Hunter," I said, "where up here can you live?"

I followed him to a closed plywood door. It was covered top to bottom by a poster of a grinning Rastafarian, a jewel sunk into each of his front four teeth. Hunter opened the door with a rope that hung from where the knob should have been. He switched on a fluorescent desk lamp.

"My office, if the slumlady asks," he said.

The twin bed wedged into the corner of the cubicle took up half the space in the room. There was a tiny desk, painted what someone probably thought was a cheery yellow. The walls were made of rough dark wood that didn't seem to line up. I could see a second layer of wood through knotholes and gaps where the boards didn't meet.

"Must be toasty in the winter," I said.

"November to February," he said, "home base is Tail's couch."

Marley appeared in the doorway, dove onto the bed in a single leap. He circled once, twice, curled up in the center on a heap of blankets. He laid his head on his paws and peered up at us, like he was asking whether he'd get ousted soon. We both looked around the room for another focus of conversation.

"More buttons." I pointed to a cluster of them, stuck on the wall over the desk.

"Check it out," he said, and we both leaned toward them. He pointed at one along the edge of the cluster. "There's old August, on his birthday last March. You believe that guy's only fifty-eight years old?"

"No kidding?" I said.

"No kidding," he said.

I wondered why we were suddenly so short on topics.

"That bed," I said, "takes up a lot of this room."

Hunter stood up straight. When I looked at him, he smiled. "You know," he said, "you don't have to be here."

Yes, I knew, there were no have-to's in Hunter's world; he was good and true enough to love, strong enough to stand up to Tom. I also knew better than to rate myself on goodness or truth or strength right then. I put my arms around Hunter's chest, leaned all my weight against him.

Hunter touched my shoulders, pulled my face up to his. "Let's talk a minute, okay?"

I laid my head on his chest, waited for him to say something. I slid my finger in a trail around one freckle, to his nipple, around another freckle and back again. Yes, even his chest smelled different. Like oak, or maybe it was the room. I could hear Marley's toenails clicking up and down the stairs.

"What are you thinking about?" Hunter said.

I shrugged. He shook my shoulders, lightly probed my ribs for spots to tickle. I held his wrists till he stopped, then let them go.

"It used to be you were always fighting me," he said. "Now it's like being with a blowup doll."

Marley started whimpering outside the door.

"That's flattering," I said. "You're a lion in bed yourself." I sat up, spotted my jeans on the floor and dragged them toward me. "Where's my sweater," I said, more a statement than a question. Marley was pacing the stairs again, the pitch of his whine peaking in sobs.

"Marley!" Hunter screamed from behind me. "Shut the goddamn hell up!"

"My eardrums enjoyed that," I said.

Hunter sat up. "Look," he said, "I like you, Annie. I just want to be nice to you, I swear to God."

I pulled a leg of my jeans right side out. "I know that," I said. "You're a nice guy."

"You say it like that's the problem," he said.

I stuffed one of the pockets back inside. Hunter reached around me and yanked the jeans away.

"I'm going to ask you again," he said, "what you've been thinking about."

I turned around in the bed to face him. He put a pillow under his head and leaned against the wall.

"The name was, let's see," he said. "It was a last name first and a first name last."

I laughed. It hadn't been Carter I was thinking about, but letting him think so was simpler than trying to explain: I don't really want to be here, and I don't know why.

"Smith Sam," he said.

I shook my head.

"Green Jim," he said. "Farbstein Bob. MacGillicuddy Joe."

"You're getting colder and colder," I said.

"Well sure I am," he said, "what with you way, way over there." He circled his arms around me and pulled me close against him. "Washington George," he whispered. "Ruth Babe. Scott Walter Sir."

I nestled my nose in his hair, traced the outline of an ear with my tongue. "You're a fine one to talk, Mr. Hunter X," I said. "Hunter whose last name I don't even know."

Marley's whimpers were turning to wails, his floor pacing getting faster. Hunter hugged me, then pulled away and stood up.

"You and I are starting over," he said. "Dog out, music in."

Outside the bedroom door I heard Marley dash up to him. Hunter led him to the far end of the floor where the shoes were stacked, then a door opened and closed. Hunter went down the stairs and some music came on, soft reggae with nobody singing.

The first drag off Hunter's pipe sent me into a coughing fit. "What is this stuff?" I asked as soon as I could get breath.

"Just some calming, friendly hash. Relax." He took a long hit, then sat behind me and started rubbing my shoulders. "Take it slow," he said. "A steady stream."

My lungs ached from the first time, but I wanted to do something to help me lighten up about being with Hunter. I drew in slow, loosened my lips to take in some cool air along with the smoke.

"Hold it for a while," he said.

I lowered the pipe, felt the burning smoke in my lungs. Soon the burning turned to a cloud of heat, spreading through me like a fever. He was a nice guy, a kind man, who liked me and wanted only good things. I let out the smoke and the fever stayed.

His cheek was smooth and cool against mine. I kissed lightly along his neck, across his throat, down his chest. His body all over was smooth and cool, like new sheets, like swimming. He pulled me up beside him, rested my head on his pillow while

235

he kissed my breasts. Yes, I thought I could get to like this. Yes, it could be enough, pillows and sheets and niceness.

The room was smelling more and more of smoke and wood and fireplaces. Hunter was nudging my legs apart, kissing the tender skin on my thighs. I opened my eyes.

"There's steam coming up from somewhere," I said.

I felt him nod slowly without lifting his head. In the beam of the desk lamp, smoke seemed to be swirling the dust in the air. I propped myself onto my elbows, squinted, focused hard.

"Hunter. Really. Look at the lamp."

Hunter went to the lamp and turned its hood to the wall. Smoke was rising from the cracks and knotholes, like fumes from a manhole cover. I touched the wall behind the bed.

"It's kind of hot," I said.

I looked at Hunter and he looked back, like we were each sure that the other would come out with the simple, easy answer. After a few beats, we jumped into our pants.

"Where's my sweater?" I said. The lamp flickered twice, went out. Hunter pulled a shirt from a desk drawer and tossed it to me.

Outside the room, the smoke was seeping in from between boards, from knotholes, from where the wall met the floor. Hunter reached back for my arm. It was only then, seeing his hand in the light gathering force inside the walls, that I heard my heart race, felt the breath in my lungs.

We sprinted to the staircase that led down to the store. Flames small enough to have come from a cigarette lighter licked at the knotholes in the low ceiling over the stairs. Hunter and I bent into a crouch, and he nodded for me to go first. I had crept down two steps when I heard the beam above me start to give. I sprang against Hunter, and we both fell onto the top landing, scrambling backward like crabs. The beam made almost no sound until it crashed. Flames skidded down the beam to the staircase, spilling down the steps like pudding from a kettle. None of the sounds of fire were like I'd've thought. There were none of the fireplace noises—the crackling of the wood, the hisses and pops.

While Hunter looked from one wall, one doorway, one exit to another, the building seemed to rumble, like an earthquake coming.

Hunter led me to a door beside where the shoes were stacked. He pressed his hands flat onto it, turned to me and shook his head, it was too hot to risk opening. I heard myself laughing, put my hand to my own mouth till I didn't have to laugh anymore. "Okay," I said. "Okay."

Across the room I watched Hunter wedge his fingertips between two boards. He gripped the edges of one, pried it away from the wall in three hard jerks. Through the window underneath the wood I saw stars and a streetlight, or maybe the moon.

"Annie," Hunter called, "come help."

My lungs were scorched and dry; each breath stung the lining, stretched it raw. Count on me, Hunter, I wanted to be saying, I was raised on the streets, I was born for this. I was made to rip the boards from the window. I was hatched whole from a hard, tough place in the earth.

The rumble was louder, something in the ceiling whined over my head. Breathing through my nose helped slow the coughing. I looked down at my hands that were holding each other. I was shaking inside and I couldn't pull them apart.

Hunter had all four of the boards pried off, then he was hoisting a bucket of paint, heaving it up and through the window. I was thinking about why it took so long for me to hear the glass shatter, about whether my shaking inside slowed sounds from being heard, then Hunter yanked at my arm, pushed me up to the window. I looked at the sparkling triangles of glass that still clung to the frame where the window had been. Part of the room behind me crashed into itself. The room was sucking the wind inside.

"We've got to jump." His mouth was next to my ear and he was yelling, "Annie. Now."

I sat on the windowsill, something pierced the back of my thigh. I tried to raise myself off it, it sliced in deeper.

"Go. Jump."

I lifted myself on the heels of my hands, turned and faced

237

the building, started to lower myself down. Hunter was crouched in the window. My hands gripped the sill next to his feet.

"Just let go," Hunter was yelling. I hung from the sill with my arms stretched, my cheek against cool, rough plaster. His hands were locked around my wrists.

"Push away," he called.

I bent my knees, kicked my toes against the surface of the wall. In the long seconds of falling, I felt the wind and the grit pull through my hair, like on Tom's bike weaving down Lombard Street. When it was blowing the hardest, the wind turned to earth, hurling like a blow meant to slap the child out of me. I didn't hear Hunter land, though wood and glass flew up around him. I could hear only the rumble of the burning and the wail of the sirens. There were so many sirens I couldn't separate one from another.

– 17 –

Hunter had been across the street with his buddies ever since I told him to leave me alone. I just wanted to sit on the post office steps and watch my fire.

The police had strung rope between sawhorses to block off Hunter's building. The pavement was slick like after a rain, and I could hear water rushing up the hoses, crashing through floors and walls. The sky glowed orange, and it felt like daytime out. Down the street a crowd of young women sat, stood, and crouched in front of one of the dance bars. Some of the men on the other side had brought out lawn chairs, were sitting with their feet propped up like hotel guests around a pool.

Hunter sat next to me on the stairs. Though the post office steps raised us over people's heads, my view of most of the building was blocked by fire engines.

"You should go back to your buddies," I said. My voice was low and scratchy, and it tickled to talk. Across the street Marley was leaping for something Noosebaum held high over his head.

Hunter kept staring toward where the smoke wafted over the building. "They said it climbed up inside the walls," he said.

"They said it could have surrounded the room without us even noticing."

I pulled Hunter's shirt tight around me. I noticed for the first time that it was a dark green plaid. It itched my breasts whenever I moved and sent the smell of the fire to my aching nostrils.

"I hope you understand," I said, "if I ask you again to please go."

There was a boom at the back of the building. The men on the lawn chairs clapped.

"There goes my Peter Tosh collection," Hunter said.

There were chopping sounds, then an eerie echo. I pictured firemen axing through mountains of shoes.

"My Mighty Diamonds," Hunter said. "My General Saint, my live Big Youth, my bootleg Wailers."

"I mean it," I said. "Don't make me ask you again."

Hunter turned to look at me. I watched a thick jet of water arc over the roof.

"Look," Hunter said, "I can't just leave you here. If you won't come to Tail's place, you got to call your family."

"They're not my family."

"Don't start," he said. "I seen that movie a couple times already."

While Hunter was in the phone booth, a tall blond cop with a face like a yield sign knelt beside me, the third time that night.

"Just some cuts," I answered. "No need for a hospital."

"I'll take you home then." He stood up, adjusted his belt, his holster. "We'll drive up to your house with the lights spinning and the siren on. The royal treatment." He smiled, winked.

I stopped myself from explaining about not having a home.

"My father's on his way," I said.

Hunter stood in front of me when he came back. The holes he'd cut in his shirt made him seem ridiculous now, after all that had happened.

"Your people are duly freaked," he said.

Hunter was still facing me, like there was no fire behind him at all.

"I had to call the Chateau Rude," he said. "They got the home phone number off your application."

There was another boom from the back of the building.

"I'll bring the shirt back to..." I paused. "Well, I'll find you," I said, "and give back the shirt."

"I don't care about the fucking shirt," Hunter said.

Hunter passed his buddies and kept on walking. Marley galloped after him, and his buddies gave him a block head start before they turned to follow. I leaned against the building and closed my eyes. Now there were pops and crashes and crackling sounds. Now it was sounding more like fire.

"I hear your daddy's on his way," Tom said.

I wanted him to know that his voice didn't faze me. I didn't move or open my eyes.

"That'll teach you," I said, "to go talking to cops."

I heard the leather in his jacket creak when he sat down next to me.

"I love a roaring fire, don't you?" he said.

Tom's face startled me when I looked at him. His cheeks were bright red, like he'd been sitting on a beach. He was grinning like someone was about to snap a picture.

"So how'd you do it?" I said.

He kept grinning.

"Gasoline?" I said. "That's the only way I've ever heard.

He reached up and gripped my shoulder, started rubbing it, massaging my back.

"I'm glad you're all right," he said. "You don't know how worried I've been."

I closed my eyes again, felt the tingling warmth shoot through everything he touched.

"Next time you're worried about somebody," I said, "you might think twice about setting them on fire."

He was rubbing harder under my neck, between my shoulders. "Think," he said, "about all the people who ever claimed

241

they cared about you. Who's ever really done anything for you? Anything big, powerful?"

I shook my head, no one, never. Tom rubbed harder and harder.

"I know," he said, "what you've been thinking."

"You know?"

"I do." He was working down my shoulders to the hard muscles of my arms. "You been thinking it's all Jotta still. Everything I've done. All of it."

He was moving down my arms and my fingers fell open. "I love Jotta," I said.

"Yes," he said. "You do, Orphan Annie."

It seemed like a long time passed, then Tom stopped rubbing. I opened my eyes. Five steps below me they were lined up: Marie, Gloria, Sam, Jotta.

"Quite the coincidence," Tom said. "Y'all come here every season?"

Nobody moved.

"Listen, you son of a bitch," Marie said, then stopped.

Tom held up his hands. He turned to Gloria. "I believe congratulations are in order. The nuptials looked very festive, though I can speak only as a passerby."

Gloria turned to Jotta with a look that said, Does he really expect to carry on this conversation?

"And you, I presume," he said to Sam, "are the current paramour of choice."

"Jotta's my wife," Sam said, then seemed to feel uncomfortable about it. I could see he didn't know what kind of pose he should strike, whether to smile and try to smooth things over or puff out his chest and defend the women. In his heart, Sam was more diplomat than soldier. He took a step toward Tom and held out his hand. Over his shoulder I saw Marie roll her eyes.

Tom went back to rubbing my shoulders. "My hands are full just this second, good buddy."

Sam stepped backward, clasped his hands together. It was

that action that made Jotta and me look at each other: it was just the two of us again somehow. Nobody else could save us. Like before, like always.

"Annie," she said, "come home."

We looked at each other; I didn't answer, but I didn't look away. Marie walked a few steps down and turned her back. Gloria and Sam followed and put their arms around her, then Sam turned back to check on Jotta. Jotta didn't look at him, or Marie, or even Tom. She looked at me while the tears spilled down her face.

Tom reached over my shoulder and aimed a finger at Jotta, cocked his thumb and squeezed a trigger.

"Bang," I heard myself say.

Sam walked up next to Jotta, fixing a glare on Tom. "You and I should talk," he said to Tom, but no one seemed to hear. Then he wrapped an arm around Jotta to pull her away. She was staring so hard at Tom's hand, at the pretend pistol, that she didn't seem to notice Sam at all. I knew from her face that nothing mattered as much as that pointed finger. Not the fire, not Marie or Gloria, not the garden or the house, not Sam, not the baby.

Sam led Jotta down the stairs to where Marie and Gloria were huddled.

"When the hell you going to leave her be?" I whispered to Tom, leaning hard against him.

Nobody made me talk on the ride home. Sam and Jotta drove my Mustang, while I rode with Marie in Gloria's rental Peugeot. I couldn't hold back my coughing. My clothes, my hair, my pores, my lungs all seemed to exhale smoke and ash.

I took a hot shower, then ran a steaming bath. I lay with the water to my chin, feeling the sting on the cut at the back of my thigh, watching slow drips fall from the faucet. It had seemed like they'd made him back down, Hunter and his friends, but Tom had something much bigger in mind. It was in the long seconds of falling from the window that I'd understood the fire was for me. The drips from the faucet were heavy, slow, I tried to hold my stare on each one till it was lost in the splash it made. I got tired of staring, but it was too scary to close my eyes. If I did, I'd see not fire but water—tidal waves, dams collapsing, rivers swelling up and covering land, smothering flames.

— *18* —

I got dressed again after I dried off. I knew just walking down the hall that nobody had gone to sleep, though it must have been close to two A.M. Every light in the house seemed to be on. All the bedroom doors were open, and though I couldn't hear any talking, I could tell everyone was downstairs.

Gloria was lying on the couch in her pink housecoat, a magazine unopened on her lap.

"What's up?" I said from the stairs.

It took her a second to look at me. "Up?" She took the magazine and opened it to the middle. "Marie's making coffee."

I walked down the rest of the stairs. "I could stand to eat a little something," I said.

She didn't look up.

"Been thinking all day about that bread of Sam's, with maybe a little jam slathered on it."

I waited, watched her, still no answer. In all the years I'd known her, I'd never seen Gloria so cold, so far away. I thought of the last time she and I had been alone, the last time we'd really talked. Helping her fasten all those overstrained hooks on that fragile wedding dress, I'd asked her to talk to Marie about my leaving, to tell her I'd be safe. She could never do that, she'd said, unless she believed it was true. And I'd known by the way she'd looked at me that she loved me for being smart and strong. Which was what I'd hoped she'd tell Marie, and in those very words.

I walked to the couch, put my hand on Gloria's shoulder. "Could I talk you into some bread and jam?"

Gloria turned a page. "I got nothing to say to you, child."

Marie was pouring a pan of water into a filter resting on a glass coffeepot.

"Making enough for me?" I said.

Coffee flowed from the filter in a thin stream. Marie took the pan to the sink and filled it again.

"Funniest thing," I said. "You almost die in a fire, and nobody talks to you."

I heard a clatter of tools outside. Through the window in the back door I saw Jotta on her hands and knees in the far end of the garden. Sam stood ten feet from her, his arms crossed in front of him, looking up at the moon.

"Sit down," Marie said. She poured coffee into three cups, added milk to one and took it out to Gloria. She put the milk and sugar in front of me, sat down with our cups and crossed her legs.

I tilted the sugar and watched it slide to one side of the bowl. "Did Gloria say anything," I said, "just now?"

Marie poured milk into her cup, slid the carton over to me. She stirred her coffee and didn't say anything. For the first time I noticed how neatly she'd dressed to come to the fire. She was wearing a sweater and a skirt, like she used to back in California. Her hair was clean and styled, and she had her best necklace on. It was like her jeans and messy hair had been part of her fighting, but now there was something more grown-up and serious at stake.

"You look nice," I said. I scooped in sugar, though it hadn't been my habit just lately.

246

"Jotta was pregnant once before," Marie said. "Just before she married Tom. She was nineteen years old."

"I didn't know," I said. But then lots of girls got knocked up young. I was pouring milk in my coffee, pulled it away too late.

"She didn't want him to know," she said. "It was years ago, before you lived with me. Jotta made me promise not to let on to Tom about the baby."

"He didn't want to get married," I said.

"He married her afterwards," Marie said. "But you're hurrying my story." She got up and opened a cabinet over the stove. She pulled down a liter bottle of whiskey, poured a long shot into each of our cups of coffee.

"I didn't mean to hurry you," I said, but she sipped the coffee and paid my apology no attention.

"As it turns out," Marie said, "Tom got a physical at Jotta's doctor's office. He wormed the information out of some nurse or other. But we didn't know that at the time."

"He's pretty good," I said, "at that kind of thing."

"Out of the blue," she said, "he comes up with this trip to Mexico. Just him and Jotta, he said, on the road—like Kerouac, like Cassady."

I took a sip off the top of the coffee where the whiskey was floating.

"They were four hours south of the border," she said. "She'd wanted to stop hours earlier, her back was aching from leaning forward against him on the bike. He said no. He said they had reservations."

I took Marie's spoon and was stirring my coffee. "Reservations where?"

"It was dark when he led her into this tiny house." Marie took back the spoon, was now stirring in the same rhythm as I'd been. "I don't remember the particulars—the smells and all that kind of thing, though Jotta told me about it over and over. But everyone was talking in Spanish, and Tom held her down while they gave her the shots. What I remember best is what he said to her while she was going under."

247

"Before the operation," I said.

"Slipping under," Marie said, "she felt as if her brain was shrinking tight as a seed, so small it didn't have any power at all. Tom was stroking her arms and face so sweetly, brushing the damp hair from her forehead. That's when he leaned in close to her and said, 'Whoever had a mother called Jotta? You'd never ever get away with that.'"

We each took a slow sip, set our cups down, took slow sips again.

"It's different now," I said. "I'm seeing to that."

Marie didn't seem to be listening. "That was story number one," she said.

"She'll be fine this time," I said. "You wait and see."

Marie sighed and took another long drink. "Story number two," she said, and looked at me. "I wonder where to even start."

Gloria leaned in the doorway and waved to Marie. Marie said good night, and Gloria blew her a kiss.

"Sleep tight," I said. Gloria froze in the doorway, looking at me, then she blew me a kiss too.

Marie and I listened to Gloria's footsteps heading up the stairs. I poured another shot into my coffee.

"You want to hear about the fire?" I said.

Marie leaned across the table, dipped the spoon in my coffee and stirred. "No," she said.

Jotta burst through the door and dropped an armload of greens into the sink. She turned the water on hard, splayed the stream with her fingers to shower everything. Through the open door I could see Sam in the moonlight, slowly walking the path around the garden. It hurt too much to think about what Marie had just told me, about Jotta being held down and feeling no power.

"Midnight snack?" I said. "Twelve pounds of rhubarb?"

"I don't grow rhubarb," Jotta said, matter-of-fact. She was plucking spiny okra from their vines, washing each pod with special care.

"You supposed to pull up the whole vine?" I said.

248

Marie touched my hand, forced an airy laugh. "What Annie knows about gardening," she said, shaking her head.

I waited for her to finish the sentence. Her mouth was tense, and she sat straight in her chair, alert, almost nervous. I wanted to be able to say: Relax, Marie, here we are, all together, watching Jotta wash some of her vegetables. But we both understood that things weren't right in that kitchen, that it was two A.M. and Jotta was stripping whole okra plants, one by one, and dropping them, root and all, in the kitchen trash.

"We've got enough," Jotta was saying, "for pickling this year. They have to be washed, cooked, washed again. The crock has to be clean too, and salted, of course. People don't know sometimes, or they forget maybe. Or they use *iodized* salt. Imagine." She talked without turning to face us. "Imagine," she said again.

– 19 –

When I heard Jotta downstairs at dawn, I imagined her every step as she moved about the house. I decided it was my being afraid that made the pictures so sharp and vivid: I saw her making tea, buttering bread, checking her bag for keys, pills, checkbook. She looked no more surprised to see me standing at the door, dressed to go, than I was to see her come out of the kitchen, overcoat on and car keys in hand.

"Where do you think you're going?" she said.

"You stole my line," I said.

She looked down at her purse as if she needed something there but couldn't think just what.

"I've got a lot of errands today," she said. She opened the purse, moved some things around.

"Jotta," I said. "Don't pretend with me."

She let out a long, slow breath, closed the purse. "You've no right," she said, "to think anything about this. You don't know"—she was shaking her head, starting to tremble—"and I can't explain anything, and I don't, don't want to talk." Her chest was heaving, but no tears came. She wrapped her arms around her belly, then seemed to catch herself and jerked them away.

"How far is it?" I said.

She looked at the floor. "Boston," she finally said. "There's a clinic where if you convince them it's an emergency, they do it that day."

I sat on the couch. "Just rest a minute," I said.

Jotta hoisted her purse onto her shoulder and opened the door. "I'm going." She said it with a cold, hard force that made me shiver. I stood and walked next to her.

"They dope you up, Jotta," I said, trying to match her tone. "You'll need a driver."

I brushed past her and walked to my car without looking back, opened the passenger door, waited. The front door shut, and I heard her steps coming toward me. The fear I felt then was worse than that heart-pounding fear of the fire. What could happen seemed worse than what falling beams could do, and now it was me behind the wheel.

As I eased out the driveway and onto the graveled street, Jotta pulled a slip of paper from her coat pocket and held it in her lap. I could see the first line in her neat handwriting: Take Tremont to Cambridge, turn left.

"Ought to be a good hour and a half before we need directions, don't you think?" I said.

She stared ahead without answering, folded her hands in her lap with the paper pressed between them.

We didn't say a word till the Sagamore rotary. I asked her if she wanted coffee. She shook her head and I took the off-ramp north, crossed the bridge and headed up the mainland.

"So," I said. "What do you guys do for fun out where you live?"

Jotta turned, slowly, to face me. "Annie," she said, "we're not driving to a prom, you know."

"So that means we can't pass the time of day?" I said. "So we have to sit in silence like we're going to a funeral?"

I gasped a little at hearing the word. It wasn't concern

for some person or soul inside Jotta that made me want to choke back what I'd said. It was a fear of the death of something else, something trying to take root in her for the first time in her life.

"Silence," Jotta said. "Maybe that would be best."

A station wagon passed us on the left, loaded with glum-faced kids, probably driving home after a week of splashing in the warm Atlantic. We passed a sign—only forty-three miles to Boston, with Jotta not even letting me talk.

"I was trying to think," I said, "about what we used to do for fun back in California, back when I was little."

"I don't remember anybody having fun when you were little," Jotta said.

"Come on," I said. "You used to take me places. The haunted house, the circus."

"And we all had so much fun," she said. "The haunted house made you cry hysterically. The smell of circus animals made you throw up. The clowns gave you nightmares."

"You're making all this up," I said.

"I used to ask you about the clown nightmares," she said, "just to hear you tell me about them. You used to dream that little clowns the size of mice would crawl onto your pillow and hold your eyelids down so you'd never wake up again."

"Wow," I said. "I'd forgotten those dreams."

"Some of the clowns," she said, "were dressed like clowns, with bloomers and floppy shoes. The scariest ones were dressed like the lawyers from the Hall of Justice—suits and ties and starched collars, with those big clown heads laughing at you while they tried to make you sleep forever and ever."

"That does sound scary," I said. "But I don't remember the dreams so much as I remember how you begged me to tell you about them."

Jotta laughed, and then we laughed together—the full, loud laughing of a couple of scary clowns without the right equipment to cry.

"Oh"—Jotta sighed—"it felt good to do that."

"You're pretty good at it," I said. "Or you were until very recently."

"This is what I meant," she said, "by not wanting to talk."

"You've *got* to talk to me about this, Jotta," I said. "You wanted this kid." I felt the speed picking up, saw the speedometer edge over seventy. Getting there faster was not what I needed. I let up on the gas and pulled into the slow lane.

"You couldn't possibly understand," Jotta said quietly.

I watched the speedometer drop to fifty. A van whipped around me on the left, honking as it passed.

"I knew this girl," I said, "when I was sixteen. Her name was Sandy—she spelled it funny I think, but I can't remember how."

Jotta cut in, "And she missed her period and she didn't tell anybody, then four months later went to a butcher in Mexico and regretted it for the rest of her days."

I gripped the wheel at the mention of Mexico. I swallowed and slowed to forty-five.

Jotta looked at the speedometer. "I'm due there no later than eight," she said.

"This girl Sandy," I said, "used to come to school every few weeks with her eyes black. Instead of hanging her head or trying to cover it with makeup, she'd strut into the cafeteria, let her books drop onto the table so we'd all look up. When somebody finally asked her what happened, she'd lean in close to all of us and whisper louder than her normal voice, 'I got Lenny so mad, God, he almost *killed* me.' She talked about getting beaten the way the rest of us talked about kissing."

"There are girls like that," Jotta said.

"Here's the thing," I said. "I never knew why, but when she talked like that, Jotta, I felt electric, alive. I laughed behind her back with all the others, but I always wanted to say, Sandy, you're a fool to trust regular people to understand about that. And then I wanted to ask her everything about it. Not the beating part, but all the rest—the thrill of not knowing what would happen next."

Jotta was folding her slip of paper in half, then opening it

254

and folding it tighter again. I thought there might have been tears in her eyes, but I didn't want to look and risk her feeling me watching her. "No matter what happens," she said, "no matter if he does something and gets put away again, he'll always, always be out there."

"He won't," I said.

"He *will*," she said, "and that'll always be true, and a baby would only be pretending."

"Pretending what?"

"That I'm not what I am, what I've always been. That there's hope, Annie. Don't you see?"

"I'll tell you what I see," I said. "I see a big guy with a beard who loves you. I see a house and a cupboard full of jars of things I'd never even *seen* before I came out here. I see you having a life here, *making* things." I thought of the sweater she'd given me; I would never tell her the truth about what happened to it.

"I like"—she paused—"I *want* those things." She put her hands around her belly and held them there.

"What if," I said, "Tom didn't come back?"

"But he's still here," she said.

"That's not what I asked you. I said, 'What if.' "

Jotta leaned back, closed her eyes. "Then maybe I could keep it all," she said. "Everything. If I believed that could happen, that he'd go away."

"What if he didn't turn up," I said, "for a few days, a week."

"He always turns up by then, once he's made me know he's wherever I am. Or he gives me some kind of sign, so I know to be always waiting."

"One month," I said. "What if he didn't show for a month?"

"A month." She was rocking very gently now, her arms still around her. "I'd take it to mean he'd gone."

"Promise me," I said. "If he doesn't show. Give it one more month of your life."

When I pulled off at the next exit, Jotta didn't say a word.

255

On the overpass headed for the southbound lanes, I took her hand.

"Promise me," I said.

She squeezed my hand and nodded. I screeched onto the highway, my window rolled down, pulled Jotta's directions from her lap and whipped them into the salty wind.

– 20 –

The first hours of waiting, I went through all the highway songs. I thought of as many as I could and put them in groups: Lonely and On the Road, Free and On the Road, On the Road Hungry, On the Road Looking. But there was no highway song for me. This was part of what I knew different now. As homely and low as they thought they could be, songs were made of charm and air, of faith in someone listening. I wanted to make something out of words while waiting, but it wouldn't be a song. It would be something just said:

I grew up among women, and left everything I knew. I followed a man to a world full of men, where I could have lived out a life without ever belonging. I learned I wasn't the kind of strong I wanted to be, and that I hated weakness more than fire. I loved another woman best. So I left her, and waited.

I waited on the post office steps, across from where he'd set the fire. I waited in the phone booth where he'd come when I'd called Carter the night before. I saw us gunning full throttle, siren wailing, onto the highway and over the bridge. I saw us gliding with the engine silent, his motorcycle glistening like a toy. Those things I saw while waiting were more important than what it was like to leave. What mattered most was my having been there, and then, even more, my having gone.

FOR THE BEST IN PAPERBACKS, LOOK FOR THE

In every corner of the world, on every subject under the sun, Penguin represents quality and variety—the very best in publishing today.

For complete information about books available from Penguin—including Pelicans, Puffins, Peregrines, and Penguin Classics—and how to order them, write to us at the appropriate address below. Please note that for copyright reasons the selection of books varies from country to country.

In the United Kingdom: For a complete list of books available from Penguin in the U.K., please write to *Dept E.P., Penguin Books Ltd, Harmondsworth, Middlesex, UB7 0DA*.

In the United States: For a complete list of books available from Penguin in the U.S., please write to *Dept BA, Penguin, 299 Murray Hill Parkway, East Rutherford, New Jersey 07073*.

In Canada: For a complete list of books available from Penguin in Canada, please write to *Penguin Books Canada Ltd, 2801 John Street, Markham, Ontario L3R 1B4*.

In Australia: For a complete list of books available from Penguin in Australia, please write to the *Marketing Department, Penguin Books Australia Ltd, P.O. Box 257, Ringwood, Victoria 3134*.

In New Zealand: For a complete list of books available from Penguin in New Zealand, please write to the *Marketing Department, Penguin Books (NZ) Ltd, Private Bag, Takapuna, Auckland 9*.

In India: For a complete list of books available from Penguin, please write to *Penguin Overseas Ltd, 706 Eros Apartments, 56 Nehru Place, New Delhi, 110019*.

In Holland: For a complete list of books available from Penguin in Holland, please write to *Penguin Books Nederland B.V., Postbus 195, NL–1380AD Weesp, Netherlands*.

In Germany: For a complete list of books available from Penguin, please write to *Penguin Books Ltd, Friedrichstrasse 10–12, D–6000 Frankfurt Main 1, Federal Republic of Germany*.

In Spain: For a complete list of books available from Penguin in Spain, please write to *Longman Penguin España, Calle San Nicolas 15, E–28013 Madrid, Spain*.